Praise for *Secrets* [barcode: D0942514]

"Anyone seeking a different Regency setting and non-royal characters is certain to find Romain's novel a bright light… Expect to shed some tears of joy by the wonderful conclusion."

—*RT Book Reviews*, 4 Stars

"Cat-and-mouse games are augmented by spirited repartee."

—*Publishers Weekly*

"By far one of the best romantic novels that I have had the pleasure of reading."

—*Night Owl Reviews*, Top Pick

"I would highly recommend this brilliant yet stunning novel… It's the most captivating romance readers will ever find."

—*Romancing the Book*

"This was a delight."

—*Smart Bitches, Trashy Books*

"Beautifully written…a must-read for anyone who enjoys romance."

—*Long and Short Reviews*

Jun 2016

Praise for *To Charm a Naughty Countess*

"Utterly charming plot and sprightly dialogue... The intelligence of the writing, coupled with well-drawn and appealing characters, pulls readers into a love story that is not just enchanting, but joyous."

—*RT Book Reviews,* 4.5 Stars

"The latest in Romain's Matchmaker trilogy will wow readers with its perfectly imperfect protagonists and emotionally compelling plot. With this superbly written novel, it is easy to see why Romain is one of the rising stars of Regency historical romance."

—*Booklist*

"Romain's characters are raw and honest... Amazingly refreshing."

—*Emma's Miscellaneous Maunderings*

"The writing is good, the plot is original, the characters are engaging, and I enjoyed reading every page."

—*LaDeeta Reads*

Praise for *It Takes Two to Tangle*

"A delightful romance. Its intriguing plot, replete with unforeseen twists and coupled with a set of passionate characters, quickly make this a page-turner."

—*RT Book Reviews,* 4 Stars

"Romain's ability to draw me into the story that deeply is impressive. If you're a Regency fan who likes unconventional heroines [and] the Tragically Wounded Hero...pick it up."

—*Smart Bitches, Trashy Books*

"Theresa Romain has a rare ability to blend beautiful writing, great characters, delicious banter, and a lovely romance, all in one perfect package. Her writing is gorgeous."

—*TBQ's Book Palace*

"Tender romance, passion, witty banter, secrets, healing, forgiveness, and love make this story absolutely delightful."

—*Romance Junkies*

"Romain uses strong characters, witty banter, and a Cyrano de Bergerac type situation to bring her story to life...definitely a must-read for Regency fans."

—*Debbie's Book Bag*

A GENTLEMAN'S GAME

THERESA ROMAIN

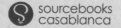
sourcebooks
casablanca

Published by Sourcebooks Casablanca, an imprint of Sourcebooks,
Inc.
P.O. Box 4410, Naperville, Illinois 60567-4410
(630) 961-3900
Fax: (630) 961-2168
www.sourcebooks.com

Printed and bound in Canada.
MBP 10 9 8 7 6 5 4 3 2 1

One

NATHANIEL CHANDLER SOMETIMES THOUGHT HE HAD traveled every road in England, and he liked them all. He liked the stony walks of Cornwall that fell away sharply to the salt-scented sea. He liked the wagon paths through endless, shifting Yorkshire moorland. He even liked the ramshackle corners of London's rougher bits—where a man had to keep one hand on a pistol and the other on his purse—as much as the wide, smooth paths of Mayfair, where the houses were large and the coal smoke hung less heavily in the sky.

The only road he did *not* like was the one he was on now, which wound from the high street of Newmarket through his father's lands. Because when the rotunda of Chandler Hall appeared above the trees like a gleaming middle finger to fate, Nathaniel's journey—wherever it had taken him—was at an end.

Not for long, though. Not if he could convince Sir William that his plan was a good one.

When grooms scampered from the grand stables to take charge of the horses and carriage, Nathaniel hopped down and strode off toward Chandler Hall. He crossed the glassy marble floor of the entry hall, turned the handle of the study door, and nudged his way in. "Hullo, return of the prodigal son and all that. How is everyone this afternoon?"

The baronet's study was a slim semicircle that, with the entrance hall and a few other chambers, made up the echoing rotunda of Chandler Hall. Tall windows and a set of glass-paned doors alternated with book-shelves, all stuffed with heavy bound volumes.

Spare and unadorned, it wasn't a pleasant room, exactly. But it was efficient. Which, Nathaniel supposed, suited his father much better than a study full of burled walnut and red velvet tapestries.

Sir William Chandler sat behind the stretching mahogany table he used as a desk. The feathered barb of a quill lay in picked-apart shreds across a series of papers before him. "Nathaniel." When he looked up, his heavy slate-gray brows were furrowed. "Right, right. You were meant to be back today."

"Well—yes. I *am* back. And I bring good news from London."

The baronet ran skeptical hazel eyes over his younger son. "Did something odd happen? Your clothing is filthy."

Was he? Nathaniel glanced doubtfully down at his coat and waistcoat.

Oh, yes. Right. He was spattered with mud and was all-over grimy.

This was due to a cracked carriage wheel. After

crawling on the ground and hammering things, being covered in dirt was inevitable.

But he had learned long ago not to speak to his father of things like cracked wheels—or thrown horseshoes, runaway horses, or thieves who didn't realize Nathaniel carried a pistol. When one traveled the length and breadth of England buying and selling horses, one had to be prepared for unusual occurrences. Still, it was best if Sir William thought everything went smoothly on Nathaniel's journeys.

"It was a milkmaid." Nathaniel leaned against the study wall. "Caught me just after dawn today. She was overcome by lust and wrestled me to the ground. I barely escaped with my dignity intact."

"I wouldn't be so certain you did." The baronet's heavy brows lifted. "You encounter a remarkable lot of milkmaids on your travels." *I don't believe you*, said the tone behind the words.

Nathaniel shrugged. *You don't have to. I'm back, and so is the carriage.* "There's a saying about that, isn't there? 'Some are born milkmaids, some achieve milkmaids, and some have milkmaids thrust upon them.' I seem to be the latter sort of person."

A laugh, quickly smothered, reminded him of the room's other occupant. At the short end of the table sat Sir William's secretary, a young woman named Rosalind Agate.

Nathaniel had met her only once before, when she had been in his father's employment for no more than a month. Sir William did not mind a female secretary after being aided so long by his daughter Hannah— especially when his three previous male secretaries had, as he put it, "hardly known the arse end of a horse from the front."

Miss Agate made a neat ruddy-haired figure in a print gown that covered her almost from chin to wrist and down to the floor. Nathaniel had an impression of forthright green eyes, wide cheekbones, and a quick twist of a smile before she returned to her work, quill racing across a sheet of foolscap.

He smiled back—but a tense silence fell, and after a moment, so did his grin. "All right. I can tell something is wrong. What is it?"

Sir William scrubbed a hand over his face, making a deranged tangle of his stern brows. "The colic."

Nathaniel cursed. With the Epsom Derby a few weeks away, ill horses were the last thing a stable needed. "Which horse? Or horses?"

"Sir Jubal's colt, Epigram."

"*Epigram?* How can that be?" If ever a horse was, well, healthy as a horse, it was the strapping colt that had recently won the Two Thousand Guineas Stakes. The elderly Sir Jubal Thompson had transferred his champion to the Chandler stables to join the company soon to travel south for the Derby.

"Not only Epigram." Giving the mahogany wheels of his chair a little push, Sir William angled himself back from the desk and pulled a watch from his waist-coat pocket. "I need to meet with Sir Jubal in the stable in a few minutes. Miss Agate, please acquaint my son with the latest happenings while I see to my brandy. Taking it early won't hurt just this once."

About Miss Agate were arranged industrious islands of paper, ink, and quills, of ledgers and correspondence and waxes and seals. With her brows puckered, she sifted through papers.

"Two other animals have developed colic," she explained in a low, calm tone, her accent as tidy and crisp as the angled streets of Mayfair. "All three were to travel to Epsom in a fortnight to await the Derby. Other than that, they've little in common. Epigram does not belong to the Chandler stable. Pale Marauder is one of your father's racehorses, but the third is not a Thoroughbred at all."

"Do you mean Sheltie?" At the secretary's nod, Nathaniel grimaced. The fat little pony had kept the Chandler Thoroughbreds company for twenty years, soothing fractious tempers—human as well as equine—with her stolid presence. "Poor little Sheltie. Sick at her age; that's rotten luck." Nathaniel sank onto the edge of the wide table, resting his weight.

"Off. Off the desk, Nathaniel. I tell you this every time." Sir William looked up from his fussings with the brandy decanter. "Do you think it's a matter of luck, then? Sheltie's illness?"

Nathaniel slid from the table and planted his feet. "Do you think it's *not* luck? What else could it be?"

"That," said Sir William, "is a question against which we've been beating our brains for some time." He indicated the papers before him. "For the three ill animals, we have reviewed exercise schedules, stable care, water sources…"

"Currying supplies, the tack," continued Miss Agate. "And feed."

"They shared feed," said Sir William. "That's all. When

Smith last delivered lucerne hay, did you remember to check it for mold?"

The baronet's tone was mild, which was far worse than when it rang out sternly. Mildness meant disappointment. Mildness meant *I should have known better than to trust you with this.*

"Of course I did," Nathaniel replied. "I cut a sample from the center of a few of the bales, and the quality was perfectly acceptable. Since my childhood, I have known how to tell good hay from bad."

"I suppose," granted the baronet. "And Lemuel Smith has been supplying this family's stables and stud farm with lucerne for decades. Which means the colic can't be caused by feed either."

"There is some common cause," said Miss Agate. "And we will find it."

We, she said easily, as though she had already become an indispensable part of the household. It had been thirteen years since Nathaniel had spoken or heard that effortless *we*.

It had been longer still since he'd felt the certainty reflected in her words.

Sir William eyed his glass, then poured in a few more drops of brandy before resealing the decanter. This ritual was performed at the same time every day. It was always a half inch, never more and never less.

In the slanted sunlight of late afternoon, the brandy glowed like liquid gold. Half an inch was no more than a taste of heat, a splash of sharp, buttery warmth on the tongue. At the end of a journey, Nathaniel wanted that brandy as much as the carriage horses had wanted their stable and hay.

But there was always a reason to want brandy. Or whisky. Or port. Or claret.

Nathaniel turned away, squinting toward the west-facing windows and their glimpse of the stables. "Have you time to hear my news of London before your meeting, Father? I had some success there."

"Did you? We could use some good news." *We* again, and Nathaniel had no idea if the pronoun included him or not. The baronet twisted his empty glass, the crystal making a heavy sliding sound on the table. The sound of luxury, of a half inch of brandy that was enough, that had to be enough.

Nathaniel swallowed the craving. "Yes. The chestnut and bay colts sold for much more than expected."

When he named the price, Sir William's heavy brows lifted. "Not bad. Those two could never win one of the classic races, but they'll be quick after the fox if they're gelded and trained up as hunters."

"I also purchased a broodmare named Helena for the stud farm. Sothern is bringing her up to Newmarket." At the name of the trusted groom, Sir William grunted his approval. "And," Nathaniel continued in a rush, "Sothern will remain with her until she is settled under Jonah's care, which means I—"

"Of what line is she?" Sir William broke in.

Nathaniel bit off the rest of his sentence. The most important part. "I beg your pardon?"

"Of what line is she? The broodmare?"

"Through her dam, she is of Matchem's line." One of the finest Thoroughbred bloodlines of the past century.

Sir William tipped his head toward Miss Agate. "How does one know that?"

Was this a test for her or for Nathaniel himself? "Because the horse told me so," he muttered. "She's a Houyhnhnm, just like the talking horses in *Gulliver's Travels*."

The secretary's mouth twitched. "A great piece of luck," she said. "In cases involving a nonspeaking horse, I believe one would be required to consult the *General Stud Book*?"

This book of reference was practically the family bible. Hundreds of pages of illustrious names and *begats*.

"Good, Miss Agate," Sir William approved. "You're learning the racing world quickly."

Nathaniel rubbed at his unshaven chin. "Right. Well, that's how it's done if one hasn't the good fortune of meeting a Houyhnhnm. Check the *Stud Book*. Trust Nathaniel. Buy fine horses." He took a deep breath and began his request again. "While Sothern is occupied at the stud farm—"

"It was wise to have him walk Helena there. There is no one more trustworthy, and she sounds like a very fine broodmare," Sir William interrupted for at least the thousandth time. "Jonah will welcome the addition to the stable. He thinks Matchem's descendants are sturdy. Healthy too, and good-tempered."

Nathaniel agreed. "That's why I chose Helena." An extravagant purchase that he was nevertheless confident would pay dividends. Dividends even more precious than gold coins; dividends in the form of fleet-footed, race-winning foals.

Jonah, huge and inscrutable, was the oldest of the

four Chandler offspring. He oversaw the operations of the stud farm north of Newmarket. On those spacious acres, Thoroughbreds were born and received their first training.

Far more at ease with horses than people, Jonah had an eye for racing potential and a knack for bringing it out. The stud farm, like the stables at Chandler Hall, housed not only the family's horses but also horses belonging to many others. Hopeful owners betting that the fees they paid the Chandlers would bring not only the best care and training, but also success on the turf.

Sir William glanced at his watch again before stuffing it back into his waistcoat pocket. "I must be off to the stables. Sir Jubal is expecting me. If we're to have a prayer of getting these horses to Epsom in time, they'll need to be physicked quickly."

"I shall accompany you." Both Nathaniel and Miss Agate spoke at once.

Nathaniel blinked at the secretary with some surprise. She smiled at him tentatively. "*We* shall?"

"You both ought to join me," decided Sir William. "Nathaniel, you must learn more about the situation so you can acquaint Sothern when he arrives."

I have asked him not to come. It was on the tip of Nathaniel's tongue to say so, to blurt it out after so many interruptions. *I want to take the horses to Epsom instead, to lead the one journey I have never yet made for this family.*

Trust Nathaniel.

But it was a great deal to say all at once, especially when worry over ill horses was poking at the ever-tentative peace between father and son.

"I would be delighted to see the horses," he replied. This was always true.

He pushed himself away from the wall. The brandy decanter winked at him as he walked by the table.

He turned away, instead sidling around the table to unlatch the French doors leading out from the study. As he reached them, he somehow jostled Miss Agate, who was moving in the opposite direction. She caught her balance on the table's edge, scattering a batch of quills.

"I beg your pardon," she said. "Sir William, I shall set this to rights and join you directly."

"Allow me." Nathaniel reached for the quills.

"No need, thank you. It will take only a moment to tidy this." She was already crouching, her face hidden. Only the smooth back of her light print gown was visible, and that great crown of russet hair picking up golden-red sunlight.

Nathaniel hesitated, half crouching himself—but Sir William made an impatient sound. "Sir Jubal awaits. If you're coming?"

Nathaniel unfolded himself, cracking an elbow on the underside of the table and smothering a curse. He always felt a bit out of place in Sir William's world, wrongly sized and out of step.

It hadn't always been that way. But it had been that way so long that Nathaniel had almost forgotten that things had once been different.

Maybe Sir William had too.

Holding open the glass-paned door with one boot and an outstretched arm, Nathaniel made way for his father. With the agility of long practice, the baronet steered his cumbersome chair out from the study onto a stone path paved smoothly for wooden wheels.

And Nathaniel followed in the lines his father had so carefully laid out.

❧

Rosalind kept her face turned demurely toward the floor until the French door had swung shut again. Crawling forward one tiny nudge at a time, she peered around the legs of the large table.

The Chandlers were moving steadily down the path to the stable. Away from the study. Good.

It only took seconds to tidy up the mess of quills she had created by way of excuse. Rubbing at her elbow to reduce the tightness of her old scars, Rosalind then took up a fresh sheet of paper and dipped the quill again. After folding the paper and inking the direction, she smoothed it out and scrawled:

> *Anweledig,*
> *Several horses have fallen ill. They might not be able to race in the Derby.*

Should she say more?

What more could she say? She considered the possibilities, quill poised over the paper.

Alpha and I have no idea what is causing the illness.

Nathaniel Chandler—no, she called him Gamma in letters to Aunt Annie. *Gamma returned from London with good news, muddy boots, and an unlikely tale of a milkmaid.*

Gamma's blue eyes are full of mischief and plans. I should like to know what is on his mind.

This last thought was as sweet as it was irrelevant. Rosalind's snipped and abandoned friendships and posts lay about England like a shawl full of dropped stitches. She had been a housemaid time and again, a governess for family after family. There was no sense in regretting any of these departures when each hole, each break in the pattern, was only one among many.

But she did regret them. All of them. She was tidy by nature, and she would rather knit than unravel.

No, she would add no more to her brief letter right now. She wiped the quill and set it aside.

After sanding the paper to dry the ink, she folded the note to Aunt Annie and slid it into the bodice of her gown, along with a gummed wafer. Once she knew more, she would complete the letter. Tonight, in her small bedchamber, with the stub of a pencil.

When she had an opportunity, she would shuffle her letter into Sir William's others and take it to the post. Just one bit of correspondence among the many she had written for the man who thought he owned her loyalty.

Just one, to the person who truly claimed it instead.

Two

BEING IN THE STABLE AMID THE HAY RAKES AND shovels, the scents of oil and leather from tack, and the grassy-sweet scent of feed always smoothed the edge of Nathaniel's temper when it began to fray. A horse needed help. He could give it, and he would.

He filled a bucket with heated water, hesitated, then splashed a bit on his face. *Not* to tidy up for the sake of Miss Agate. Not that. He really did feel dirty from his travels, and there was no time to scrub off just yet.

Steadying the bucket against his side, he made his way toward the rear of the stable where Epigram was kept. When he passed the first stall, a gray poked forth a curious muzzle.

"Hello, Jake, old boy." Nathaniel patted the velvet nose, then combed through the animal's tousled forelock. "Keeping an eye on things? Behaving beautifully?" The gelding blinked his long-lashed eyes, then ducked his head for Nathaniel to rub behind his ears. With a laugh, Nathaniel took the unmistakable hint.

Sir William believed such chats and pats were a waste of time. Horses were workers, just like grooms and stable boys. They must be treated fairly and well, and in return they must give him their best.

Nathaniel was of the mind that everyone—man or beast—could use a little scratch behind the ears sometimes. Or the preferred equivalent.

But a sick horse waited. "Back later, Jake. I have to take care of our illustrious visitor now." The gelding snorted, and Nathaniel left him with a final pat.

The other stalls in the block were empty because the Thoroughbreds were being exercised on Sir William's short training track or cooled down with a walk. At the end of the row was a loose box in which ill horses were given room to recover. Here the pleasant scents of horse and feed were damped by the odor of sweat. A compact, dark-brown colt, Epigram stood with his head hung low and his hooves splayed wide as though his balance was upset.

Sir Jubal Thompson was crammed into the stall alongside Sir William, and the elderly knight and steely baronet were arguing.

Had the horse not been in such need of help, the argument would have been amusing. Mindful of the skittish beast between them, baronet and elderly knight tore into each other in the most soothing voices imaginable.

"It has to be the feed," crooned Sir Jubal, stroking the horse's neck. "He was perfectly fine when I turned him over into your care." His white hair was tied back in an old-fashioned queue, and his face was lined deeply, as much with worry as with age.

Again with the feed. *Had* Nathaniel checked the hay well enough? Surely he had. And Smith would have done so too.

Surely.

Sir William shot a veiled glance at Nathaniel, who paused just outside the stall. "It is not the feed. All horses are given the same, and only three of them are ill."

"What is the cause, then?"

"I have not found it yet." Sir William might have been singing a lullaby, so gentle was his voice. "But the treatment—"

"—will be carried out according to my preference—"

"—you turned the horse over to my care, and therefore my judgment is to be—"

Their voices continued, blended and faded into a calming harmony as Nathaniel squeezed into the stall, making a fourth body in the small space.

He saw what the two older men had already seen: the colt's latest ration of hay had gone untouched. A prickle of apprehension touched Nathaniel's neck.

While so many Thoroughbreds were flighty and fractious, Epigram was like a steam-powered boiler. Once fired up, he ran as steadily as churning pistons, and he consumed massive amounts of feed. No fuss over hay or oats for this one. Whatever was put before him, he ate it, and before he exercised, he tried to crop the grass on the turf too.

Usually. When he was in good health.

Nathaniel kicked aside a bit of straw to set down the bucket of warm water before Epigram's lowered head. This won him a *whuff* of humid breath over his fingers, and he rubbed at the colt's soft muzzle.

"They're worrying about you," he murmured. "Are you going to get well so they can stop?" One never knew if an appeal to a horse's finer feelings would work. It certainly couldn't hurt.

At the approach of swift, light footsteps, Nathaniel stood. Here came Rosalind Agate, cheeks flushed and hair loosening from its pins as though she had run. In her hands she carried a cake of salt.

She caught Nathaniel's eye and explained, "A stable boy told me you had brought warm water. If it's for the horse to drink, I thought salt might encourage him."

"To make him thirsty," Nathaniel realized. "A good idea. Let's see if it helps." Thus far Epigram had politely ignored the warm water—which was the best thing possible for prodding along a halted digestion.

Crouching in the doorway of the stall, skirts trailing in scattered straw, Miss Agate murmured something quiet that made the colt's ears swivel toward her. She moved with smooth calm, working free some crystals of salt and dabbing them at the mouth of the dispirited animal. Epigram whiffed and sniffed and licked, then stretched his head to drink the warm water.

Success. Nathaniel grinned—and when he caught the secretary's eye, she was smiling too. "Again," he said.

While she administered the salt, he pressed gently along the animal's side. Epigram's barrel was distended, but there were no obvious tender spots. The colt continued to behave as placidly as ever, taking a drink when it pleased him. The surface of the warm water rippled as he dribbled into the bucket.

The mild patter between the baronet and Sir Jubal had turned to a discussion of further treatments to try.

"Nux vomica," suggested one, and the other asked for mineral oil as well.

"Miss Agate, fetch a stable boy and have him locate those," Sir William said in a voice of infinite kindness.

Yes, the tone was for the horse's benefit. And there was a tiny corner of Nathaniel that found himself envying a sick horse.

"I know where the nux vomica and mineral oil are located," said the secretary. "I'll collect them and return in a moment, Sir William." She sprang upright, wincing as she did, then slipped from the stall doorway to carry out the errand.

The older men were silent for a moment. Then Sir Jubal spoke: "How you turn these mad arrangements to your advantage, Sir William, I'll never know. I wasn't the only one who thought you were a fool for engaging a female secretary, but she's capable enough."

"That's all I require. The last three secretaries I hired had a neat hand, but they knew nothing at all about horses. I don't mind a female as long as she knows her way about a stable. You'll recall that my daughter Hannah was my secretary until she married." Sir William's gaze caught Nathaniel's, and he added slowly, "All I expect is loyalty and hard work."

And was that some sort of criticism? Or praise so veiled it could hardly be recognized?

Nathaniel returned his attention to Epigram, though his jaw could not seem to come unclenched.

The secretary returned soon enough with supplies, and Sir William rolled toward her to take the requested bottles. "Thank you, Miss Agate. That will be all for now. Make way, Nathaniel."

Nathaniel slid around the edge of the stall, out of his father's path. Sir William executed a neat, tight spin, but could not edge his wheelchair into the right position. "Jubal, pull your horse forward a tick."

But as the horse edged forward, the right wheel of Sir William's chair remained locked. Nathaniel spotted the problem: a fallen halter, almost hidden by straw.

"Father, allow me." He stepped forward to pull the halter free. When it proved trapped, he eased the chair back a few inches and bent to remove the obstruction.

When he stood again, halter in hand, Sir William's hands were tight on the rims of his wheels. "You may go, Nathaniel."

"But I can help Epi—"

"Go. Now. You've done enough." The baronet's gaze was stern—but after a moment in which Nathaniel blinked at him, startled, it dropped to fix on his hands instead.

Though a protest was at the tip of his tongue, Nathaniel understood: *You've done enough* meant *I don't want you around right now.*

There were reasons Nathaniel had traveled so many roads across England. This was one of them.

He sketched a curt bow. "The salt is encouraging Epigram to drink. His barrel seems sound. Please alert me if I can be of further help."

And then, hanging the halter over the open stall door, he left.

❧

Rosalind followed Nathaniel Chandler from the stall and back down the main passage. The stables were less than a decade old, like Chandler Hall itself, and were built on the same wide, smooth lines. The cobbles here were as snugly laid as the tiles inside the house. Away from the crowded confines of Epigram's stall, the stable was quiet. To Rosalind's ear, the pair of human foot-falls echoed from stone floor to high ceiling like those of penitents walking the nave of a church.

When they reached a stall from which a gray horse peeked—a sweet gelding named Jake, who loved noth-ing so much as radishes—Nathaniel stopped. Petting the horse's long, straight nose, then scratching behind its ears, he spoke at last. "Miss Agate, you could stay with Sir William. He'll find some use for you."

"I don't want a use *found* for me. I want to *be* of use." This was quite true, and not only because her letter to Aunt Annie required her to look at the other two horses that had fallen ill.

"Is this the sort of way you think a secretary ought to be of use?"

"By caring for horses? If one works for Sir William Chandler, certainly. We're in the stables as often as the study." She stroked Jake's smooth neck, wishing she had one of his favorite treats in her pockets. "And I wouldn't keep my post long if I began every conversa-tion with 'secretaries don't.'"

Nathaniel darted a sidelong glance at her, an odd smile on his features. "Under many circumstances, that *would* be an appropriate thing to say. But in this case, if you want to help the horses, I'm glad for the aid. Find two more buckets, will you?" He straightened the gray's forelock, then gave the horse a final pat. "I'll get more salt from the feed room."

All business, he was, as he started walking away. A long line of snug buckskin and fine wool, the quality unmistakable beneath spatters of mud and the dust of straw. He had the look of a man who could fit in anywhere, confident and capable.

For a moment she gazed after him, distracted by a quick stab of wistfulness. She had met him the week after beginning her employment with Sir William. It had been a quick introduction and quicker good-bye as he exchanged one set of luggage and horses for another before setting off to London.

Secretaries don't was true for her when it came to personal desires. Just as *governesses don't* and *housemaids don't* were before that. She was twenty-three years old, and she'd been alone for the last ten years, even in a crowd.

And that was fine. It was the way matters had to be. She was accustomed to it.

But when she had met Nathaniel Chandler, and he'd smiled at her as though she was truly worth meeting…well, maybe she wasn't as accustomed to it as she'd thought.

She allowed herself one final glance at the tall figure walking away, then got on with her work.

A nearby stable boy directed her to unused buckets. Grabbing two, she hurried toward the front of the stable. She caught up to her employer's son at the door of the feed room, where he was working on the difficult latch. It had to fit so tightly that no rodent, no matter how small, could slip within.

Without looking up, he said, "You are out of breath."

"This is Newmarket. Everyone runs." Rosalind extended the buckets. "I have what you wanted."

She flushed a little at the words.

He flashed a quick smile at her, then returned his attention to the latch. "Good. We only need the salt then." He paused. "I am going to check the hay for mold."

When he shoved the door open, Rosalind set the buckets on the clean-swept floor and stepped into the feed room after him. "But you said you were sure. That you trust the man who supplies the hay."

His pause was long. "No harm in checking again, is there?" The feigned lightness in his tone did not fool her.

The feed room was dimmer than the wide stretch of the stables, though a high-cut window let in daylight. Grain bins with tight-fitting lids held—curious, she peered into them one by one—oats and barley. The maligned hay was stored in a loft reached by a narrow wooden ladder, though a single bale had been pitched down.

Nathaniel Chandler stared at it as if it were a beast.

"I could check it if you like," Rosalind suggested. "So you don't have to. I could be a cruel, shrewish harpy who refused to take your word on trust. Here, I've found a hay knife."

As she crouched before the hay, looking up at him, his gaze seemed to snap into focus. "Nonsense, Miss Agate. You'll dirty your pretty dress. I'll check the hay."

You look pretty.

This was not what he had said, of course. The tight scars webbing her side were a reminder. When he sank to the floor of the feed room beside her, she turned the hay knife over to him. "Please do not pay me false compliments, Mr. Nathaniel. I am a secretary, not one of your imaginary milkmaids."

He rose to a crouch, regarding her with eyes that were very blue and just a little wicked. "Why imaginary?"

"The sheer number of them. There cannot be so many cows in all of England."

He granted this with a shrug. "And why must compliments be false?"

The words were practiced and smooth, like a sauce poured over a dish to mask its true flavor. This was a habit of his, doubtless, and she must remain proof against it. "Compliments are…" She tipped her head, sending a cursed lock of hair falling from its pins. "They are not relevant when we have sick horses to care for."

"Or hay to check for mold, I suppose? Come now, Miss Agate. One can look for mold and pay compliments at the same time."

She raised a brow.

He laughed. "All right, maybe not. No compliments, then, Miss Agate. As you wish. Er—am I permitted to be friendly, or ought I to be serious all the time?"

"Can't you be both?" She was beginning to ache, crouching on the floor, and with a wince she straightened up.

"I really don't think I can." With the long-bladed knife, he began to slice at the bale of hay.

"Just be…" She frowned. "I don't know. Just be yourself, Mr. Nathaniel, and we'll do fine."

He turned his head to look up at her, an odd

expression on his features. He looked as though something had clubbed him in the head and he wasn't sure whether or not he needed to fall over.

"I'll try," he said at last, turning his attention back to the hay. "But you don't know what you're asking of me, Miss Agate."

As he sliced at the bale, she located two cakes of salt and tucked them under one arm. Two more animals needed treatment. She was ready.

"Damnation." Behind her, Nathaniel Chandler inhaled deeply. "Ah—sorry about that. Shouldn't speak so before a lady."

"Quite all right. My parents keep a coaching inn, and as a child I heard much worse from drunken customers."

She bit her lip, cutting off further speech. When faced with a pair of twinkling blue eyes and a stable full of horses needing help, she was ready to drop every guard. She needed to be more careful.

And then she realized that he had cursed because he had got a good look at the inside of the bale.

"*Is* the hay moldy?" Dropping the salt blocks, she lunged to his side and grabbed for a handful of hay. Lucerne hay was among the finest types available, its scent pleasantly grassy and tangy when it was clean and well dried.

And this was. "It's perfect. You're not pleased?"

"Of course I'm pleased." He rubbed a hand over his jaw, where thin sunlight caught the golden glint of stubble. "Sort of. It means we still don't know what's wrong with the horses."

"Sir William said it was colic."

"True enough." Rolling to his feet, he extended a

hand to her and pulled her up as well. "But colic is a word that means everything and nothing." From the floor, he picked up the two bricks of salt. "Colic can involve the gut or the lungs or even the hooves. The sort Epigram has can be due to a poison or simply to the horse not drinking enough water."

"A poison," murmured Rosalind. No…surely that was impossible. Aunt Annie had never destroyed anything without first making a plan for Rosalind's departure. "How could someone have poisoned the horses?"

"It wouldn't have to be a poison as we think of it. As something introduced with malice," he said. "It could simply be something that disagrees with horses. Just as oysters should not be eaten during the summer months, but that's not because they wish to hurt people."

So he said. But some people *did* wish to hurt. "Could you tell if someone had intentionally poisoned the horses?"

His dark-gold brows lifted. "I can't decide whether you're the most conscientious secretary my father has ever had or the most suspicious."

"Both, probably."

"Probably." He grinned and tossed a salt brick to Rosalind, who caught it in worry-cold fingers. "I don't think Epigram has eaten something toxic. He didn't have that look, and his belly didn't have that feeling."

"What is the look or the feeling?" She wanted to believe him. She wanted this all to be chance. Coincidence. She wanted to be just a secretary, doing exactly—and only—the work she was expected to complete.

Or a milkmaid, eager and confident. As long as she was wishing.

"I don't know exactly," he admitted. "I just… know them when I see them. You can tell the difference between a person with a rheumy cold and a person with her nose in everyone's business, can you not? Both are disorders of the nose, but they show up differently."

"Hmmm." A question tumbled through her mind, only to fall from her lips a moment later. "Why *did* you check the hay again?"

His lips twisted. "Horse racing is a gentleman's game. It's a house of cards on a foundation of trust."

This she had learned at once in her few weeks as Sir William's secretary. So much of horse racing depended on trust. The trust that a horse was who his owner said, the trust that the jockey would race his best, trust that the odds would pay off and that bookmakers would honor the wagers scribbled in their little notebooks.

Such trust was a luxury for the wealthy. It was far too costly for those who could little afford to lose. At Rosalind's father's inn, travelers paid their expenses in advance.

The block of salt was dry and scaly on her hands. "'Trust Nathaniel,'" she murmured. "You said it in your father's study."

"Exactly," he said. "And I've got to make sure it's a worthy thing to say, even if that means checking something I've checked before. Nothing's too much trouble when the health of a horse depends on it."

He waved a salt brick at her. "You might as well

call me Nathaniel. Since you're going to be trusting me and all that delightful stuff."

"And you may call me Rosalind," she said. *Trust Rosalind*, she wanted to add in echo of Nathaniel's phrase.

But the letter hidden in her bodice poked her through her shift, and she dared not say another word.

Three

"NATHANIEL. YOU'RE DIRTY AGAIN."

At Sir William's words, Rosalind looked up from the dazzling array of cutlery surrounding her dinner plate.

Nathaniel had just entered the dining parlor, a gray-walled room as sprawling and unadorned as Sir William's study. Nathaniel had exchanged his travel-worn clothes for elegant dinner garments, but his cream-colored waistcoat was splotched dark.

"Wet, rather. Sorry about that," he said easily as he pulled forth his chair. "Could have changed my attire again, but I didn't want to be late for dinner."

"Did you encounter another milkmaid?" Rosalind could not resist asking.

"Naturally." He seated himself facing her across the broad table, which was covered with a cloth starched to such stiffness it could probably stand on end.

Sir William served himself a heap of boiled asparagus over toast. "In the house? I long to hear this tale."

"She upset the water pump in the bathing room to get my attention. So that would make her a water maid, I suppose."

"A nymph?" Rosalind suggested. "A naiad?"

Nathaniel snapped his fingers. "The very creature. You've seen her too, then."

"No wine for Nathaniel," grunted Sir William when the footman approached to fill his glass. "He is hallucinating."

"Oh, surely a *little* wine for Nathaniel," his son replied. "Half an inch?" He took the bottle from the footman and sloshed a careless amount into the goblet.

Sir William frowned but held his peace. "Miss Agate was just about to tell me what the pair of you thought of Pale Marauder's condition."

Was she? She had thought she was trying to pick the right fork. A girl raised in a coaching inn with a tavern was used to one size of fork for everything, and in her posts as governess for various households she'd never dined in company with the family.

"You can tell us about Sheltie too, if you had time to check on her," added Sir William.

Nathaniel's easy grin slipped. "Tell you. The two of you. Right. Sheltie has little strength, but I did get her to take some water. This was after you returned to the study, Miss Agate."

Yet he did not look at Rosalind. He regarded his father with lowered chin and unblinking eyes. Almost as though he were daring the baronet to take issue.

This was not the first time Rosalind had seen tension flicker between father and son. Why was this? Of Sir William's four grown offspring, Nathaniel was the only one who ever lived at Chandler Hall. Yet the two men were wary with each other. Like two horses that weren't sure whether they were supposed to pull in tandem or race one another.

And there was no trainer for them. There was only Rosalind.

So she broke the weighty pause by picking up the stack of papers that had accompanied her almost everywhere within Chandler Hall—yes, even to meals—since the horses developed colic. Setting the stack down again with a flamboyant shuffle, she said, "You asked about Pale Marauder, Sir William. Your son's treatment of the horse was like that of an experienced nanny with a misbehaving child. I could have watched them for hours." She deepened her tone. "'Now, then, my boy, you're causing too much trouble. You need a bit of a walk. No, no biting. No kicking either.'"

Nathaniel coughed. "Is that *really* what I sound like? All froggy and odd?"

Rosalind waved a hand. "Close enough. What matters is you got that horse to obey you." Pale Marauder was the most fractious of Sir William's colts, as quick-tempered as he was curious.

"So you got him to walk." Sir William served some roasted beef from a platter in front of his plate. "Good. Jubal prodded Epigram into a walk as well. And Miss Agate has begun another search through records related to the ill horses." He indicated the pile of papers atop the snowy tablecloth, his expression grim. "This time, we seek to discover which servants cared for Epigram, Pale Marauder, and Sheltie before they took sick."

"We," sighed Nathaniel. Or maybe that was *oui*,

and he was speaking French. Rosalind regarded him, puzzled.

He met her gaze after a moment, and his devil-may-care grin was back in place. "Miss Agate," added Nathaniel, "I note that your appearance suffered no ill effects from the time in the stable. Which is *not* intended as a compliment."

Time in the stable. That was one way of describing slipping to one's knees in used straw when one tried to put a halter on that stubborn Pale Marauder. Or coaxing that irritable colt from his stall with carrots and a half-remembered drinking song.

"I possess remarkable gifts," said Rosalind. "One of which is to change my clothing before dinner."

The spacious bathing room, with its piped hot and cold water, was a luxury at which Rosalind thought she would never cease to marvel. And yes, all right, she had washed her limbs and neck and face and tidied her hair when she changed her clothing. The dark-blue gown she now wore was her favorite. Though the style was plain, the fabric held a silky sheen that hinted at its original use in a much wealthier woman's garment.

Sir William beheaded a stalk of asparagus. "Doesn't anyone want to praise me? I was in the stable too, and I managed to get myself tidy before dinner, even though the pump mechanism in the bathing room was upset again. *Honestly.* Let's all give ourselves a medal."

Rosalind coughed to cover a laugh. "I'd love a gold one."

"Make mine of lead. Like plumbing." Nathaniel gestured toward the baronet with his fork. "Which reminds me, Father, that the pump is working again. You'll get as much hot water as you wish."

Aha. This must be the true cause of the supposed naiad's splashes on his waistcoat. Rosalind had been wondering what the imaginary milkmaids across England represented. With no small sense of relief, she decided that they too were repairs and complications.

Not that it mattered if Nathaniel Chandler was regularly waylaid by lustful milkmaids. Or if he entertained a kept woman in every town.

In fact, it was better if he did, because then it would be easier for Rosalind to keep her head. The more she allowed herself to like him—and his father, of course, and the house and her work and the stable full of horses—the more she would hurt when she inevitably left.

And she already bore so many scars. She would rather not collect another, even if it were hidden within.

As Nathaniel began some carefully polite thread of conversation with his father, she noticed that his glass of wine had been left untouched.

∾

Nathaniel had not remembered Rosalind Agate being so pretty. Now the realization was becoming rather distracting.

It wasn't the sort of prettiness that came from some detail of form or feature or fashion. No, it was more that she was…*bright*, somehow. Her smile teased out his own, and even that of his gruff father. Her eyes were green, even in this giant candlelit cell of a room, and with a noticing look to them. He had the feeling everything that went into her eyes and ears stayed within her brain.

Maybe this was why noblemen usually kept male secretaries: so when their sons came home from a journey, unshaven and dirty, there were no lovely, noticing eyes in front of which to look like a fool.

He regretted the splash of water that had marred his waistcoat, but there was nothing to do about it now. Finishing some anecdote about his latest trip to London, he added, "You might be imagining, Miss Agate"—at table they must be formal again—"that since horse racing is the sport of kings, I dine with dukes and marquesses all the time."

"I was hoping you dined with the king and the Prince Regent, actually. Now you have left me disappointed." There was that smile again.

"If you dined with the Prince Regent," Nathaniel said, "you *would* be disappointed. The man has no more manners than…"

"Pale Marauder," suggested Sir William.

"Exactly. Anyway. When I'm in London, I often buy a meat pie off a street vendor and get on with business. And the grooms and stewards and others in the business of buying and selling horses are the same way."

Though Nathaniel had dressed today for dinner in Hoby's and Weston's finest, in a cravat whiter and stiffer than meringue, he found the habits of the gentry more difficult to don. Only a highly leisured class could afford to waste time or money on the preparation of food no one would eat.

At this table, no one had yet touched the clear soup.

Or the salad of spring greens. Or the boiled chicken with cauliflower, or the sliced jellied tongue.

This space could not have been more different from the one in which the Chandler family had dined throughout his childhood. That dining room had been warm, full of the tasty scents of freshly cooked meat and pickle and bread. Sir William had been striding about then—and actually, he hadn't even been *sir* yet. Mrs. Chandler had been alive; Nathaniel's elder brother, Jonah, had smiled sometimes; sister Abigail thought herself blissfully in love with one swain after another; and little Hannah clambered from lap to lap. The room had been too small for six people and a serving maid, so the red-walled space always roiled with people popping up and down from chairs, fetching this and that.

Here, a footman entered with another platter, each step of his shining shoes echoing over the stone floor. As he set down the dish, Nathaniel requested tea in place of wine. "Well, enough about my sad lack of dinners with the Prince Regent. Father, how did Epigram go on after I left his stall? You said he walked?"

Sir William sawed at his roast beef. "He did, and had a massive evacuation. Cheered him right up. It cheered Sir Jubal too, to see his horse lifting its head again."

Rosalind looked up from the papers she had begun reviewing. "That is excellent. I am sure Epigram's condition will improve rapidly."

"It needs to, for I've promised Jubal a victory. Only Smolensko has won both the Two Thousand Guineas and the Derby Stakes, and Sir Jubal is determined Epigram shall be the second double champion." With his knife, the baronet counted the sawed-off bites of beef, then pushed aside the rest on his plate. "For my part, I'm determined his faith in us won't be misplaced."

In us. In Epigram and Sir William?

This was as good a time as any to shoulder himself into that company. "May I hand you any dishes, Father?"

The heavy gray head looked up. "Hmm? Oh—yes, the soup."

Nathaniel rose to slide the porcelain tureen within reach of his father, then took a deep breath as he seated himself again. "So if the horses seem to be recovering, we might begin to speak about how they'll get to Epsom."

"Sothern always takes them." Sir William eyed the ladle, then served out a bit more soup.

"But Sothern is on his way to the stud farm. With the new broodmare."

Sir William dropped the ladle back into the tureen with a *clack*. "He can be recalled."

"Or. Well. I rather thought"—Nathaniel thanked the footman for the teapot and cup the servant set beside his plate—"that I could take them."

He didn't breathe while Sir William swallowed three deliberate spoonfuls of soup. "No need for that," the baronet finally decided. "I shall find someone else. Jonah, maybe."

"With a new horse to care for? He won't want to go. Father, really—I travel to London more often than the Royal Mail. I think I can make it a bit farther to Epsom."

"Bart might be able to go." This was Sir Bartlett

Crosby, the new husband of Nathaniel's younger sister, Hannah. "He and Hannah could—"

"Father, Hannah is with child. She cannot make the journey. And Bart has his own estate to manage." He considered his next words carefully. Pausing. Laying hold of his teacup. When he poured out tea, steam rose in the cold air. "I can do this, Father. I know you would not deny me simply because this is not the way things have been done in the past."

"True. So I'll simply say no." Sir William counted bites of vegetables before forking up two more. Thus it had been for thirteen years: the baronet's every bite and drink measured in an attempt to return his body to his control. "Nathaniel, you are good at—at the sort of thing you are good at."

"High praise," his son muttered. Shooting a glance at Rosalind Agate, he found her absorbed in her papers. Lifting a glass of wine to her lips as she turned a page.

He traced the swallow of it, the movement of her smooth throat, the way her tongue touched her lips to catch a leftover drop. How delicious it looked, and not only the wine.

He poured out a cup of tea and took a cautious sip. It was not what he wanted, but he drank it all the same.

"Surely you understand." Sir William set down his fork. "You're a flirt. A—a charmer of milkmaids. You have an easy manner that wins people over."

Across the table, Rosalind made a choking sound and avoided his gaze.

"Again with the high praise," Nathaniel said. "I feel a blush coming on."

"It is praise in a way. It's good at a horse sale or in a tavern. It's not right for a trip of this seriousness when anything might happen. Our family's reputation is at stake."

Well, hell. Hoist with his own petard—was that the phrase? For years, he'd tried to earn Sir William's trust by painting his every journey as effortless. And it had worked for a while, allowing those journeys to spin out longer and longer, covering much of England.

"I'm sure I can cope with whatever arises," Nathaniel said. "I fixed the pump in the bathing room, you know."

"Ah—yes, all right. Thank you. But there won't be any bathing rooms along the road."

"Then I'll fix chamber pots and cisterns. And I'm extremely serious-minded. Or I can be. Hypotenuse? Philosophy? Er…a little help, Miss Agate."

She looked up from her papers, a frown of concentration creasing her brows. "Iron gall ink. Penny post. Budget. Stitchery."

"My thoughts exactly. See, Father? *So* serious."

Sir William shook his head. "Also serious? Colic. I can't risk further endangering the health of these horses." He rubbed at his chin in thought. "Perhaps if trusted servants went with you. Miss Agate could—"

"Oh no, Sir William." She sat upright, eyes wide. "I could not dream of leaving my work. I am sure Mr. Nathaniel will do quite well on his own."

"Hannah could take your place as secretary for the time you are gone." The baronet mulled over the idea. "That might work. You know my preferences,

Miss Agate, and you could see that they are respected during the course of travel."

Astounding how much a casual remark could hurt. Surely Nathaniel ought to know his preferences too, having been Sir William's son for twenty-eight years.

But this trip to Epsom would, Nathaniel hoped, be enough to blow a hole in the wall between them. It would be a grand gesture of competence, a way to say, *See, I can be trusted! I am not the same terrible person I was at fifteen!*

"Trust Nathaniel," he murmured, catching Rosalind's eye.

A knock sounded at the dining room door.

"Enter," Sir William called. Was Nathaniel imagining it, or did his father sound relieved by the distraction?

The handle turned to reveal a groom, hat in hand, boots anxiously shuffling. "I beg your pardon, Sir William, but you said to tell you at once if anything changed in the stables. And another horse is down with the colic."

A dreadful silence blanketed the room.

"But how—" Rosalind shuffled madly through the papers beside her plate. "The hay…we know it cannot be."

"No, it's not the hay," Nathaniel said. "Or the grain or the salt. There is no problem with anything the horses have eaten."

"There's no problem with it by chance or accident." Sir William shut his eyes. "Someone must be tampering with the stables."

Four

THE FOLLOWING MORNING, ROSALIND CUT ACROSS the grounds from house to stable, ignoring the tidy angles outlined by Sir William's crushed stone paths.

I'm tracing the hypotenuse, she realized as her feet slipped over neatly trimmed grass, green and full from spring rains. She could thank her last position as a governess for that bit of geometry. Nathaniel's "serious" subjects of yesterday's dinner had brought it to mind again.

In preparing for each of her posts, she had tipped a slurry of random knowledge into her head. Her current post as Sir William's secretary was the best of them all, or it had been as long as she could pretend it was what it seemed. That her letters to Aunt Annie were just the correspondence of a young woman to her curious benefactress, and that her real work was organizing Sir William's papers and occasionally venturing where his wheelchair could not.

The sick horses were a sign that those days of pretending were over. Rosalind had tossed and fidgeted for hours, waiting for sleep to cover over that knowledge. She had no idea what would come next.

Her strides grew faster, as though she could slip ahead of this thought, until she finished crossing the grounds at a run.

Nathaniel Chandler was already waiting at the stable door, swinging a silver watch at the end of a fob. He grinned. "Rosalind Agate, three minutes past the hour. Tut-tut. No gold medal for you."

She bent over, tried to catch her breath. The ropy scars on her back tugged, a sharp physical reminder to pull herself together.

Wincing, she straightened. "It was a gift to you. I suspected my slight lateness would allow you to win a medal instead, which would put you in a marvelous mood."

"Indeed not, for it deprived me of your company." His blue eyes crinkled as he stuffed the watch back into the pocket of his nut-brown waistcoat, trim and practical with a dark coat and snug buckskin breeches. "Or was that too much like a compliment? Forget it. Go away and be even later."

"And cause the horses to wait? For shame, sir. If we don't go in together, we cannot go in at all."

Sir William had decided on this security measure the previous evening, after returning to the stable to examine the fourth animal with colic. Until the cause was identified, he stated, no one was to be alone in the stables. Anyone who wished to enter was to find someone else with whom to keep company.

When they returned to the house, Nathaniel Chandler had requested the aid of Miss Agate the following morning. Sir William, of course, agreed. He seemed to trust his secretary implicitly, a realization that came buttoned to a pang of guilt for Rosalind.

"Then in we go." Nathaniel slid one of the great doors to the side, nodding a greeting to the pair of stable boys who stood on indolent watch within the building. "I shall ask you to carry far more than buckets today."

"Because I am being punished?"

"Should you be? Have you done something scandalous?" He shot Rosalind an odd look. "Actually, it's because you said you wanted to help."

She had to shake off the cobwebby remains of her nighttime worries. "Right, yes. Of course. I—yes, I shall do it."

"So agreeable." Another odd look, this time with a knowing smile. "You probably want a bucket of coffee right now, do you not? I know that expression well. You passed a sleepless night, and not the pleasurable sort."

That comment woke her up. "I'm all right." She tried to smile. "Which animal first?"

He blinked down at her, as though deciding whether to press the matter—then let it drop. "Pale Marauder. He will need the least attention, I believe."

After retrieving the now-customary bucket of warm water and cake of salt, they made their way to the cream-colored Thoroughbred's stall. Sir William's stables were made up of linked, winding rows, all constructed for the ease of their owner's navigation in his wheelchair. Everything was the most modern, the most costly, the widest and largest and smoothest and finest.

The scent of horses—that unmistakable combination

of hay and dust and sweat—drew Rosalind back to the stables at the Eight Bells, though she hadn't seen them for almost ten years. Her parents' inn was cramped in comparison to Chandler Hall, and the stables were built on the same slight lines. Five stalls could have fit in the space two of Sir William's stalls occupied, and they never drained quite right. But if sweeping could clean a floor of packed dirt and straw, that one was made clean. New animals arrived at every hour of the day and night, and there was always someone to see to their needs and those of the people who brought them in. Her father had sometimes joked that he'd needed a large family so his children could serve as his staff.

Maybe it hadn't been a joke at that. But he had always smiled when he said it.

Pale Marauder was as little like the job horses for which Rosalind had once cared as the royal princesses were like Rosalind herself. Sinewy and tall, the colt had fine bones that spoke of generations of breeding for speed.

He also had a fragile temper, as the talented and coddled often did. Today the colt laid back his ears at the sight of them.

"Don't be a brat, Roddy." Nathaniel unlatched the stall door. "Come on, boy. You know us."

"He knows *you*," Rosalind corrected. "He must not remember me. Or he didn't like my song for him yesterday. I'll wait out here until you get the halter on."

"Cowardly?" Nathaniel tossed back with a smile.

"Prudent," Rosalind replied.

"He's all right." Nathaniel approached the horse slowly, voice calm and low. "If he felt worse, he would be listless. I think his temper is a sign he's recovering. He might even be hungry. I see he kicked a dent in his feed bucket."

"I certainly get in a temper when I haven't been fed."

"Yet he still has some hay." At the horse's side now, where a stray hoof could not catch him, Nathaniel laid a hand on the colt's coat. "You're hungry, aren't you? Look, silly fellow. You have food right before you."

The horse's flattened ears pricked up at the sound of this soothing voice. With Nathaniel nudging him forward, he deigned to take a mouthful of hay.

"He likes your company," Rosalind said. "He must have been lonely."

"Maybe he was at that. I might be in a temper too, if I were three years old and sick and left alone all night."

If you only knew. "I could feel that way at far more than three years old."

"Let's see if we can get him to walk again. That will help him to feel more like himself." He looked around. "Which would be much easier if we had a halter. Which we don't. Will you fetch one?"

"Can I, while following your father's instructions? We wouldn't be together."

"Oh. You're right." He gnawed at his lip. "All right, take this handful of hay and hold it out to him. Walk back to the tack room, and with any luck he'll follow you. Sing that drinking song again—the one you thought I didn't hear yesterday."

"You have the ears of a bat." She filled her fists with sweet-smelling lucerne. "And what will you do?"

"I'll follow him."

Had anyone been present to observe, they would surely have laughed at the spectacle thus made: a young woman in a capacious gown of riding-habit green, singing a bawdy song as she walked backward, her outstretched hands full of hay. A colt, dancing on light hooves and stretching out its fine head. At its side, Nathaniel keeping a hand on the horse's withers and a stream of half-overheard chatter in its ear.

"That's right, she's a chestnut. Chestnut hair. You like chestnuts, don't you? You've met chestnuts before. Be calm, now, Roddy my boy. Just follow…follow. You'll get the hay soon enough. Almost there."

The colt snapped his teeth, catching some of the hay a mere inch from Rosalind's fingers. She bit back a yelp. "I *am* being punished," she muttered. "You denied it, but I know it's so."

"Oh, I don't think I denied it," Nathaniel said with a cheeky grin. "I just reminded you that you wanted to help. Ah, look! Here we are at the tack room, and I am sure this fine pair of stable boys would be glad to fetch Pale Marauder a halter and take him for a bit of exercise."

As he explained to the youths what he intended for the care of the horse, Rosalind found herself…confused.

As Nathaniel had guessed, she had slept badly the night before, her mind turning over the surprising events of the day. What did it mean, so many sick horses all at once? What to do next? She'd had no letters from Aunt Annie in a week. Now she might be sent to Epsom, entirely the wrong part of the country—unless she could convince Sir William that Nathaniel ought to travel without her company.

Should she fight to stay? How hard could she fight

without arousing suspicion? Or ought she to go, if the information she was meant to find had to do with the horses themselves? *Whatever you can find from Spain, 1805.* Aunt Annie never gave much guidance as Anweledig, but this latest instruction was more vague even than usual.

Nathaniel finished his conversation with the stable boys, then returned to Rosalind with his fine mouth pulled into a grim line. "Epigram is in better health today, but Jake is bad off."

"Jake?" For a moment, Rosalind thought he meant one of the stable boys, but then she understood. "Oh no. He's one of the sweetest creatures in the stable."

"Indeed he is." Beckoning Rosalind to follow, Nathaniel retrieved their salt and bucket from Pale Marauder's stall. "My father and a groom are with Jake now, so you and I can check on Sheltie."

"But you were a help to Epigram yesterday. Would you not like to see Jake?" The memory of the gelding's curious muzzle poking over the stall door, friendly and puppy-like, gave her a pang.

"My father would rather handle the horse's care himself. I'm sure you noticed yesterday that he doesn't welcome my help." He hoisted the filled bucket and held out a hand for the salt.

"In Epigram's stall?" At his nod, she said, "It wasn't the help with Epigram he minded. He was upset when you moved his chair."

Nathaniel dropped the block of salt onto his booted foot. "I beg your pardon?"

Shuffling her feet in the straw bedding of Pale Marauder's stall, she folded her arms across her chest.

Her scarred right elbow protested the angle. "You did not ask before rolling his chair. For you, it would be as if…" She struggled for a comparison. "As if someone picked you up from behind without asking whether you wanted to be lifted."

Without removing his gaze from her face, Nathaniel bent to fumble for the brick of salt. "He did not like being helped?"

"In that way, I think not. He knows best how to move his own chair."

She paused, then decided against saying more. It seemed odd that Nathaniel would not know such a thing about his own father. But maybe it was Rosalind's own understanding that was odd, born of her long recovery from the burns that had nearly taken her life. She had been so helpless for so long that she was determined never to be again.

When she met Sir William, she had, of habit, rubbed at her scarred elbow before taking up a quill. He had recognized the signs of an old injury, had commented on it. She wondered whether that was the reason he had hired her.

It certainly wasn't because of her illustrious references, because for once Aunt Annie's forger had failed to deliver a product on time. Rosalind had come to Chandler Hall with no references at all—which she didn't altogether mind. She had used false names for past posts, serving as governesses named Davis and Hall and Burdock, but this time she could go under her own name.

By the time Rosalind met Lady Crosby—Sir William's younger daughter Hannah, who had been his secretary before she married—her employment had been secured. All Sir William had asked of Hannah was that she give Rosalind a bit of instruction, since the man who had preceded Rosalind had hared off in a flurry of incompetence and temper.

No, she said none of this to Nathaniel, keeping a safe silence instead.

"You must think me an incredible arse," murmured Nathaniel at last.

Again, she declined to reply. *You meant well* was perfectly true, but she had never found the phrase to be comforting.

He straightened up, handing the salt block back to Rosalind. It felt heavier than before, as though she now held the burden of all their unasked questions.

He asked just one. "But what kind of arse would I be if I could help my father and I did not?"

His expression was troubled, and she sensed he referred to much more than the rolling of his father's wheelchair.

"I cannot say." She exited the stall. "Maybe just a different sort of arse. Maybe not an arse at all, if he wanted the help."

He followed before latching the stall door behind them both. "Well, there's no point to discussing it further. Come, let's see how Sheltie does today."

❧

Before encountering Sheltie, Rosalind had never been close to a Shetland pony, though she'd had girlhood dreams of riding one around a village fete with a crown of flowers in her hair. Because it was too small to work, a pony seemed a living luxury to one who saw job horses rented out like the rooms at her father's inn.

There was no luxury surrounding Sheltie today, though. "She usually shares a stall with any animal that needs calming," explained Nathaniel as he knelt in the straw piled as padding over the stone floor of a storage room. "With the stable full of Derby horses, well…"

"There's no room for her to have her own stall."

Not that the pony seemed aware of her undignified surroundings. Her little barrel of a body, all shaggy splatters of brown and white, lay prone as only a horse in the deepest slumber could rest. The long-lashed eyes were closed.

Without thinking, Rosalind sank to her knees beside the pony and tucked a hip against the swayback of the elderly creature. The pony's eyes blinked, showing deep brown irises, and her ears flicked forward.

"She doesn't seem to be in pain," Rosalind said.

"She doesn't anymore," agreed Nathaniel. "Thank God for that. Before you arrived, I got a quick report from a stable boy. Sheltie was up all night rolling and twisting as though her intestines were hurting her. This peaceful sleep is a good sign." He sat down by the little animal's head. "So is her movement. Look."

Eyes now half-open, the pony was shifting to press closer to Rosalind. "She's herding me." A smile spread across her features.

"She's comforting you. You're part of her stable now."

The simple sincerity of his words, of the pony's actions, made her heart squeeze. Rubbing her fingers over the salt brick, she reached over Sheltie's large head to dab salt on the pony's muzzle. "She's so small." Unlike the leggy Thoroughbreds, the pony had short and sturdy limbs. Would she reach Rosalind's waist? She would be a bit taller, maybe.

"Poor old girl." Nathaniel, seated by Sheltie's head, dribbled water over the pony's mouth. "You're tired, aren't you? You passed a bad night."

For a moment, Rosalind thought he was speaking to her. Then Sheltie sighed and put forth her tongue to catch the drops.

"Good girl." More water. "Wait, Rosalind—no more salt just yet. Let's see how much water she'll take first."

Rosalind searched for something helpful to do. "Would she like to be groomed?"

"I'm sure she would."

Rosalind found a currycomb and returned to her spot behind the pony's withers. She began with the mane, teasing tangles and straw from the coarse chestnut hair. It was almost the same color as Rosalind's own. *Chestnut*, Nathaniel had called her to Pale Marauder. "How old is Sheltie?"

"She's at least twenty years old. She's been trotting in and out of Chandler stalls since I was a boy."

The image made her smile. "Like a hound."

"In a way. Some stables keep dogs or goats. We keep Sheltie. She's steady enough to calm any nervous horse. The Thoroughbreds like having her around." *Drop. Drop.* More water. "My younger sister and I used to find our way to Sheltie's side too. Hannah, now Lady Crosby—you've met her. She was only ten when our mother died. The months after that were…"

"Difficult," suggested Rosalind.

"Yes. Very." The light was low in this corner of the stable, and Rosalind couldn't read the expression on Nathaniel's face. "If I couldn't find Hannah in the house, I'd always look for her in the stable. Once I found her asleep in a pile of hay she had pitched down from the hayloft. Sheltie was standing right next to her. Not eating the hay; just keeping vigil."

The simple memory, sweet and everyday, stood in contrast to the Eight Bells. Horses there were for working, not affection. Rosalind had never had the opportunity to love an animal as much as the Chandler children loved Sheltie.

But instead, the Agates had a mother and father to give them love. Busy though her parents had been, they smiled. They gave hugs. They did their best.

Nathaniel had gone silent for a moment. "Well, now you know a great deal more than you wanted to, I'd guess. You have the sort of face people want to talk to, Rosalind Agate."

She looked up, a blush heating her cheeks. "What sort of face is that?"

"What I just said. It's the…" His hands flailed shapes in the air, then settled. "Devil take it, I don't know. You look as though you don't mind listening."

"I don't. Though I hoped you'd say it was my charm or persuasive ability or something like that."

"No compliments, remember?"

The treacherous blush deepened. "No *false* ones," Rosalind said primly.

Slowly, his gaze swept over her from top to toe, from unpinned hair to her folded-up legs beside the back of the drowsy pony. "In that case," he said, "I like telling you things."

It was both less and more than what she had hoped for, and all she could say was, "Oh."

Then a memory made him smile. "Hannah was only six years old when we got Sheltie as a yearling. She's the one who named her." He chuckled. "Naming a pony 'Sheltie' is like naming a hound 'Doggie.' But how can one correct a six-year-old who thinks everything has to have a literal name?"

"You could have called your sister 'Girl,'" Rosalind suggested.

"I'm sure I called her a lot more than that."

"I can imagine. I don't think there's a single name I haven't been called—or called one of my brothers or my sister."

"Brothers, plural? How many Agates are there in the world?"

"I'm one of nine children." Idly, she plaited a section of the pony's mane.

"A crowded household. And you grew up in a coaching inn, you've mentioned?"

"Not *grew up*, exactly. I haven't lived at home for a decade, since I was thirteen." The pony's coarse mane slipped through her fingers, the plait unraveling at once. She had once found talking about her family a comfort, but it was never wise to reveal too much. And now those memories were so old they'd gone gray and indistinct.

But she supposed she liked telling Nathaniel things too, even though—or because—she'd been trained for the past decade to be ever alone.

Distraction. That was what she needed. She would help; she'd find something that would help the pony drink more rapidly.

She pushed herself upright, biting her lip against the usual tiny tugs and aches across her back. Nathaniel handed her the currycomb, which she replaced where she had found it—both conscientious, they were— then skimmed the storage shelves for something useful. A dented funnel? That might do.

Resuming her place, she tried dipping the funnel and stopping its stem with her thumb. She had no desire to feed her thumb to a pony, though. Somehow she managed to slip it away and let the water dribble into Sheltie's mouth.

"I could say the same," Nathaniel spoke up. "As what you said when we came into the stables."

Rosalind squinted at him, trying to remember. "What, that you…ah…called your siblings all sorts of things?"

He snorted. "That I am being punished."

"Oh. No, I was joking." Turning toward the bucket, she hid her face as she dipped up more water. "A secretary's job is not all organizing papers and sharpening quills—at least, not if one is Sir William's secretary. I'm glad to spend so much time in the stables."

"Yes, but do you expect to watch over a grown man?"

"It's not what I'm accustomed to, though I *was* formerly governess to an earl's children."

"And now you're being asked to govern me." He sighed. "I need your help. I need you to come to Epsom with me, because I have the distinct feeling that's the only way my father will agree to hand the horses into my keeping."

So he too had noted that Sir William's confidence lay in unexpected places. It made her uneasy, as did the idea of leaving Newmarket without permission from Aunt Annie. So instead she seized upon a young woman's most hackneyed excuse. "It would be improper for us to be alone on the journey to Epsom, wouldn't it? Surely it must take days."

He laughed. "Is that what's worrying you? We wouldn't be alone at all. There are outriders and grooms and—oh, you could even take along a lady's maid for propriety's sake."

"I don't have a lady's maid."

"Well, a footman, then. Whatever sort of company would make you feel that your virtue wasn't in danger."

She dipped some more water, mulling over his staccato suggestions. "You speak as though you don't even consider me female."

Now, why had she said that? It was an invitation for him to look at her—the sort of thing Anweledig's agent, slipping in and out of different posts, ought to discourage.

Water rippled in the bucket, turning her reflection into a dizzy spiral. When she looked up, Nathaniel was gazing at her.

Just as she had feared. But she was not afraid, even as he traced her, line and angle and curve, with his shadowed blue gaze. She could almost feel it drifting over her like a whisper over skin. Her stomach gave a little flip; her hands became unsteady.

"I suppose," he replied at last, "I have been trying not to think about it."

"Why should you try to—not to…" She stumbled over the words, her tongue shy. Unable to say *think of me as a woman.* Everyday words, but somehow very personal ones.

"Don't you think that's wise? A man who travels England and meets milkmaids everywhere he goes?" The corners of his mouth turned up.

"All well and good, but you have no idea of the sort of people *I've* met." Her voice was husky, a little breathless.

"How you rouse my curiosity." He looked around the secluded corner. "I should have been more attentive to the demands of propriety. I should be thinking of that even now. If we were hanging about the *ton,* they'd consider us unchaperoned. Your reputation would suffer."

"Anyone who could manage impropriety beside a colicky pony is more determined than I am."

He grinned. "Well put. This is hardly a spot for seduction."

Now, why had *he* said that? Because once he said the word, her thoughts took wing. Where *could* one pursue a seduction, if one were perfect and unmarred and blithe? Ought it to be in a bed draped with silks? On the velvet squabs of a bespoke carriage? Would there be perfume and rose petals?

Curled against Rosalind, Sheltie took another drink, then let out a low animal sigh—and a shuddering burst of flatulence.

Such was always the fate of rose-petal dreams, was it not? Rosalind had to smile.

Five

WHEN SHELTIE AGAIN FELL INTO A PEACEFUL DOZE, Nathaniel called an end to the morning's work in the stables. Though Rosalind hadn't mentioned the passage of time, he knew she still had to complete her usual tasks in the study.

"I am the one with the watch"—he made a show of pulling it from the pocket of his old brown waistcoat—"so it must be up to me to dismiss us. Shall we meet again at three o'clock? You, me, bucket, salt, Sheltie: we make a formidable team."

"Don't forget the currycomb," she added. "Yes, all right. As long as I am back in the study when it's time for brandy."

Sir William's brandy. One of the only rituals that had changed over the past thirteen years. He used to take it after dinner; now he took it before. Nathaniel couldn't argue with that. He would be fortifying himself all day, if—if only he could trust himself to *be* himself.

He helped Rosalind to her feet. Then, following Sir William's edict to the letter, Nathaniel and Rosalind found a pair of grooms, and as a foursome they walked to the exit.

Rosalind began to slice an angle across the grounds. Then—with a glance back over her shoulder—she hopped onto one of the smooth stone paths instead.

Nathaniel stood in the doorway to the stable and watched her get smaller, though somehow she still loomed large for him.

Not for the grooms, though. They took advantage of this interlude to slouch against the wall and gossip. "They've been eating sand, them sick horses," said Peters, a large red-haired man. "I've seen the signs before, and that's a fact. There's no kind of colic that looks like a sand colic."

"Sand colic, pah." Lombard, who always chewed at a straw, spit on the stable floor. "Where'ud they get sand? This ain't a desert."

"And it cannot be in the hay," murmured Nathaniel. "Miss Agate and I checked it ourselves." Rosalind was dark and spare against the white crushed stone of the path. In another moment, she would be out of sight.

He turned to face the grooms. They both snapped to attention, uncle and nephew. Lombard's gulp and grimace was a sign that the grizzled older man had been about to spit again.

Grooms were as gossipy as old maids, and these two had served the Chandlers for long years. "What are the other grooms saying about this run of illness?" Nathaniel asked.

Lombard rolled his straw from one side of his mouth to the other. "Some were sayin' it was moldy hay."

If Nathaniel had been closer to the wall, he would have beaten his head against it.

"But it ain't the hay. No, and it ain't sand neither." The wiry man elbowed his large nephew, who looked as though he wanted to speak up. "If you're askin' me, Sir William was right to keep a closer eye on this place. Can't be too careful durin' race season."

"So you think someone poisoned the horses."

"Could be." Lombard's shrug was as elaborate as a ballet. "Time was I'd a-blamed the Crosbys. But with Miss Hannah married to one—nah, they wouldn't hurt their kin. It could be anyone else though. Plenty of people don't want Sir Jubal to be winnin' two classics in the same year." He spit again, then wiped his mouth with a muttered apology to Nathaniel.

Nathaniel nodded. "Such as?"

"The Two Thousand Guineas and the Derby," piped up Peters.

Spit. "Not the races, you clod." Lombard spoke with affection. "I mean the bookmakers, o'course, Mr. Nathaniel. The whole lot of 'em don't have the conscience of a snake."

"Bookmakers," Nathaniel repeated. They could be ruthless, with their livelihoods at stake as odds tipped and tilted from horse to horse. But why would they bother to hurt Sheltie and Jake, who had never raced in their lives?

Lombard ventured a comforting clap on Nathaniel's shoulder, though the slight groom had to reach up to do it. "Don't you be worryin', Mr. Nathaniel. I've worked for your father longer'n you've been alive, and there ain't no problem yet he han't solved."

When, though? And what would the answer be?

Even if Sir William's new strategy for protecting the stable worked, that still meant that someone had intended to harm the horses. Would they recover? The pride-puffing opportunity to guide and train a double champion might already be destroyed.

The grooms' chatter was just speculation; they had no more answers than Nathaniel himself. But just in case, he told them, "Come to see me—the pair of you together—if you find out anything more definite."

When he left the stable, spring sunlight made him squint. A breeze teased and rumpled his hair. He felt as if he had exited a cave, his system shocked by the reminder that there was such a thing as daylight.

The shaded moments he had just spent sitting with Rosalind Agate in a corner of the stable, dribbling water into the mouth of a tired pony, were some of the most pleasant he had experienced since leaving London.

Rosalind did what needed to be done. She helped. She even smiled, even laughed.

When she did, it was difficult to remember that she was Sir William's secretary. Sir William's choice, trusted above Nathaniel. What was he to make of her? How could he get her to agree to journey to Epsom? What did she want?

She had a way of diverting his questions with quips. He knew that she had been raised in a coaching inn, that she'd been governess to an earl. But what were the steps in between, or the ones that led from the earl to Sir William?

Again, he had nothing but questions. And he

couldn't ask his father; it would be unwise to bring up Epsom before the arrangements were completed. Otherwise, Sir William might decide to make his own plans. Plans with no place for Nathaniel in them at all.

But Hannah might know the answers. Nathaniel's younger sister had met Rosalind before she was hired.

Until three o'clock, Nathaniel's time was his own. So he decided to take a walk.

◈

No one in Newmarket lived far from the racecourses, which meant none of the horse-mad members of the Jockey Club were far from each other either. The Crosby estate was no more than an easy ride or a mildly strenuous walk from Chandler Hall, yet Nathaniel could count on one hand the number of times he had ventured onto Crosby land.

Over the span of a few generations, the Crosbys and Chandlers had developed a proud tradition of detesting one another. They hired away stable staff and jockeys; they bet against each other and bribed and undermined the other family's success on the racecourse. No one was sure how the rivalry had started, but all good Chandler children had been raised to hate the Crosbys.

With her marriage to Sir Bartlett Crosby the year before, Hannah had been a very bad Chandler indeed.

Though her new home hardly appeared that of a gothic monster. The brick pile of the Crosby home was worn and archaic compared to Chandler Hall's shining modernity, but it had the elegance of a home that had been loved and built onto over generations.

Sir Bartlett's mother had been a slave to the betting book, and to pay off family debts, the young baronet had sold almost everything—except his best horses. Hannah had brought a generous dowry to their marriage, and she had replaced the household staff and begun to furnish the house anew. As Nathaniel was shown into the drawing room, he saw that his favorite sister had worked a small miracle in the weeks since he had last visited.

Gone were the bare walls he remembered from his brotherly *I can't believe you married a Crosby, though I suppose if you press me, I'll admit he seems a decent enough fellow* post-nuptial visit. The bare floor was now covered by a carpet, its softness a contrast to Chandler Hall. There the marble floors felt like sliding over ice. This made for a nice change, these patterns and colors like curling wheat underfoot.

Hannah had changed too. Usually brisk and active, she was reclining on a sofa, bolstered by cushions behind her and beneath her feet.

"Nathaniel! I'm so glad you've come to visit. I've been bored today."

He dropped a kiss on her head. "You look lovely, sister dear."

"Liar. I have turned into a decorative person who lolls around all day wishing for sweets." She wiggled her slippers. "My feet started to swell as soon as the weather turned warm. Until then I felt all right."

She had told the family she was with child a month before; since then, her belly had puffed out all at once. Instead of the riding habit she used to wear daily, she was dressed in one of those filmy gowns that *ton* ladies wore in the afternoons.

Nathaniel had seen more pregnant horses than humans, and he suspected that if he made any comparison, he would find out how hard a swollen foot could kick him. But if she were a mare, judging from the state of her belly, she would be nearly done with her pregnancy.

"Not much longer until we get to meet the spawn?" This was, he hoped, diplomatic enough.

"Says you. I have three more months, I think. I'll have the pleasure of swollen feet and a huge belly through the hottest months of the year."

"You can come sit in the icehouse at the Hall." Nathaniel settled into a chair opposite her.

She began to laugh—then considered. "That sounds pleasant. Huh. Trust a brother to come up with an idea that sounds stupid but actually might not be."

"I am not sure why I've got into the habit of thinking of you as my favorite sibling," he murmured.

In truth, it was because they had grown up together. Jonah and Abigail were only two years older than him, but the twins had always seemed ages ahead. Jonah was the only one of the Chandlers who had gone away to school, and Abigail had always had some beau or another before running off with an Irish lord at the age of seventeen and settling in County Tipperary.

Hannah, of course, had an answer of her own. "It has to be because of my kind nature, which matches your charming one."

"I *am* charming."

"Which implies that I'm not kind? *Phoo*. Of course I am." She winked. "Also good-looking."

Hannah and Nathaniel shared the same straight hair that fell somewhere between blond and brown, though she had inherited Sir William's hazel eyes and Nathaniel their mother's blue ones. To Hannah's dismay, she also had freckles, which faded each winter and speckled her anew each spring and summer.

"Watch how kind I am. I'm about to feed you." She rang for a servant. "What would you like after your walk to visit me? Scotch? Brandy? I know how you love them."

Yes.

But Nathaniel clutched at his resolve. If he could never have enough spirits, then he ought to have none. "Tea would be fine," he said. "It's a bit early in the day for the sterner stuff."

"Very well. I never used to imbibe, but Bart has this newfangled notion that I ought not to drink spirits until the baby is born, and it makes me want to gulp an entire bottle of brandy."

"How contrary you have become. I see marriage agrees with you."

She wiggled her feet again. "I wouldn't *do* that, of course. Maybe Bart thinks I would pickle the baby."

Nathaniel reared back in horror.

"*Maybe*, I said. *Maybe.* You turned squeamish spending all that time with your fancy friends in London."

"Is that what you think I do?"

She shrugged, which took a great deal of effort considering the number of cushions stuffed around her. "Well…"

"Hannah, honestly. I buy drinks, and then I buy horses. It's between friends, yes, but not fancy ones. A duke's man of business doesn't get nearly enough to drink when one considers the amount of ridiculousness he has to put up with in his post."

"I believe that. Serving as Father's secretary was challenge enough, and since we're related, he could hardly give me the sack."

"Perhaps that was why it was so difficult. You couldn't leave."

Except she had, hadn't she? Somehow Hannah had managed the conversion from secretary to daughter. Then she had married and set up her own household. True, it was with a Crosby—but even so, Nathaniel's younger sister had leaped ahead of him, when once she had looked up to him.

When their mother died, Nathaniel bore it stolidly so he could comfort Hannah. When Sir William went to Spain, he bore that too. But when his father returned because his body had been wasted by palsy, Nathaniel couldn't bear it anymore. He'd been fifteen years old, alone with his younger sister and their servants. And Sir William came back to his family only when he was unable to walk away from them anymore.

That was when Nathaniel began to drink, because to drink was to forget. And when Sir William asked for—no, demanded—help, he said no, and he drank some more. Whatever he could find in a decanter or in the wine cellar. New bottles, vinegary old bottles. Bottles covered in dust, bottles with sediment he accidentally disturbed. He drained them all dry, and he drank the sediment too.

Nothing made Sir William come closer to him. Maybe nothing would. Once the doctors were sure the baronet would never walk again, he would certainly never draw his children near.

So Nathaniel was as good to Hannah as he could possibly be, because she had no one else. He taught her as much as he could about horses. Riding. Stables. Pedigrees.

And then one day when he went to fetch her from the study, there was Sir William with her. Perched in his new wheelchair with the smooth wooden rims. Hannah standing at one side, looking at a ledger with him. She didn't notice Nathaniel in the doorway, but Sir William did.

He did not welcome Nathaniel in. And Nathaniel did not ask to enter. At this distance in time, he was not sure which of them had turned away first.

More than a dozen years later, their cordiality often seemed like a truce, with every request the negotiation of a treaty with ever-changing terms. Hannah's amiable relationship with their father still mystified Nathaniel.

Fortunately the tea arrived then, the tray set on a table beside Hannah's sofa. She poured, and Nathaniel gulped at his tiny cup.

Hannah sipped at her own, then crunched a biscuit. "I love this baby, but I miss all the Chandler sorts of things I used to do."

"Like what? Arguing? Hating Crosbys?"

She rolled her eyes. "Those *are* Chandler-ish things to do, but remember, I'm the kind sibling. No, mainly I miss riding. If I put on a huge cloak, I can still visit the track and watch the promising colts and fillies exercising. But it's not the same."

"The best colts won't be there this week." Aha, he was leading her around to the subject at last.

"Because of the colic in Father's stable?"

"Gossip, gossip." Nathaniel nestled his tiny cup back into its saucer. "Newmarket is the largest tiny town one could possibly imagine. Do you know which animals are down?"

She listed them off. "And I won't insult you by asking what you've tried to help them, because I know you'll have done everything." After a pause, she set her teacup down, fists clenching. "Ah, curse it. I have to say something. Water. Walking. Call a physician if you must. Do it for Sheltie, please."

"Hannah. Stop. I'm not here for advice."

"I didn't figure you were. But it's all I can do to help right now." She looked ruefully at her round belly.

"There is something you could help with." Nathaniel leaned forward to place his cup and saucer on the tea tray with what he hoped was a casual air. "I want to know whatever you can tell me about Rosalind."

"She is 'just as high as your heart.'"

Somehow his finger got stuck in the teacup handle, and it made an unholy clatter on its saucer as he freed himself. "She—what?" That selfsame heart gave a little leap.

"Rosalind? Heroine of *As You Like It*? It's somewhere around here." Hannah pawed at several of the cushions. "The library was stripped almost bare, so there's nothing to read here but Shakespeare and Milton, and I'd rather a comedy than damnation. *As You Like It* is the play in which the hero falls in love with Rosalind at first sight, and they wander around in a forest in disguise and he sends her love poems by nailing them onto a tree."

"A tree?" Nathaniel's brows yanked together. *Love at first sight?* Nonsense. "Never mind all that; I wasn't talking about Shakespeare. I meant to refer to Miss Agate. And if you tease me about calling her by her first name, I shall—"

"Threaten a woman who is with child? Maybe *you* need to read about damnation. Milton is the morocco-bound volume on the floor behind the sofa." She coughed. "I don't know how it happens to be there."

Nathaniel folded his arms and sat back in his chair.

"All right, all right," Hannah gave in. "What do you wish to know?"

"Whatever will make her agree to do what I ask."

Hannah's jaw dropped. "Are you *blackmailing* her?"

"What? No! The opposite of blackmail, whatever one might call that. I want to...to...sparkle-mail her." He ignored his sister's snort. "Father almost granted that I could take the horses to Epsom if Miss Agate came along. Now I need *her* to agree so *he* will agree."

"Ah, it makes perfect sense."

"Good. So you see, I want to make the journey sound so delightful that there's no way she could bear to refuse." He considered. "Did the Rosalind in the play like her poems?"

"You would write a love poem to our father's secretary? This day has taken an interesting turn."

"Not a love poem. More like a 'Please agree to accompany me to Epsom' poem."

Hannah finally stopped fiddling with her cushions. "Let's hear one, then."

Uh. "All right. Something like…
'*Please agree*
To accompany me
To Epsom for the Derby.'"

"That's rotten," said Hannah. "She would stay behind just so she'd be certain not to be subjected to any more poems."

Sisterly honesty was horrid, but in this case he had to agree with her. "I know, I know. I've always been more handy with things than with words."

"Well, then give her a thing instead."

"I…" Nathaniel cleared his throat.

"Oh Lord. I didn't mean it like *that*." Hannah turned pink.

"Of course you didn't. And I most certainly didn't either. I was just clearing my throat."

Right. Except that now he wondered whether Rosalind Agate would like to be touched, to be stroked.

If they were talking of *things*, *handy* was all Nathaniel had been lately. Once the race season began, there was no time to pursue pleasure, no time for anything but work.

Well, work and thought. Thought of a wry smile, of a ready sense of humor. Of clear green eyes and hair the color of new cedar. Of silky deep blue and pale print gowns that… Honestly, they covered so much that Nathaniel had no idea of the shape beneath them. But as long as Miss Agate had the usual parts, she would be lovely.

Fortunately, Hannah was oblivious to the fact that Nathaniel's mind had gone exploring. "There's not much I can tell you about her," Hannah said. "By the time I met her, Father had already decided to hire her. I asked about her references, and he said he had learned everything he needed to."

Oh. So Hannah hadn't been privy to the decision to hire Rosalind. He hadn't realized that. "You didn't see the letters of reference, then?"

"No, I didn't. Why, what are you getting at?"

"I just wondered who had provided them. Rosalind Agate was raised in a coaching inn and now talks like the Queen of England."

"With a German accent? I don't remember noting that."

Would it be unkind to hit a pregnant woman with an embroidered cushion? Probably. "I hope your baby kicks you hard in the ribs."

"Wish granted." She smiled. "'Do you not know I am a woman? When I think, I must speak.'"

"Yes, so I noticed."

"Idiot. That's more of Rosalind from *As You Like It*. Ah, you were never bookish."

"As I said, I'm better with things."

His education had been patched together by tutors and grooms. He knew the Latin names for every bone in a horse's body and could figure any sum that might be involved in the running of a household. But calculus? Literature? If they didn't have a practical use, he had never crammed them into his head.

"Why don't you ask Miss Agate what she likes, or whatever else you want to know?" Hannah suggested. Reasonably.

And yet. "She has this cursed way of slipping away from the subject."

"Maybe you need to ask her in a poem." Hannah's freckled nose scrunched in a wicked smile.

Nathaniel stretched out his legs. "I'll write one for you. 'Dear Hannah. When you make suggestions like that, I wish you were on the savannah.'"

She pretended to dab at her eyes. "That was so beautiful! I may weep…for your lack of skill." Struggling to sit upright, she added, "All right, be off with you, wretched brother. Unless you want to come to the stables with me?"

"No, no. You go on and talk to your husband about…whatever it is."

"The stud farm. Jonah and Bart have some plan to lease buildings to each other, or horses, or maybe both. It's changed so many times that I've threatened to step in and make all the arrangements for them." Her brows knit. "Secretly, I think they like writing to each other. Bart has no brothers, you know."

"I know he hasn't. But Jonah has." Nathaniel felt a bit stung. He couldn't remember the last time his taciturn brother had sent him a letter.

"I never said he didn't." She held out a hand. "Come, help me up. I have become terribly unwieldy, like a pumpkin stuffed into a crepe."

He stood. "Why those two things in particular?"

"Because I'm hungry."

She held out a hand, and Nathaniel heaved her to her feet.

"I hate visiting the stables and not being able to ride," she said. "Bart knows it, and he would spend more time with me indoors—but there is always so much to do. I don't want to sacrifice anyone's well-being just because I become maudlin at the sight of a saddle."

I hate visiting the stables and not being able to ride.

Nathaniel had never considered such a thing before, but would it not apply to Sir William too? Once upon a time, he had taught all his children to be as comfortable on horseback as on their own two feet. Now he himself could neither stand nor ride.

Sir William had never complained about no longer being able to sit a horse—but that did not mean it didn't bother him. He hadn't told Nathaniel he hated having his chair pushed, either.

If Rosalind was right, such things ought to be understood without having to be explained.

Nathaniel hesitated. "Hannah. Do you think Father likes to have his chair pushed?"

She rolled a fist in the small of her back. "I don't know. Maybe. If he asked for help. I can't say I remember it ever coming up."

"But you were his secretary for years."

"Yes, but I'm a woman. And his daughter." She linked her arm with Nathaniel's and dragged him toward the doorway to the drawing room. "A father doesn't ask a daughter for help. And a man certainly doesn't ask a woman. Why, what brings on this question?"

Rosalind Agate had brought so many uncertainties to his mind that Nathaniel could hardly untangle enough thoughts to reply. "Oh…just wondering."

This was not an answer, but Hannah knew when to let a small idiocy pass without comment. "Shall I come over some day soon? I'm not allowed to ride, but I can walk."

He blinked himself back to the dark entryway of Hannah's home. "That might be a good idea, yes. If Miss Agate agrees to go to Epsom, Father will need your help again. But"—he had to drop a brotherly hint—"have a servant walk over with you. Bart and Father will take turns shooting me if I encourage you to venture over alone in your condition."

"That's how they show their love," Hannah said.

Nathaniel knew when to let a small idiocy pass too. He only embraced her—tentatively, so as not to bump that human foal she was growing—and bade her farewell.

"When you come again, bring some novels with you," she called after him.

He nodded, leaving her with a parting wave. Then he walked back to Chandler Hall with even more questions than before, and the suspicion that he wanted them answered as much to learn about Rosalind Agate as to lead a traveling party to Epsom.

Six

A FEW DAYS GALLOPED BY. LONG SPRING DAYS THAT still seemed too short as Rosalind ran from study to stable and back again; days of water and walking and mineral oil and nux vomica and more of all of them, again and again. Of radishes to tempt Jake's appetite to return, and plaits in Sheltie's mane as the little pony leaned hard against Rosalind, each soothing the other.

Rosalind welcomed the exertion. If it weren't for the fatigue that knocked her into bed, deeply and dreamlessly asleep at the end of each day, she would have wasted her nights in wakefulness and confusion. And the reason was Aunt Annie—and so much more.

The day after Sir William had decreed that everyone entering the stable must remain in pairs or groups, Rosalind had finally managed to slip into town to collect the post. "Our master is expecting some confidential letters," she lied to the footman whose usual errand it was, and he gratefully accepted her offer of an hour of freedom while Miss Agate carried out his work.

Within the usual shuffle of business was one sealed note for Rosalind.

> *Stay where you are. I am giving you the opportunity to search.*
>
>   *Anweledig*

The Welsh signature made the letter seem more like a secret and less like an edict. Anne Jones was neither Rosalind's aunt, nor did she truly bear a Welsh name meaning "invisible." When Rosalind had begun to work for her a decade before, she had been young and raw and frightened of everything, her burns hardly healed, her muscles weak from her long recovery. Then Anweledig was the counterpart to Rosalind's Cyfrinach, or "secret." The two of them stood against the world that had taken so much from them both. Together they would conquer.

Now, at twenty-three, Rosalind went under her own name. She knew better than to think she would conquer, but she was determined not to be beaten.

Aunt Annie had told her about the man known as Tranc who had bought up the debt the sainted Widow Jones incurred to save young Rosalind's life. The name Tranc meant death—and worse than that, *Welsh* death, which was somehow more intimidating than the English sort. Tranc could hire anyone anywhere. With a shilling's worth of poison and five minutes unobserved, he could kill thousands of pounds of horseflesh. And what could be done to an animal ten times Rosalind's size could easily be done to Rosalind herself.

Though this letter, brief though it was, implied

that Aunt Annie—not Tranc—had arranged to sicken Sir William's horses. That she had arranged for the animals to be ill so that Rosalind could search the baronet's papers in the resulting confusion.

The only thing that would take Sir William from his house was his stable. If Aunt Annie knew this, then Sir William was more than a stranger to her. And this was, perhaps, why Anweledig was so certain the answer lay at Chandler Hall. The answer to whatever had happened in Spain in 1805.

Year after year, each of Rosalind's positions had included secrets and searches. And each seemed to have pulled Aunt Annie closer to the answer she sought. Rosalind had no idea what it might be, or even of the question. She had asked, but queries sent by letter could be easily ignored.

She always wrote to Aunt Annie in care of the foundling home the woman had helped to establish in East London. Return letters came from different parts of the country. Among all her charitable works, perhaps Anne Jones pursued a hunt of her own.

If she did, Rosalind did not know the purpose of that either. She knew only that once she found the right papers, Aunt Annie would turn them over to Tranc, and they would both be safe.

In darker days, Rosalind had wondered if her life was worth the layers of debt she had incurred to save it. But now, for the first time in a decade, she saw the promise of choice ahead of her. Of a life free from secrets and spying. A life that was *real*.

She just needed to carry out one last betrayal, and then she'd be an honest woman.

❧

"You look like a half-laundered cloth that someone forgot to wring out," came a familiar voice. "Are you all right, Rosalind?"

She hadn't heard the study door open—but then, Sir William's latest order had hit her with an unexpected force that left her ears ringing in disbelief.

With a quick tug of breath, she tried to pull herself together before looking up from her usual litter of papers. Nathaniel Chandler crouched next to her chair, blue eyes at the level of her own. "I'm fine." She turned away with the excuse of neatening a stack of paper. "I think I just ate some moldy hay."

"Very amusing. Ten points for wittiness. But I think"—he stood, then rested his weight on the corner of his father's long table-turned-desk—"that you spoke to my father, as I did just outside the study. And that what he told me, which put a smile on my face, has put a frown on yours."

A broad, tanned hand came down on the stack of papers. "Rosalind. Truly. Will it be that bad to come to Epsom with me? I had hoped you'd be happy to receive such a sign of my father's trust." His tone was dry; they both knew that trust in Rosalind was a sign that his father's confidence in Nathaniel was lacking.

If only she had what they had: the fraught pairing of parent and child, so near at hand that they could be wary of each other. Test one another in everyday ways.

But if she had that, she wouldn't be wary. She would be grateful if her father were near.

She rummaged for some explanation that might serve as an adequate excuse. "I don't feel that I can leave my work. Or travel. At this time. To Epsom."

"Your short sentences. Do not. Convince me. Of anything." He hopped himself up the rest of the way, sitting atop the table and letting his booted feet swing free. "What about a poem instead?"

Rosalind looked up into his face. "Happy to oblige. 'Roses are red. Nathaniel, I wish you would get Epsom out of your head.'"

"I'm impressed. Your poetry is even worse than mine."

Despite herself, she smiled. "Why, what are your poems like?"

For some reason, he blushed. "Never you mind."

A thought struck her. "If you just spoke to your father outside the study, why were you originally coming this way?"

"To tell you. And gloat."

"Try again."

"For the pleasure of your company?"

She swallowed. "Try again."

"Because I wanted to hunt through my father's papers for anything that would tell me more about you."

A *why* almost escaped her lips; then she brazened it out. "Try again *again*."

Nathaniel sighed and slid from the table. "I can see that I am never going to get it right. Why don't you tell me the answer instead? I'll be over here flipping through the *Stud Book*, ready to consult the pedigree of any horse you mention."

She turned in her chair to follow his progress across the room. "When does Sir William want us to leave?

He did no more than poke his head in and tell me I was to join the traveling party."

"That's odd even for the name of a racehorse. Hold for a moment while I look that up." Balancing the book on his knee, he turned pages.

Rosalind hid a smile. When Nathaniel looked up, she managed to narrow her eyes.

He slammed the book shut. "All right, all right. You are so serious."

"Yes, well. Hypotenuse. Iron gall ink. Naiad. I am at work, you know."

All buoyant energy, he paced from bookshelf to bookshelf and back. "We're to leave the day after tomorrow. Whit Monday. Sir William's plan of keeping to pairs and groups seems to be working, for no other horses have developed colic. But that means—"

"It was no accident." Her fingers felt cold.

"Exactly." He drummed his fingers on a shelf, then kept pacing. "I was so certain it wasn't an intentional act. However, I guess it doesn't much matter since the tampering hasn't happened again."

"It still matters." How faint her voice sounded.

"Sir William agrees with me—can you imagine?— that we ought to get away from the stables as soon as possible. Whit Monday is earlier than I would usually wish to depart, but Epigram and Pale Marauder aren't at their full strength and will benefit from a slow pace."

"Slow paces don't win races."

"I was wrong: You *are* a better poet than I am. And you are also quite correct. I've no idea how they'll do on the journey, but I do know they've no chance to win the Derby unless they are in Epsom. Once we arrive, I will send an express updating Sir Jubal and my father on their horses' conditions."

"You said you're wrong," she repeated, "and I'm right." He said it with such confidence, as though another rightness would come along any moment.

"This time, yes." He stopped his pacing. "So. What sort of work has you in such a mental flurry? Maybe I can help, so you can run off to Epsom with a clear conscience."

Conscience was exactly the right word to hit upon, though she couldn't let him know that. "Maybe you can help at that." She fumbled to frame a reason. "I need to find a...a sale record. For a horse Sir William bought in 1805. Where would papers from 1805 be kept?"

"For 1805?" He tilted his head, gaze searching the ceiling as though clues were hidden in the plaster. "He was hardly in England that year. Any horses he bought were probably on behalf of the military, so the papers would be held by the government. Why would he need that now?"

The best way to deal with a question one did not want to answer, Rosalind had found, was to ignore it. "Where would Sir William's other correspondence be stored?" If her understanding of the family chronology was correct, Chandler Hall had not yet been built in 1805. Yet surely they would not have destroyed papers when moving households.

"Other correspondence?" Now Nathaniel's searching gaze was turned to Rosalind. "I've no idea if there is any. His secretarial difficulties have been of long standing—with the exception of present company and my sister Hannah. And he was never the sort to send long, newsy letters home."

"Could anything be stored in the attics here?" She might almost be pushing too hard. But she trusted the son not to tell the father, *Your secretary was acting odd earlier. What sort of information could she need from 1805?*

Nathaniel paced back to the table, then pulled the stopper from the brandy decanter. "I doubt it. There's nothing in the attics that Sir William might need again. He was reluctant even to have attic space constructed. He doesn't like the idea of a part of the house he cannot reach." He held the crystal stopper to his nose and breathed deeply, shutting his eyes.

"Half an inch, no more," Rosalind murmured.

"No more," he echoed, replacing the stopper. "If it helps, 1805 is the year he was granted his baronetcy. Though it's not the exciting sort that came with new lands and estates and tenants. It's merely a title."

Merely, he said, as though a hereditary title were of little importance. "How did he gain it? Some sort of military service?"

He nodded. "Horses. Supplying cavalry horses for the Light Dragoons. He used his connections across Wales and Scotland and Ireland to find horses that were sturdy and healthy and quick."

Wales. Rosalind's thoughts went fuzzy all of a sudden. When she jolted back to the present, Nathaniel was still explaining, "—worth quite a bit to know one's horses were going to travel calmly across the Channel and recover their land legs quickly. Sir William—not that he was quite Sir William yet— traveled with many of them. Then he went to Spain."

"Spain." Rosalind blinked.

"You are surprised?"

"No, no. Only curious. For me, Spain is a place in books, not a place I might ever go." Surely it was a place with days and nights like any other. But in her imagination, it was drenched in sun, a sun so warm and lasting that one need never light a lamp or drop it or go up in flame.

"Why was your father in Spain?" she wondered. "He cannot have been a soldier himself."

"Lord, I don't know. He was always traveling somewhere or other, even before our mother died. He was in Cádiz for months, blockaded when sea battles were going on. That's where he contracted the palsy that paralyzed his legs, but I don't know much else about it." His hand strayed to the decanter again, fingers trailing down its crystalline side. "It wasn't the best year for this family. I was a scruffy, resentful youth, left behind with a tutor I never obeyed and no parents."

"And your brother and sisters?"

"And them. But somehow we never had much to say to one another. Not then."

Another possible path to the information blocked. She sat back in her chair, brows knit tight with strain. "How can I get what I need?"

He looked over his shoulder at her, his expression all roguery. "Well, Rosalind Agate, that depends on what you need."

Her lips parted, but no ready retort fell from them. Though he doubtless meant the statement lightly, it was much more than that to Rosalind.

What did one need? Food, drink, shelter, safety. She had the first three; she wanted the latter.

No, she wanted more than that. She wanted the right to beam back when a man like Nathaniel Chandler grinned at her. To take his compliments, to allow something deeper than flippant flirtation.

To allow herself a touch of excitement at traveling to Epsom, a road that would lead her through London and might permit a visit to her family.

And for now, she wanted him to keep smiling at her, just like that, and for the smile to stay as he learned more of her. To stay and never to fall, until the expression became as familiar to her as the shape of her own scars.

But she couldn't admit that to him. She could hardly bear to admit it to herself.

"I need to carry out my work," she replied at last. "That is all."

Nathaniel picked up a sheet of blank foolscap from the stack before Rosalind. "Very commendable, of course."

Right. If only she felt *commendable* as she watched the swift movements of his hands, folding the rectangle of paper at odd angles. Those hands had fixed a water pump; they had soothed skittish and ill animals. He was quick with his hands, a sort of quickness that intrigued Rosalind. Could those hands soothe her own worries? Would he touch her if she asked?

She wanted to ask, so desperately that she could taste the shape of the impossible words on her tongue.

He made another fold. The result was a sort of flattened paper pyramid.

What had Rosalind's hands done that was good? For every horse she had helped, she had sent a prying letter.

She balled her hands into fists and stuffed them beneath the tabletop. The question she allowed herself was hardly urgent, though she'd wondered about it for some time. "Nathaniel. Why has Sir Jubal entrusted Epigram's care to your father?"

"And to us now?" His grin was a quick flash before he returned his attention to the…whatever he was making. "Everyone knows of Sir Jubal's dream to follow a victory in the Two Thousand Guineas with a triumph in the Derby. He has only a small stable, and he's too frail to travel himself. So he trusted his… Well, I'm not sure Sir William is his friend. Doesn't that seem like too warm a word? Like *puppy* or *chocolate*. I can't imagine my father with either of those."

With a pointed toss, he sent the flat pyramid-like thing gliding across the room.

"What is that?" Rosalind asked.

"I don't know. Just something I made, wondering if it would work." He stood still, poised like his gliding pyramid just before it was thrown. He was ready to leave, maybe. He *would* leave for now. Unless she gave him a reason to stay.

"Fly it again," she said. "I want to see it fly."

This time, when he gifted her with a smile, she returned it—yet she felt she had kept it too.

And after all, there was more than one way to pay a debt. The information for Tranc was in exchange for Rosalind's medical expenses, which had piled and grown with interest over the past decade. Aunt Annie had paid them to save Rosalind's life, then turned the debt over to Tranc.

But what if Rosalind paid the expenses with coin instead of stolen papers?

"I have a suggestion." Her throat caught on the words.

A paper pyramid winged across the room and smacked into the wall. "What is that?"

"I will go with you to Epsom, and I will be as helpful as possible. And as long as the horses reach Epsom safely, I will write glowing letters of your progress and conduct to Sir William all along the way."

He slid across the glass-smooth floor and scooped up his fallen paper. "I'm hardly going to argue with a suggestion like that. It sounds ideal. But you sound nervous, so there must be more to come that will not be ideal. What do you have in mind?"

She took a deep breath. "I want one hundred fifty pounds."

He tripped, catching himself heavily against a shelf. "Say that once more."

It was even more difficult to say the second time, but she kept her voice steady. "I *need* one hundred fifty pounds."

"That is what you need? And I thought you needed only to carry out your work."

He drew closer, and for the first time, Rosalind was heartsore at the way he looked at her. With suspicion.

She lifted her chin, thinking of her sister Carys. If Rosalind did not pay off her debt, Tranc would take Carys into his employment, making another Agate his puppet. And Carys was far too pretty, too whole, to lose her future through someone else's failure.

"One hundred fifty pounds." This third time, as she thought of her sister—only six years old the last time they had met, but now a young woman of sixteen—the words came more easily. *One hundred fifty pounds*. This time it sounded like a real sum rather than an impossibility.

Nathaniel was frowning deeply. "You think I can be bought for such a sum? There are many in the *ton* who would consider that nothing."

"I don't think it's nothing. I can be bought for that amount." She tried a smile. "As I said, though, the horses have to be safe. I won't lie."

He turned away, gazing toward the brightness outside the French doors. His coat-clad shoulders rose, then fell in a great sigh. "And if I cannot or will not pay you? Will you tell my father I am not to be trusted?"

"Of course not!"

"So if we make a safe journey—"

"I will say so." A sinking feeling made her feet grow cold, her head pound. She really had no influence at all, no means of persuading him.

He turned back to face her. "I have a different idea." The usual warmth had returned to his eyes, his voice. "I shall stake you for a wager once we get to Epsom. If you lose, no harm done. If you win, you can pay me back. How much you choose to wager, and on which horse—I'll leave that up to you."

"You will leave it up to me," she repeated. "Why?"

"Encouragement, maybe? You'll see the horses in good health to Epsom if you've a financial interest in their safe arrival."

"I would do that all the same."

"I suspect you would." His blue eyes were warm. "But I can't just *give* you the money, you know. That would be bribery. At least, it might seem so to people less ethical and honest than we are."

"That makes sense." She paused. "Then why did you agree at all?" Hers was a ridiculous request. A life-changing request.

He held out a hand, and she grasped it with her chilled fingers, uncomprehending. "Because there was no reason on earth that I had to. Which tells me, my soon-to-be-traveling companion, that your need is genuine." Gently, he drew her to her feet. "And that you are a terrible negotiator."

"Not so terrible." Had she ever stood this close to him? He seemed so tall with her eyes at the level of his heart, and he smelled of salt and sweet hay. "Since you agreed to give me what I asked."

He laughed, releasing her hand. "You could not have persuaded me with an argument that was any less terrible." As she looked up at him, he turned serious. "It is not for anything illegal, is it? For any reason that could hurt someone?"

"Quite the opposite."

"And you will let me know if there is anything I can do to help?"

There was nothing he could do to help, so this was an easy promise. "Of course I will."

Again he extended his hand. She stared at it. "What?"

"We have an agreement. So we shake hands."

"Oh. Right." How scattered she was today. But relief bloomed in her and buoyed her. At last, she had the promise of freedom. She, who had never earned more than fifteen pounds in a year, would buy back her debt, and she need never betray anyone's trust again.

Trust Nathaniel, she remembered him saying when he arrived from London. A heartfelt plea cloaked in flippancy.

Trust Rosalind. She had never had right or reason to ask such a thing before now.

His hand was warm and calloused. The hand of a rider, a driver, a man who knew how to make and fix things.

Too soon, she drew her hand away and took a brisk step back, bumping her calves against her chair. "I won't disappoint you."

"I don't make promises I am not sure I can keep. But I shall do my best to make sure you get—and give—your money's worth." The silence that followed was long enough for one beat of her heart, one fidget of her feet, and then he smiled. "Don't look so worried, Miss Rosalind Agate. You might find that keeping company with me is rather pleasant."

In every line of his handsome face, in every angle of his body, there was the promise of adventure. Escape. Exploration.

Pleasant? She had never heard such an understatement. The incoherent reply she made could best be transcribed as "Humnah."

"My thoughts exactly. A journey always transforms me into a Houyhnhnm. Pack something pretty for Derby day, will you? It's a day of celebration." And with a bow, he unlatched the French doors and strode out, whistling.

Her fingers tingled, still feeling the warmth of Nathaniel's clasp.

Which made her wonder: did she owe a debt to herself too? And if so, how—and by whom—ought it to be satisfied?

Seven

For Nathaniel, Whitsun passed in a flurry of preparations for the journey to Epsom. Early the following morning, when the sky was still sunrise-pink and the humid air of this May morning was honey-sweet in his lungs, he and the band of travelers set off on the road south.

It was a road he knew well from his frequent trips to and from London. Back and forth, back and forth. That in-between time, that unfettered time on the road, was his favorite. Just then, he was exactly where he needed to be, and the next stop was all perfect potential.

Nathaniel was mounted on a stolid bay cob, a calm stepper named Bumblebee that he sometimes drove in harness. Lombard and Peters walked, leading Pale Marauder and Epigram in halters. Armed outriders—a quartet of Sir William's burliest servants—kept pace ahead and behind. Another armed servant and coachman followed separately in a carriage filled with racing tack and travel trunks.

Riding at his side, Rosalind wore a gown the green shade of a riding habit—and, he thought, her eyes.

For her, Nathaniel had borrowed a gentle mare from
Hannah. His sister had lent Farfalla with many sighs
of envy at the idea of riding for an entire week. "If
you have a wonderful time, do *not* tell me. I cannot
bear it."

This would not be a problem. Far from having a
wonderful time, Rosalind appeared to be concentrat-
ing almost too hard to breathe: clutching her reins
tightly in gloved hands, tense in the saddle. "Miss
Agate, if you cannot relax a bit, you'll ache from head
to toe before we stop for luncheon."

"I am not able to relax right now. Perhaps later."
Her voice sounded like a pianoforte someone had
tuned too tightly.

"You're perfectly safe." With gentle pressure on
the bit, he slowed Bumblebee to match the shorter
strides of Rosalind's mare. "We're surrounded by
men with guns."

"That sounds like the beginning of a horrid tale."

"Er—well, perhaps, but they're our men, not
highwaymen, which makes a difference. And I'm
armed too."

Her exclamation was faint and, he thought, profane.

"Just with a pistol," he added. "I'd be a fool not to
carry some sort of firearm. Hundreds of thousands of
pounds are at stake in each classics race, and we're in
the company of two potential champions."

If he could see through the leather of her gloves,
he was sure her knuckles would be white. "That was
all I needed for perfect calm. A reminder of the level
of trust heaped upon us." Quickly, she darted a glance
and a tight smile at him. "Truly, that's not why I'm

tense this morning. I have not sat a horse for ten years, and I fear I've lost the feel for it."

A decade—about the time she mentioned she had left her parents' home. What had sent her out into the world so young? Where had she spent her time since?

This was hardly the time for such questions, when her shoulders were squared with brittle determination. So he only smiled with reassurance—not that she was looking around to see his expression. "You'll soon get the feel for it again, though I won't take back what I said about you being sore as a—" He cleared his throat. Best to spare her the colorful similes. "We shall have a week on the road, and by the end of that time, you'll be riding as well as a jockey."

She looked unconvinced. He tried again. "Seven days, if you'd rather think of it like that." A bit of quick arithmetic, and he added, "One hundred sixty-eight hours. The time will pass quickly, and you won't have to sleep outdoors or anything of that sort."

He explained the plan of shifts he and the grooms would take, stopping at the selected lodging houses where he stayed on his many trips to London, and where he trusted the owners to care for both human and equine guests.

She didn't seem to be listening, so he finally gave up the explanation. "If you had attended to any of that, you would have been impressed by the organization and planning."

She swallowed, flexing her hands on Farfalla's reins. "No, no. I was giving my full attention to every word. I was very impressed."

The mare sneezed, shaking her head.

"My thoughts exactly," said Nathaniel.

There was more to Rosalind's tense posture than the stiffness of a woman who had not sat a horse in a long while. Maybe she was worried about spending so much time in this company of men. Their number was so large that they effectively chaperoned her, but still he should have brought along a maid.

Or maybe this company of men and the unexpected freedom from work had set her to thinking of someone else. Someone special who lay heavily on her mind.

The idea that Rosalind had pledged her heart had never occurred to him before, and now he wished it would un-occur. Though that was hardly unlikely. As governess to an earl's family, she had doubtless encountered every level of society from night-soil men to dukes. Raised by a horse breeder turned baronet, Nathaniel saw his own place as somewhere between trade and gentry.

Unfortunately, there was nothing between trade and gentry except a void.

"You must be missing someone," he ventured.

"Hmm?" Her grip on the reins had slackened a bit since Farfalla's emphatic sneeze. Beneath the shallow brim of her straw bonnet, Rosalind bit her bottom lip.

"Missing someone." Unwise to poke at this snake of a subject, maybe, but he couldn't resist. "You seem distant. Are you thinking of a loved one?"

"Unless you think I love my worry that I shall topple off this horse, no."

Poke. Poke. "No suitors left behind you in the earl's household? Or ahead, maybe, somewhere on the road to London? You must tell me if there's someone dear to you we ought to visit."

"Secretaries don't have suitors." She ventured a pat to the withers of her mare.

"This from the woman who swore that 'secretaries don't' would not fit into her vocabulary."

"This from the man who assured me there was a time and place for such a phrase." Her lips crimped with amusement. "If this is the sort of conversation you're to threaten me with over the next week, I shall ride ahead and talk to Pale Marauder instead."

Fifteen or twenty lengths ahead, the cream-colored colt let a dropping fall to the road.

"Or perhaps not," Rosalind added. "I'll keep company with you if you promise continence—"

"Done."

"—and tell me about your own pursuits."

"Not much to tell, really."

"Because you are pure and monk-like, or because you don't want to share your scandalous stories with me?"

"Ah…whichever one will get me in less trouble with you."

She laughed, her shoulders relaxing for the first time since she took to her sidesaddle. Sensing the change in her rider's grip, Farfalla eased into a trot.

"Oh!" The first jolt surprised an exclamation from Rosalind, bouncing her in the saddle.

Nathaniel clucked to Bumblebee, who was eager to lengthen his own strides, and they again kept pace with the other pair. "Do you like trotting?"

"I'd…rather…keep…my teeth." Rosalind's jaw jarred as she was tossed by each trotting stride rather than posting smoothly. Before Nathaniel could offer further instruction, she murmured something and gave a little tug on the reins. Farfalla's ears swiveled back, listening, then she slowed to a walk.

Bumblebee's ears pricked with interest. Given a bit more rein, he touched noses with the little mare.

"Making friends?" Rosalind wondered.

"Something like that." Bumblebee might be a gelding, but he was still a male who appreciated a pretty female of his own kind.

Which reminded Nathaniel: Rosalind had asked him whether he'd ever played the suitor. He suddenly wanted to give her an honest answer. "You asked about my romances, Rosalind. Leaving aside the milkmaids—"

"Oh, must we?"

"—I courted a lady, but it came to nothing. Curse of a younger son, I suppose. The lady thought she could do better, and in the end she did. I've no real ties in either London or Newmarket."

This would be a delightful time for her to say something like *How could such a thing be possible* or *No one could be better than you.*

Instead, when she spoke, she sounded puzzled. "Do you not wish for attachments? Even those of friendship?"

"Can you possibly be wistful? Rosalind Agate, who embraces the role of a secretary and lives in unfettered independence?"

Her little mare walked on a way before Rosalind answered. "I didn't say I was unfettered. Or independent."

"With a gambler's fortune in your pocket, you'll have all the freedom you wish. Settle down in a seaside cottage…keep sheep and cats…pickle vegetables…"

She made one of those Houyhnhnm noises. "What an idyll you describe."

"It's not for everyone, of course. But since I made that particular vision up in about three seconds, I could easily come up with a different one."

"I don't know what my vision would be." She turned her head toward him for an instant, and he noticed something shadowed and soft in her gaze before she looked away again. "Let us reach Epsom before we worry about what comes next."

"Let us reach Epsom," he agreed. "And then we shall worry."

That sounded too much like a promise, and the pistol felt heavy in the pocket of his coat. He flailed around for a new subject of conversation. "I started reading *As You Like It*," he said. "Do you know the play? My sister Hannah told me it has a Rosalind in it."

"Yes, I do know it." She accepted the turn of subject readily. "I was bedridden for a time when I was younger, and to pass the time, I read whatever I was given. I made my way through all of Shakespeare and was delighted to find a heroine with my name. It's not my favorite play though."

"No, it's awful rubbish. I'm not a scholar by any means, but I'm certain a woman couldn't cavort around in trousers and fool everyone into thinking she was a man. Not only fool them, but get half the shepherdesses in the world to fall in love with her."

"If you won't allow for women cavorting in trousers, you'll take away half of Shakespeare's plots."

"You've read all of his plays, have you?" That

was interesting. "Do publicans' daughters commonly read Shakespeare?"

"They do in my family." She ventured another pat on the mare's withers, then added, "The Agates fell into running a coaching inn rather than rising to it. My grandfather was a country squire who sold off all of his land to cover debts. After he died, his widow took boarders, and that's how it began. Eventually the house became an inn. London was growing toward Holloway by then, and there was more custom from travelers than boarders. They never sold off the library, though. No matter how the household changed, each child in my father's generation and my own got the finest education a gentleman's collection of books could provide."

A short version of what was no doubt a long tale, but it made sense. It explained her learnedness, her plummy accent. "You were fortunate," he said, "to grow up in an inn, and with so many ideas about."

"Compared to Chandler Hall, there's a sad lack of marble on the floor."

"Yes, but…" Surely if one operated an inn, one never knew what the day would bring. Which was the opposite of Chandler Hall, where everything had already been decided. Everything from the hour at which horses were fed to the number of bites of vegetable Sir William would take at dinner.

There was nothing for Nathaniel to do there. There was no need for him.

"You must have met a great many interesting people," he finally said.

"Few milkmaids, if that's what you're wondering."

When he turned, ready to protest, she winked.

And he smiled.

The rest of the morning passed in occasional conversation as the sun painted the sky pale blue and dried the surface of the road to a dusty gold. Around them, the terrain swelled into gentle slopes and open greens perfect for gallops, but the travelers kept to a sedate walk.

Mostly.

In the opposite direction, a few farm wagons passed, causing Pale Marauder to stamp with temper and Epigram to turn and follow the luscious scents of spring vegetables. Once he broke into a trot, which inspired Pale Marauder to match his stride. That one never could resist a race. But Lombard and Peters kept a capable hand on both horses, slowing them back to a walk.

One encounter with a milkmaid averted.

With about eighty miles to cover, their pace was good. If the horses could make fifteen miles today, they would reach the Dog and Pony before tonight, saving a day's travel.

Saving it for what, though? The sooner they arrived at their destination, the sooner Nathaniel would be at loose ends again.

He called an early halt for luncheon.

The party exited the road into a treed field through which a brook threaded. When the laden carriage caught up with them, Nathaniel oversaw the unpacking of hay for the horses—an edict from Sir William, who did not want the Thoroughbreds cropping grass at the roadside. Instead, he had measured out feed in careful amounts that reminded Nathaniel of the way the baronet regulated his own meals.

Testing the water of the brook with a bare palm, Nathaniel found the water too cold. With the help of Noonan, the Irish-born groom who had ridden in John Coachman's laden carriage, he hauled buckets for the impatient horses. Dill and Button, the first set of outriders, built a fire to boil water for a kettle of tea, and when it was ready, they splashed a bit into each bucket to warm the water for the thirsty horses.

The second pair of outriders to arrive were craggy, scar-faced former boxers incongruously named Egg and Love. It was unwise for a man to do so much as smile when either introduced himself, but their tenderness with animals could not be surpassed. They began removing the horses' tack and setting it aside for a quick cleaning amid pats and quiet conversation seemingly at odds with their bulk and fierceness.

As Dill and Button took over with the water buckets, Nathaniel located Rosalind in the process of serving food out of a hamper. "There's a chamber pot in the carriage," he murmured. "If you've need. There's room within for you to have privacy."

He was not sure which of them blushed more, but—he had to say *something*. She might be a lady, but ladies were possessed of bodies the same as every other creature on this journey.

Thoughtfully, the grooms had gone behind trees to piss. The horses were less courteous.

Once they had been unharnessed or their tack removed, all were watered and fed—and wasn't *that* a delight, keeping a hungry Epigram from eating everything from grass to the tender tree leaves growing within reach. Bumblebee rolled about on a patch of open ground, scrubbing his hide with sun-warmed grass. The stouter carriage horses, a pair of chestnuts named Jerome and Hattie, found shade and folded their hard-worked legs for a rest. Pale Marauder—on a longe line attached to a tree, because Nathaniel was no idiot—danced over to the brook, stepped into it, snorted his flat-eared displeasure, and stepped into it again.

The four horses ridden by the outriders were akin to Bumblebee: sturdy horses and pleasant walkers with a great deal of stamina. Nathaniel didn't recognize them, but he befriended them all—two bays, a black with a white stocking, and a dark brown—with a few of the winter apples packed in the hamper.

Thanks to the kitchens at Chandler Hall, the human travelers were supplied with plenty of sandwiches and cold chicken, along with apples and even a beautiful pie that the grooms shoveled from the tin with eager hands. Nathaniel would have the hamper packed anew at the inn where they stopped tonight. By carrying their own midday meal, they could keep to their own pace during the day.

It was pleasant to lean against the trunk of a tree as he crunched into a crisp apple. Here there were no half inches of brandy, no clocks save the watch in his waistcoat pocket. No schedules to keep unless he so chose.

For a time, he idly listened to the good-natured argument between the grooms and outriders. His apple was sweet, the horses were happy, and few other travelers passed on the road. Above him, leaves rustled and whispered in a heavy breeze, one that felt as though it carried the promise of rain.

Nathaniel decided it would be best to move along at once. Given the choice to keep to a schedule—not the obligation—he found that he was quite willing to forge ahead.

To his eye, Lombard and Peters still looked tired as they began to re-saddle the horses. Ever since Epigram had shown the first signs of colic, the grooms had been run off their feet with treatments and keeping watch, and they were not used to so much time on the road.

He approached Lombard with the offer to let the elder man ride for a while. "Or if you like, extend the offer to your nephew instead. As I have only one horse, you'll have to decide between the two of you which shall ride."

"There is no need for them to choose," spoke up Rosalind. "Lombard is of a size to ride Farfalla." She patted the neck of the mare, looking almost hopeful about the prospect of not riding farther.

Lombard of course spat, then spoke around the straw in the corner of his mouth. "Kind of you, Miss Agate, but I can't be ridin' on a sidesaddle like a little ladybird."

"There is spare tack in the carriage," she said.

"Do you wish to ride in the carriage, then?" Nathaniel asked.

As she had that morning, she declined. "I'd feel as though I were closed up, having to see the outdoors only through a carriage window. I'm willing to walk and lead one of the horses."

"Careful, Miss Agate," Nathaniel murmured. "You are perilously close to being saddled with my company again."

"Oh, I don't think the carriage holds the right sort of tack for that," she said sweetly.

But once all items were stowed and the grooms mounted up, she stood at a distance from the Thoroughbreds. "I am only too aware that I'm entrusted with a hundred thousand pounds worth of betting-book promises."

Nathaniel folded Epigram's lead line into his fist. "You are. But you're also leading a colt who once followed you all the way across a stable for the promise of a mouthful of hay."

"And fingers." As though understanding her words, Pale Marauder dipped his head.

"Ah. I'll show you where to hold him so he can't take a piece of you with teeth or hoof." Nathaniel handed Epigram's lead to Lombard, who held it in one hand and his reins in the other.

Quickly then, he sidled around the light-colored colt to show Rosalind the best place to stand. "In line with his ear and at least a foot out from his shoulder. Then, as you walk, you can see him without being in his path."

"Understood." She wrapped the long lead around her hand.

"No—hold it. If he took it into his head to run, and you had that wrapped around your hand, some piece of you would get pulled along with him. Better to lose a bit of slack than a limb."

"You do know how to persuade a lass." She flexed her hands, then rubbed at her elbow.

Nathaniel retrieved his own lead, the outriders trotted ahead a small distance, and off they all headed for the second time that day.

Rosalind still held her arm at an odd angle, and after a few minutes of walking, Nathaniel asked, "Is your arm injured?"

She hastened to bend her elbow. "Not recently."

"Ah, she dodges the question." He clucked to Epigram, who was trying to crop a tuft of grass at the side of the road. "So in fact you were injured a long time ago?"

"Yes."

"What happened?" When she hesitated, he explained, "I'm not asking for gossip, but I don't want you to aggravate a strain. If this sort of walking will hurt you, we can re-saddle Farfalla for you in an instant."

"No, I like walking. This is good."

"If you say so," was all he said, though he quivered with curiosity. He must be patient, as patient as he would be with a skittish foal. If he chased, she'd never allow him closer.

And after a minute or two, Rosalind spoke. "When I was thirteen years old, I dropped a lamp." She kicked a small rock aside. "Burning oil splashed onto my clothing, and I was burned too."

He sucked in a sharp breath. "But you were all right?"

"Eventually, yes. A…lady my parents knew paid for me to have the best treatment. I have scars, but the physician's care saved my life. My parents could never have afforded such luxury with eight other children to support."

Another large story captured in small sentences. He wanted to know more: *How long did it take you to recover? Did the wounds hurt much? Were you able to stay at home, to see your family while you healed? Do you miss them now?*

He asked only one. "Is that...lady"—Rosalind had paused on the word, but he knew no other to use—"the one to whom you owe the money you asked of me?"

"She is," Rosalind said. "I owe her my life. Money is nothing compared to that."

"No, I suppose not."

She came to a sudden halt. Pale Marauder twisted his head back and snorted. Nathaniel drew up too. "What is the matter?"

"You looked so maudlin. Please don't. We all owe our lives to someone."

"Do we?" He tried his best to look the complete opposite of maudlin, but probably succeeded only in looking confused.

She smiled. "Well, yes. Every person in the world is indebted to his parents for his existence. I simply have a few extra people to add to that usual number. As do many soldiers. Many who travel abroad. Maybe even your own father."

With a pat on the colt's shoulder, she untangled Pale Marauder's stride and set off walking again, and so did Nathaniel and Epigram.

Peering around Epigram's neck, he tried to catch her eye. Wanting to say something; to tell her he was glad she had finally told him something of import, and that he understood and didn't think less of her, but only wished her well, and...and...

As the sun hung at the height of the sky, the horses' hooves began to stir up dust. No doubt this was why his throat closed, despite the number of words he wanted to say.

"I hope," he managed at last, "that you do not feel yourself in debt to me. Or if you do, I must be in debt to you too. We made a bargain."

"Indeed? And what do you owe me if you are in debt to me?"

Interesting. "That depends on what you owe me." He cleared his throat. "Which is for you to decide."

"A man recently informed me that we had either seven days on the road or a week. Or a number of hours that I do not at present recall."

"He sounds like an uncommonly good fellow. Diplomatic, I mean. Flexible. Good at arithmetic."

"He does give that impression. So perhaps by the end of that seven days, I shall decide whether our accounts are even. And if there is a claim on either side…"

"You must let me know how to discharge it."

They had a brief competition to see who could catch the other's eye, smile, and then look away the quickest. Rosalind won.

But Nathaniel didn't feel he had lost.

As they walked on, someone began whistling. After a minute, Nathaniel realized it was him.

Eight

Rosalind awoke the following morning to a pounding at her chamber door. Sleep fogged her wits for a moment as she squinted into an unfamiliar low-ceilinged room.

An inn! They had stopped at an inn. This was her bedchamber.

The pounding at the door grew more insistent. Startled, she threw back the covers. Every muscle ached and groaned from her time in the saddle, but as quickly as she could, she crossed the room and pulled open the door. "Nathaniel! Is something wrong?"

Nathaniel Chandler peered down at her, fist still upraised to knock again. "Must something be wrong when a man knocks at his traveling companion's door at"—he dropped his fist, then consulted his watch—"half nine?"

"Half…nine?" Her thoughts tangled. "I am so sorry. I cannot imagine why I slept so long."

"Can you not?" He grinned. "I'm not a man of great imagination, but I think it was because you are no more used to traveling for a long day than a colicky horse is."

"Not the most flattering comparison." She pulled a face. "Give me but five minutes, and I shall be ready to leave." Thank the Lord she had slept in a clean change of clothing last night. Not that she owned anything else in which to sleep, save the layers beneath.

"That's fine. I'll wait." He slouched against the frame of the door.

Now that she looked at him with less bleary eyes, she could see that he was dressed rather nicely. His boots shone glossy black, and he had exchanged his usual loose dark coat for the snug deep-blue garment favored by gentlemen of fashion.

"You're going to make me shy if you keep looking at me."

Rosalind stuffed a handful of hairpins into the pocket of her gown, hoping to hide her flushed cheeks. "I only noticed that you are not dressed for travel. The polish on your fine boots will be spoiled by the dust of the road." She eyed the privacy screen three hops away in the corner of the room, then simply plumped down onto the clean-swept wooden floor and jammed her feet into her boots. "Has your plan changed? Are we not continuing with the journey?"

When he didn't reply, she looked up. He had taken a step into the room and was grinning down at her. "What's so amusing?" she asked.

"Nothing. It is not at all funny to watch you rush around after being awakened late." The mirth in his expression gave the lie to these words. "Although you've got that boot lace in a terrible snarl. I should have brought you a maid after all. I would cheerfully pillage my father's staff if it would remove that pucker from between your brows."

"Oh…" Her cheeks went still warmer. "Not necessary. I've been shifting for myself for ten years. Although if one groom or footman is fit to chaperone a fine lady, then the size of our traveling company must make me the finest there ever was."

"I am sure everyone will think so at the fete. Which, by the way, is why I'm dressed so unsuitably this morning."

The knot in her boot lace finally gave way. "Wait. What? We're going to a fete?" Rosalind rolled to her feet, pushing back her unruly mass of hair.

"I thought we could. It's Whit week still. Everyone is celebrating because…well, really, just because they can. And we're a day ahead of where we're meant to be on the road, which is something to celebrate too."

She must have looked uncertain, for he added, "We can afford the day. It won't benefit us to arrive in Epsom before we are expected."

She bit her lip. "No, but it won't benefit us to be late either."

"Spoken like Sir William Chandler's secretary," he said with a lofty sigh. "There is something between earliness and tardiness, you know. Today, that marvelous *something* happens to be a Whit Tuesday fete in Kelting."

"Where is Kelting?"

"So many questions." He held out his hand. "Here, hand me some pins and I'll help you put up your hair. Kelting is a village about a half mile farther down the road. I don't know it well, nor have I used its inn and stables, so we'll leave the horses here and walk."

Still a bit fuddled by the remnants of sleep, she handed him a few pins and turned to the side. "Don't jab me in the head, please. Will—will it be only us two?"

"Of course not. You know how proper I am all the time. I have insisted that Lombard and Peters come along. Double chaperonage for a doubly fine day." Quick fingers made a plait in her long red-brown hair, the tiny tugs at her scalp an unexpected pleasure. "There, you can pin that up into some sort of coronet."

With a smile and a thanks, she finished the work he had begun. "I only hope the day will be as fine as you say." After the previous day of good progress, they had finished their ride in the cold drizzle they had outpaced for several hours. The whole party had thrown itself on the Dog and Pony's hot supper and dry bedding with gratitude. And since Nathaniel had covered the cost of the party's lodging, Rosalind had indulged in a bath the previous evening. A soak in hot water had done a great deal for her chilly bones and sore muscles.

Even though Nathaniel mentioned that he trusted the staff at the familiar inn, Rosalind had noticed he directed the outriders to sleep in the stable with their precious equine charges.

"If it rains again," Nathaniel replied, "you may come back and sleep the day away. And if it remains clear, you may sleep the afternoon away once we return. We have the morning, then we'll return to the

Dog and Pony so the grooms and I can spell the guards in the stable."

She poked a final pin into her hair. "That's eight bells, then."

"Hmm? How is that?"

A smile tugged at her lips. "Eight bells. My father was in the navy for a time, where eight bells marks the end of a watch. He always said that when it was time for the servants to go home." She wasn't sure why she'd said any of that, except that she liked an excuse to say *my father* as easily as others did. "He—it's the name of my parents' inn."

"At eight bells we'll return, then. Or whatever that is in landlubbers' time. And the guards can run off for a bit of wenching and feting, or take a nap or whatever they prefer."

"So we are stopping a day on the road. Just… stopping. To take a day of leisure." A morning with Nathaniel Chandler. She wasn't accustomed to either.

She found that she was more than ready to do a few things to which she wasn't accustomed.

"Yes, we are." He eyed her as she stuffed coins into the deep pockets of her skirts. "Come along, then. You promised me you'd be ready in five minutes, and it's been at least six." And with a last roguish lift of his brows, he strode into the corridor and thundered down the stairs.

After she grabbed her old bonnet and latched her chamber door, she followed.

Since he had gone ahead and could not see her, she permitted herself a little hop—just one—of glee.

❦

Kelting was an etching-perfect village through which the road ran like a brown velvet ribbon. Rosalind had never seen anything quite like it: shops with thatched roofs and glinting windows; trees new-leafed and clean from the previous day's rain; tidy pavements and a neat village green on which fiddle music guided laughing couples in a dance. Even a little elbow of a river or a canal, down which men on small flat-bottomed boats were punting to the cheers of onlookers.

"Ah, we've missed the beginning of the race," Nathaniel said at her side. "Though I notice that hasn't stopped Lombard and Peters from placing a bet or two."

Indeed, the two grooms had eased into the crowds as soon as they reached the village, their coins already tugged from their pockets.

"What would you like to do?" he asked. "Look about a bit, or try to get into the next footrace? The innkeeper at the Dog and Pony told me there's a bonnet worth thirty shillings, and his daughter intends to try for it."

Rosalind laughed. "I'm too sore to be quick on my feet today." The walk had eased the knots from her muscles, but she had a feeling a footrace would put new ones right back in.

Still, the thought of a new bonnet worth an exorbitant thirty shillings gave her a pang of longing. Imagine having something so costly and new, or of being able to win what one wanted.

No matter. Soon enough, her debts would be paid and all the money she earned would be hers. She could get an expensive bonnet then if she wanted to. Or she could spend her money on something else entirely.

For today, she wanted to try something new, to be as laughing and full of glee in the spring day and the town celebration as the women she saw here. No matter their age, they all seemed fresh-faced and light on their feet. It was difficult to tell the difference between lady and maid. Each mistress was in new garments, each maid wearing her ladyship's cast-off best from last season.

Rosalind's gowns were practical, fastening so she could dress without a maid's help. Generously cut to cover her scars.

She wondered what it would be like to be looked at with interest, even desire, as the laughing women were regarded by their husbands and lovers. *Secretaries don't have suitors*, she had told Nathaniel.

But maybe that wasn't always true. Maybe it didn't have to be—just for today.

The fiddle was joined by a harmony of trumpet and horn, and Nathaniel tapped a foot in time to the drifting music. He had removed his beaver-felt hat, holding it loosely in one hand, and she found herself staring at him. His hair was brown-gold, like sunlight through brandy.

As though sensing her gaze, he looked down at her and smiled. "Care for a dance?"

With a deep breath and a quick nod, she slipped her arm into his. "Indeed I would."

He clapped his hat back onto his head, and they ran for the green and slipped into the whirl of couples. Rosalind didn't know the steps, if there were steps to such a dance, but somehow that didn't matter. Nathaniel caught her hand and twirled her one way, then stepped and twirled her the other.

In her hurry, she hadn't picked up gloves this morning, and his bare hand within hers was solid and rough and warm. It sent a twisting curl of heat through her body, making her feel buoyant, lighter on her feet.

Then he took both her hands, spinning with her as the fiddle raced up and down the octave. Women around them kicked their feet and laughed when their partners lifted them in the air.

"Want to try it?" Nathaniel spun her close, tipping his head toward one of the high-lifted dancers. She nodded, almost breathless, and then his hands were about her waist.

The ground fell from beneath her feet while his hands spanned her and held her steady. The world was a swoop of sky, and her skirts flew about like a bell of cloth. Around, around, they turned together, giving her a quick soaring feeling. She shut her eyes and flew, just for a second, then landed lightly on her feet again.

The brass instruments drew out their final notes, followed by applause from the other dancers. Rosalind clapped once, maybe twice, but it was difficult to think of what to do now. Her feet were different for having danced in the air; her hands had been changed by being clasped by a partner.

And maybe she wasn't the only one who felt as thought something had altered, because Nathaniel Chandler was breathing hard, his blue eyes fixed on her with some deep expression to which she could not put a name. But it was good, whatever it was. It made her feel as though she were still swooping, still held by him.

She pushed her bonnet back with her free hand, catching the sun on her blushing face. Despite how unsure and fluttering she felt, she would have liked to stay there for hours. Days, holding his gaze like an embrace. But a new tune began, and the dancers eddied and changed around them, and it was time to make way.

When they reached the edge of the green, Nathaniel tossed his hat end over end in a neat flip. "All right, Rosalind Agate, order me about. What would you like to see next? The footraces? The amount of money our grooms have lost?"

"I want to buy something pretty. To wear the day of the Derby." Yet fashion was a closed book. To her, a ha'penny ribbon was as lovely as an ostrich feather that cost a guinea. "What should I choose? Not that I ought to ask you. My brothers would hate that sort of question about women's fripperies."

He replaced his hat atop his head. "I am hardly your brother," he said drily. "And my sisters would never have asked me anything of the sort. Abigail is two years older than me, but it might as well have been twenty. And Hannah is half horse herself. She never wanted anything but riding habits." He drew Rosalind's hand within his arm. "Do you actually care about my answer? I mean—will it influence what you buy?"

"Of course it will. I trust that you know what would be right for Derby Day."

"You trust that I know what would be right." His brows knit. "That's…quite nice of you, Rosalind Agate."

"I didn't intend to be nice. I mean, I didn't intend *not* to be nice either. It's simply an answer that's true."

"Then it's even better."

When she caught his eye, she felt a little more naked than her shift and stays and green worsted gown ought to permit. A little too naked for public view— yet she found she liked the trespass of such a feeling.

The trumpet called with a clear high note, beckoning the men who had finished the punting match at the footbridge just visible from the green. Their thin shirts were sweat-damp as they clambered from punt to shore. After shrugging into their coats, they accepted cheers from watching men and kisses from women amid good-humored laughter.

"Look at that," commented Nathaniel. "That fellow won a medal. Do you think it was for the punting match, or was he on time for dinner as well?"

❧

It was both easy and difficult to buy something pretty. Rosalind liked nearly everything offered for sale, so how was she to choose? She placed a hand in her pocket and let the thin coins slip between her fingers.

"I shall get a ribbon for my bonnet," she decided. "But which?"

Nathaniel pointed without hesitation to a ribbon the color of a new leaf. "This one. To match your eyes."

Were they truly that color? He had noticed, had remembered? Rosalind flushed as she took it up. "Thank you. I like that suggestion."

But oh—it was a broad ribbon of silk, smooth and bright and lovely to the touch. Something so fine would exhaust her coins. By way of excuse, she said, "Maybe something narrower would do better for my bonnet." It still hung from its strings about her neck, and she gave the straw hat a little tug.

"If you prefer something narrower, then you ought to have it. But my dear Miss Agate, if you wear the green ribbon, kingdoms will fall at your glance, and men will topple at your feet."

The ribbon seller, a goodwife with a plump, ruddy face, winked at Rosalind. "Listen to your gentleman, miss. I wouldn't mind a few kingdoms myself if they'd come my way as easily as buying a ribbon."

Now Rosalind was blushing in earnest. "A lady only needs one kingdom—or queendom. The running of any more than that will wear her to a thread."

"And how many men do you require at your feet?" asked Nathaniel.

She could not quite look at him. "None. I'd be devastated if I trod on anyone."

"The benevolent sort of queen. That settles it. You simply must have this." Before she could stop him, he had exchanged a coin for the length of sleek green silk. "Would you like me to tie that on for you at once?"

"You've—no, thank you. You've done so much. More than—you shouldn't really. I shouldn't have…" She looped the ribbon around her hand, liking the slick, satiny feel of it. She didn't want to let go of it, even to weave it onto her bonnet. "Thank you, Nathaniel. This is kind of you."

"You *did* promise not to tread on me. How could I resist?"

And did that mean he lay at her feet? For a while, she had forgot her usual warning: no false compliments.

But maybe he'd remembered, and maybe that had been a real one.

"Thank you," she said again. "I like it. Very much."

Now it was his turn to flush and look away. "Always with the short sentences." Which somehow, she knew, meant that he was pleased.

As they left the ribbon seller and Rosalind looked around, she noticed that many of the women were not even wearing bonnets. Instead, they were crowned by wreaths of flowers. For some, this had clearly been an impulse. Their bonnets swung free from strings tied over a dainty arm or had been pushed back to hang behind a smooth neck. Whitsuntide was all flowers, all new life, all celebration.

She remembered her girlhood dream of riding a pony at a fete, crowned with flowers like a May Queen. She had thought of it when treating Sheltie; before that, not for years. If pressed, she would have guessed she had outgrown this dream.

But maybe not. Maybe she had only outgrown her chance to ride a pony.

From a woman holding wreaths of flowers along one arm, Rosalind bought a circlet of carnations, red as heart's blood. There was a particular sort of pleasure in buying something for herself that she had long wanted, just because she could. She tipped her carnation crown to a jaunty angle atop her plaited coronet of hair.

"Very nice," said Nathaniel when she had done this. "You look a proper Whit-week maiden now. Shall you buy anything else?"

"I have…" *bought enough already*, she intended to say, but then she saw it. Pretty, so pretty that there was no uncertainty about the matter. Spilling atop a stall of cloths and caps and scarfs was a fichu of bobbin lace, a shade just off white and scalloped at the edges. When Rosalind slipped over and lifted it in reverent fingers, she realized it was shaped in a long thin triangle gently swooping in the middle, as though it were ready to embrace her.

"I never wear this sort of thing," she said.

"Is that why you want it?" Nathaniel asked.

He understood. "Yes. That is exactly why I want it." If she unfastened her high-necked gown at the collar, then folded the fabric under, she might feel light, rather than having something always clutching at her throat.

The fichu emptied her pocket, even after she argued the seller down to half the scandalous price first asked. It was worth the cost to fill her hands with such spiderweb-fine luxury. The passion-red crown and the lace made her feel like a different Rosalind, one who had never been scarred. She wanted to cover herself in such fineness, to carry this feeling around with her even after they left the fete.

She wanted Nathaniel to look at her with that sort of shy wonder again, as though he had found himself at her feet without quite knowing how it had happened.

"I would like to wear this lace at once," she decided. "Will you help me to find a place to change my clothing?"

Nine

Rosalind had hoped simply to duck into the village's public house to arrange her gown and fichu, but a quick conversation between Nathaniel and a random inhabitant of Kelting proved that this would be impossible.

"No inn in the village since Christmas," confirmed the villager—one George Hutchins, a broad, sturdy farmer with gnarled hands and a vinegary Suffolk accent that hopped upward at the end of every sentence. "Somehow a fire caugh' to it, a terrible loss. The Cock and Bull's nothin' bu' a shell." He indicated the handsome structure of blond and red brick to one corner of the village green, beside the main road. Though the facade was intact, Rosalind could tell that the window frames were empty eyes upon the fallen interior.

"The stables are sound enough, though," Hutchins added. "Old Toby's been serving ale from there since the new year. If yer care for a pint, the Whit ale's strong enough to grow yer a mustache." He jerked his head toward the road. "Or yer can run on back to the

Dog and Pony and roll abou' in down pillows while yer drink sherry."

Such pride in his village; Rosalind smiled as she folded away her fichu. Doubling and redoubling the fine lace, she made a packet of it as small as the palm of her hand, then tucked it into her pocket alongside the ribbon.

The color of your eyes.

"I could do with a pint," she replied to Hutchins. She felt flushed and half intoxicated already. "Though perhaps not a mustache."

"They know how to celebrate here in Kelting," Nathaniel said. "Thank you for your help, sir."

Hutchins nodded. "No one knows more abou' Kelting than me. There's been a Hutchins here since Richard Crookback was on the throne."

The stables seemed an unlikely home for a brewery, but the burly man tending the taps seemed happy to explain. The so-called Old Toby was of no more than middle age, though as he explained, he had borne the nickname since the birth of his son Young Toby two decades earlier.

"The owners of the Cock and Bull up and left after the fire," he said. "They weren't from Kelting. They'd only lived here a few decades. But they were good people. Just couldn't afford to rebuild. Couldn't find a buyer for the inn neither, as far as I know, so they sold me the stables for a song. Now, what'll yer have? A pint?"

Too late, Rosalind recalled her empty pockets. "Oh, I couldn't—"

"Yes, a pint for the lady." Nathaniel handed Old

Toby a coin. Beneath his luxuriant black mustache—it seemed Hutchins had been right about the strength of the ale—the gruff brewer smiled.

"Now that's a fine gentleman you have," he commented as he filled a pottery tankard. "Keepin' a lady in ale is the surest way to her heart."

"Is it?" Nathaniel accepted the tankard, then handed it on to Rosalind. "Like a fool, I've spent time on less liquid means of courtship."

"Ah, well. Those other ways are never wasted. Just ask the lady if yer don't believe me."

"Lady, do you share Mr. Hutchins's viewpoint?" Nathaniel was teasing her; he had to be. For he wasn't talking of her, but of someone in his past. Though they'd danced and he'd bought her a ribbon, that was hardly courtship.

Was it? Wasn't it?

She shook her head. "Secretaries are too diplomatic to have opinions about such matters." She held up the tankard, breathing a scent of grain and alcohol strong enough to pinch the nose. It pulled her back in time to the taps at the Eight Bells, where she had once seen her parents fill tankards much like this.

When she drank, the ale was like liquid bread, dark and sharp as rye. The way it fizzed on the tongue was new and interesting.

The swallow sloshed in her stomach, wary, and she recalled that she had eaten nothing yet that day.

"That's enough for me. Here, you can finish this if you like." She turned to hand the pottery tankard to Nathaniel.

"No, no. I couldn't." He slid aside as a trio of

revelers entered, clamoring for ale, and pressed himself against the brick wall beside the door.

But he was regarding the tankard the same way she had studied the fichu: covetous and determined. As though it were already in his hands.

So she pressed. "No, truly. I want you to have it." She squeezed by the new arrivals to join him at the wall.

"I shouldn't. It's far too early for ale."

"Maybe at Windsor Castle, but not at the Kelting fete. Everyone else is drinking it." Which wasn't quite true, but true enough. "Besides which, some people drink ale with breakfast."

"Not I."

She shrugged. "Of course, you don't have to have it." She tilted the pottery tankard, ready to upend it.

"Wait." He caught her wrist. "Maybe—just this one. Just one will be all right."

Was he asking her? He sounded uncertain. "I told you it was all right," she said. "Here. It's yours. You paid for it."

As he put his lips to it, she wondered: was that the same spot from which she had drunk? It was as though she had passed him a kiss—or he had accepted one. But surely the taste of ale would be far stronger than any hint of Rosalind that might remain.

He drank off the remainder of the pint in one long swallow. With eyes closed, he fumbled to hand off the tankard. Rosalind took it back, then with a few sliding steps around the others, returned it to Toby for washing—she hoped—and reuse.

When she returned to Nathaniel's side, he said,

"Let's be off at once." She made as if to take his arm again, but his hands were clenched into fists, elbows locked at his sides.

Maybe he hadn't liked the ale. She shouldn't have pressed him; getting a pint had been her idea, not his. So she accepted this odd intensity, sidling with him toward the exit, then breathing deeply of the cooler outside air. "What would you like to do now?"

"Anything. Eat. Dance. Watch a race. Play a game."

"Eat," she said. "If you are asking for my suggestion."

"Of course."

Scattered about like seeds were small stalls selling meat pies and wagons laden with spring fruits. Above all wafted a heavenly scent of sweetness and spice. Rosalind imagined the aroma soaking through every inch of her body. Something roasted in sugar; almonds, probably. The Earl of Carbury's children had gobbled them last Christmas just as poorer children might eat popped corn or rejoice over raisins.

She didn't realize she was following her nose until Nathaniel caught up to her with a running step. "You've seen something you want?"

Another deep breath. *Ah.* "Smelled it."

He tilted back his head, hand to the crown of his hat, and drew in a deep breath. "Ah. The roasted almonds have you fascinated. Have a fondness for sweets, do you?"

She nodded as she clapped eyes on the source of the scent: an open fire in a ring of stones, over which a lanky, half-grown boy was shaking a long-handled pan of the sort one used for roasting chestnuts.

"Almonds for yer?" He gave the pan another shake. Flame licked the bottom and made its contents sizzle.

Rosalind drew back a step, her skin tight and prickling.

It wasn't as though she were unaccustomed to fire. Nearly every room of every house had a hearth and—if one had the money—something to burn within it for warmth and light. But this open blaze... No, she wanted her skirts away from it.

Nathaniel must have understood why she halted. Giving her shoulder a quick squeeze, he closed the distance between them and the youth. "I think we must have some almonds, yes. How can anyone resist that smell?"

"Shoulda been here yesterdi'. I was roastin' sausages. Ma made roups of 'em out of the pig tha' we kill las' week for Whitsun."

"I'm sorry I missed it. Will you be here every day of the fete?" Nathaniel peered into the roasting pan. Rosalind rubbed at her elbow and took another step back.

The boy explained that he had injured his ankle the previous week and could not help on the land, so he was making amends by selling anything he could throughout the Whit week festivities. "If it's food, it's go' to have a fine smell. How's anyone to come buy if they can' smell me?"

"That's good sense," Nathaniel said gravely. "One must be smelled if one is to make a success of oneself. How much for a cone of your almonds?"

"A shillin'?" The youth's angular face split in a puckish grin.

Rosalind spluttered. "That's outrageous."

Nathaniel shrugged. "It's Whit week. We're celebrating." He fished out a silver coin and flipped it to the gaping boy. He accepted a paper twist of old newspaper from the boy, who scooped it full of sugared nuts. When Nathaniel stepped back to Rosalind and extended the cone, the warm almonds released their sweet, spiced scent in a blow of pleasure.

"For you." He smiled.

She took another step back. "Oh—I shouldn't accept…" It was not much of a protest, but protests were difficult when one's belly was empty and one's nose was full of the scent of warm sugar.

"If you like sweets, you should have them." His blue eyes were shaded beneath the brim of his hat. His lips curved, kind and wry at once. "And you ought to ask for what you want, Rosalind. You never know but that you might get it."

How confident he sounded, that to want a thing was to have the right to pursue that desire. For a decade she had asked for nothing she did not earn, save the money that would pay long-held debts. There was no room in her life, in her well-ordered mind, for any but the deepest claims upon her soul. What were sugared almonds next to that?

Yet he made it look so easy. If almonds meant so little, then it was but a small gesture to get them. And here they were, hot and cinnamon-scented in her grasp. All the sweeter for being a gift.

Maybe she was not right about what sort of request made sense. Or maybe this was the first time she had wanted something small enough that she had a prayer of receiving it.

He was tall at her side, and she suddenly felt shy about all the things she wanted. "Thank you," she said, and crunched an almond to paste.

The remainder of the morning passed too swiftly. First they meandered to the edge of the road, where a trotting race was to begin. After a day in the company of tidy saddle horses and stringy Thoroughbreds, the massive Suffolk plow horses seemed as thick-limbed and brawny as the elephants about which Rosalind had once taught Lord Carbury's children.

Their grizzled friend Hutchins split from the line of horses and riders, shaking his head as he tugged at a bit of tack on the long muzzle of his chestnut gelding.

"His rein has snapped," Rosalind realized. "What a shame; he will miss the race. They are to give another medal."

"A medal? We can't have him miss that. Wait here, if you will. I'll return in a moment." Nathaniel strode toward Hutchins, leaving Rosalind behind with her almonds. She savored them, sucking the candied sugar and sweet spice from each one while she watched Nathaniel cut a length from Hutchins's lead line and effect a repair.

It was so natural to him, to be the one who darted forward to help. Nathaniel Chandler was the sort of man who, when he saw something that needed to be done, would do it.

That impulsive urge didn't always serve him well, as when he'd rolled his father's stuck wheelchair. But just now, as Rosalind watched, Hutchins's gesturing turned to a grudging nod, and he mounted up and returned to the line in time for the starting signal.

As Nathaniel walked back toward Rosalind, she could not seem to stop looking at his hands. Though she wore long sleeves, she shivered. The pleasant sort of shiver. The sort that came from wondering *What would it be like if…*

When he reached her side, she managed to speak lightly. "You knew exactly how to help him. Did a milkmaid break his rein?"

He laughed. "Of course it was a milkmaid. They are the cause of every delay. Here, let me try one of those almonds, will you?"

She held out the paper, keeping her eyes fixed on the line of horses. Once he'd shaken out a few almonds, she folded the cone closed and tucked it into her pocket. "I hope no carriages are traveling the other way. This race stretches the whole width of the road."

"These horses are quick enough to keep out of trouble," he replied.

Once the starting signal set them off, she saw he was quite right. The huge animals were far quicker than the cart horses she remembered from London. Chestnuts, every one of them, they lifted their neat hooves in a light trot that soon hid them behind a cloud of dust. A minute later, a shrill whistle marked the end of the race.

"Hutchins has got it. You see if he hasn't," Nathaniel predicted. "He was so angry about that broken rein that he would have run the race himself."

And indeed the man who knew more about Kelting than anyone else was the victor. He guided his horse back to the green on a now-short lead, a shining medal about his neck.

When he reached Nathaniel and Rosalind where they stood beside the burned-out public house, he took off the medal and handed it to Nathaniel. "Yer deserve this more than I do, Chandler."

"Not at all!" Nathaniel's eyes went wide, and he held his palms out flat as if to make a wall of his hands. "You ran the race, Hutchins. You and your horse. If you don't want the medal, give it to your animal."

The farmer's deeply carved face relaxed into a smile. "They give me a guinea too. This in't the real prize."

"In that case," Rosalind interrupted, "he would be honored. He has been wanting a medal to reward him for his everyday triumphs—"

"Such as arising for the day on time," Nathaniel interrupted smoothly, ignoring Rosalind's wry glance. "I would be honored to accept it, deserving it so well."

Hutchins tugged his forelock, then replaced his cap. "Better for yer to keep it, if yer hopin' to ge' a medal for wakin' up. Not even in Whit week do yer ge' a prize for that."

When the farmer had led his chestnut away again, Nathaniel dangled the medal before Rosalind's face. "Look there, Rosalind Agate. I've finally won a medal, and I didn't even have to tidy myself up for a meal."

"Or arise early." At the end of its white ribbon, the medal turned in a slow breeze. It was a small circle of some silver metal, maybe tin, buffed to shine and catch the eye. "It's pretty," she said. "I'm glad he gave it to you. He wouldn't have won without your help at the right moment."

"Oh—well." He shrugged this off, then stuffed the medal into the pocket of his waistcoat, from which the ribbon poked out alongside his fob. "This is a pleasant village, isn't it? If home felt like this, I mightn't be so eager to take to the road."

"And how does it feel to you?" She couldn't seem to stop asking questions. Her tidy control was packed away. Today she was a woman who danced, and who owned a ribbon so green it would bring a man to his knees.

The thought made her smile as she blinked up at Nathaniel. His eyes were blue, as blue as the Suffolk sky in springtime. She had learned the shade of their brightness.

Slowly, he smiled. "It feels," he said, "like the sort of place where a man might kiss a woman with a crown of red flowers in her hair."

Her heart thudded a bit faster; her knees went watery. "It does feel that way," she whispered. "To me too."

He tipped up her chin, his hand strong yet gentle along the line of her jaw. "Thank God for that." And there in the shadow of a building once devoured by flame, he lowered his lips to hers.

Ten

ONCE THEIR LIPS MET, NATHANIEL COULD NOT imagine how he had waited so long to kiss her.

Oh, there were reasons on reasons not to. She was his father's secretary, and he had some sort of business arrangement with her about…something…

Honestly, who cared about the reasons why not? There were even more reasons why this was right.

The soft, almost hesitant curve of her mouth before he covered it with his own.

The surprised inhale that smoothed into a *hmmm* of pleasure.

The sweet-spiced taste of her as her lips parted, letting them fit together more deeply with his. As the tip of his tongue brushed hers, setting them both to shivering, he tasted the candied almonds. He tasted the heat of her and breathed in her scent. She was flowers and laughter and all the joys of a muddled morning. Of a race won. A medal for doing what was right.

Her hands wound around his neck, nails trailing lightly through his short-cropped hair. He could have groaned at the feeling, gentle and intimate, and he bent to wrap her more closely within his embrace. His hand trailed from her face to her shoulder to her back to fit her close to him. To press against her, solid and smiling and crimson-crowned and lovely.

She made another little *hmm*, and he went tense as a bowstring at the erotic sound. He laced his fingers into her plaited hair beneath its wreath of blooms. Feeling the shape of her head through her sleek hair was intimate. He almost felt as though he were holding her thoughts. Could he tell what was on her mind? How could he understand her, a woman so eager for sweetness but who had never yet claimed it?

Secretaries don't, she had said—yet she did right now, and thank the Lord for that. One kiss trembled into the next: one soft and tentative, one deep and hungry. The next shy, the following one fervent. Mouth and tongue, hand and breath and warm skin; the coolness of a shade that made him feel as though no one could see them. As though they could carry on forever, finding each other, wanting, tasting.

A breeze ruffled his hair. At some point, she must have tipped off his hat. He didn't care. He liked it. He wanted her to strip off more. To see him differently. To keep kissing him as though she had never liked anything so much, as though she were helpless to stop. As though she were drunk on the pleasure of it.

Drunk.

One drink was never enough, and so he should have none.

Kissing Rosalind Agate was the same sort of thing. He couldn't afford the distraction—not now that he had finally been trusted to lead. *Trust Nathaniel.*

She did, and he couldn't stop kissing her. It seemed the day had been made for this moment.

He had to shove her away with his hands, even as his lips refused to let go. Stumbling backward, he smacked into the solid brick husk of the burned-out inn. "I…" Should he apologize? He didn't want to.

Rosalind blinked at him, fingertips drifting to her kiss-pinkened lips. "Is this what happens when a woman wears red flowers in her hair?"

He laid a palm against the brick, pushing himself upright. "It is if she is you. And if she wants such kisses."

"I did. I—thank you. I have never been kissed like that." Her lips trembled with what was almost a smile. "It is not part of my position." Was she more surprised by their brief embrace, or was he?

"Nor should it be. A kiss should be for yourself alone."

"Oh, I don't think I could feel this way on my own. Surely the person sharing the kiss is…" She trailed off. Her fingers fluttered to the bonnet ribbon about her neck. Still the old one, faded until it was no color at all. "A kiss is made by two. And it belongs to both of them."

"It does at that." The words made his heart thump more heartily.

Her gaze was so direct that he dodged it, bending to pick up his fallen hat and brush off imaginary dust. He didn't want her to look too closely at him quite yet. Not until he assembled himself again, from hat to cheeky grin. Not until he knew exactly what they'd shared with that kiss, and why, and what it meant.

Venturing a glance about, he caught a knowing

smile from a goodwife or two. The end of a laugh between two farmers elbowing themselves. Today there was no scandal in a public kiss, not in such a festive atmosphere. It would be easy to laugh it off as a tipsy pleasure. As meaning nothing at all.

When he straightened up, hat firmly in place, he brushed the point of Rosalind's chin with a tentative fingertip. "Thank you, Rosalind."

He would not make a nothing of their kisses.

And she must have realized what he was doing, what he meant, for she smiled. It was a sunrise sort of smile, sneaking up a bit at a time until all of a sudden everything was bright and glowing. A man could lose his heart to a smile like that. A man could find himself at a woman's feet.

"Thank you, Nathaniel. For...all of it. For the morning, and the..." She blushed, a pink that seemed the prettiest shade there had ever been.

"Kisses?" He lifted a brow.

She went still pinker. "The ribbon, I was going to say. And the almonds."

"That's what you were going to say, was it?" He was enjoying this.

"It's quite a list. There might be a few other things I need to thank you for, too."

He wanted to fold her in his arms again. "There is nothing for which you need to thank me, Rosalind. Anything I gave you was because I wanted you to have it. Not because I wanted to awaken any feeling of obligation."

She lifted a hand, touching one of the carnations in her flowered crown. "I feel different this morning.

With you." Her hand fell, and when she fixed her eyes on him, they were puzzled. "But it's only for the morning, isn't it? This crown of flowers will soon fade. And I am still a secretary."

And he, her employer's son, on whom obligations were a load of bricks carried over thin ice. For the morning, she had trusted him. But would she continue?

He traced a ruffled carnation petal, wanting to touch her hair, her face again. "Maybe secretaries can do more than you allow."

"They do wear many hats." She stepped back, ducking her head as she tugged free the wreath of flowers and hung it around her wrist. "But not always of the sort one would wish."

She lifted the bonnet that dangled down her back and resettled it on her head. "It was a beautiful fete, Nathaniel. Thank you for bringing me with you." Again, the smile, though this one was more like a sunset going dim. "And I thank you not from obligation, but because I want you to know what pleasure I took. In everything."

"I didn't…" He shook his head. "Wait. What's this? Are you ready to leave?"

She gave a little shrug and an impish smile. "As though anything could surpass this morning's festivities? You have your medal, and I have been…"

He liked seeing her blush. "Thoroughly kissed?"

"Right. And so I must return to the Dog and Pony now, I think. I've much work to do."

"I'll walk with you. Let me just locate our grooms so they can return with us. As you say, we all have work to complete this afternoon." He hesitated.

"This morning—it was my pleasure too, Rosalind. All of it."

Polite words; for once, politeness and truth coincided. But he was talking about far more than a bit of company at the fete, and they had come far more than a half mile from where they had been this morning.

If only he had some idea where they ought to go next.

❧

Though the entire afternoon stretched ahead for correspondence, once Rosalind seated herself at the small writing desk in her bedchamber at the Dog and Pony, she had difficulty composing the letter she owed.

She began her daily report as she had so many times before:

> *Anweledig,*
> *Commanded directly to depart the instructed location, I could not find any excuse to remain and continue the search. The horses are safe due to Alpha's new means of keeping watch. I am in Gamma's party, journeying southward…*

What more was there to say than this? She couldn't tell Aunt Annie that she had spent a morning in leisure. Dancing, kissing, laughing. Wearing delight like a new garment tailored just for her, fitting better than she had ever expected.

It was my pleasure too, Nathaniel had said.

And she had done that? Had brought him that?

The feeling was warm and winding, wrapping her in sweet satisfaction.

A wreath of red carnations hung over the corner of the privacy screen, beneath a bonnet that hung from a plain ribbon nothing like the color of her eyes. The green ribbon was in her pocket still. A hidden luxury that seemed, now that she had left the fete, like a promise that she could return to such a time of joy. Someday. Sometime.

She drew the ribbon out and looked at its luxuriant coil. A twist of silk that Nathaniel Chandler had sworn would win her unimaginable fortune.

And was he wrong? Never had she imagined such a kiss, her first real kiss. The slow melt of it, the intimate press of heartbeat to heart. It woke her body, made her think.

Made her want more of the same and of what came next. *Trust Nathaniel*, he had said, and she knew that she did.

Too much. More than she ought. Not because she knew him too little, but because she knew herself too well.

She knew why she had kissed him back. But why had he kissed her? Because she was there? Smiling? Because the fete made him want to celebrate with whomever was near?

If that was so, then that was all right. But she hoped it was more. And that—that was a bundle of feeling she'd never had the right to entertain, nor the leisure.

Returning her gaze to her letter, she rubbed at her elbow and set quill to paper once more. She tried out a few sentences for Aunt Annie, halting and crossing out each one until her usually neat hand-writing looked like the hatch marks of an engraver's piece. Whatever she wrote sounded like excuses. Disobedience, pretexts, a cover for knowing nothing more than she should.

But surely it was all right if she neglected sending a single letter or even two. Once she reached Epsom, she could write to Aunt Annie with a promise of certain payment, not the uncertainty of the hunt for information.

Yes, surely that would be all right. Aunt Annie wanted results. Evidence. Proof. And there could be no result more valuable, no evidence of Rosalind's loyalty better, than the discharge of a long-held debt.

She took up another sheet of paper, for there was a second letter she owed.

> *Sir William,*
> *After two days of travel, we are stopped at the Dog and Pony. Progress has been more than satisfactory. Your son has seen to the safety of the horses above all, maintaining the system of two-person watches you put into place in Newmarket...*

She would not lie, but she did not have to tell him *everything*. Her fingertips drifted to her lips, where she remembered the taste of heat, of sugared almonds.

Another sentence or two completed this daily report, and she blotted, folded, and sealed it. She would ask the innkeeper to send it; Sir William would receive it the next day.

The paper on which she had begun her letter to

Aunt Annie lay atop the desk, a reproach in iron gall ink and cotton rag paper.

Rosalind folded that too. And folded it again and again, until she had a shape resembling a flattened pyramid.

Pushing back her chair and rising to her feet, she tossed it toward the fireplace. Her aim was true.

Standing at a safe distance, she watched the letter burn.

Eleven

On Whit Tuesday, Jonathan Peters, a traveler bound for Epsom, won a pair of buckskin gloves by wrestling against all takers. One cannot state whether his opponents were more impressed by his skill, or whether ladies were more impressed by the man's form after he stripped off his coat.

—Kelting Monitor

ROSALIND WAS NOT THE ONLY ONE WHO HAD ENJOYED the fete, she realized when the young redheaded groom passed the local broadsheet around the Dog and Pony's public room the following morning. It was a newer edition of the paper in which her almonds had been wrapped, and it reported the happenings of the previous day with a spirited lilt that reminded Rosalind of George Hutchins's pride in his village.

But there was little time for congratulations, even with a pair of undeniably fine buckskin gloves to admire. A day of travel lay ahead, and packing and preparations for horses and humans alike needed to be carried out with all haste.

When she took to Farfalla's saddle again though, Rosalind found her mind as free as her body was occupied. She allowed her thoughts to go wandering, far from the narrow ribbon of road along which the little mare carried her in tidy step with the other travelers. Step after step closer to Epsom, she thought back to the boisterous years before she was burned and to all the quiet years of service since, tracing Aunt Annie's secrets. Collecting pieces of a puzzle when she had no idea where they would fit or what the final picture might look like.

Before meeting Nathaniel Chandler, she had never thought that there might be a future for her beyond the next post, the next house, the next piece of the puzzle. But now she had helped horses recover from illness. She had persuaded the stake for a small fortune from Nathaniel Chandler just by being honest about her need.

She had changed the faded ribbon on her bonnet for the green one the color of her eyes. She had worn red flowers in her hair, and it had been better than her childhood dream. Even now, the wilting wreath was folded within a clean linen shift and preserved in her traveling trunk. Maybe she would wear it again before a glass to remind herself that for a morning, she had been different. More.

Perhaps it was time to think of a new dream. The tight scars that laced her back and right side need not constrain her to this sort of life forever. Once she paid her debt to Aunt Annie, and Aunt Annie paid Tranc, then…

Then she would decide what to do.

If there was one thing she had realized during her

brief time in Sir William Chandler's employment, it was that she learned quickly—and that nothing she had ever learned was wasted.

✧

As the day's travel began, Nathaniel noticed that Rosalind kept a thoughtful distance. He knew the difference between an angry silence and every other sort, and this wasn't the former. She had changed the ribbon on her bonnet to the green one he had chosen, and every once in a while her fingertips drifted to the colorful ends tied beneath her chin.

Every time she did, he tried to hide a smile, not wanting her to catch him watching.

When they passed through Kelting a short way south of the Dog and Pony, where the Whit week festivities still held sway, she waved at the boy roasting food at the edge of the green. He had brought sausages again today, and the smoky smell was rich as it drifted across the road.

The burned brick structure of the Cock and Bull seemed to watch them pass with wistful windowless eyes. *I'd like to stay*, thought Nathaniel. It seemed a pleasant village. Though of course a morning spent in festivity was far different from the everyday wheel of the villagers' lives. One could not spend one's life counting on dances and kisses.

He slanted another glance at Rosalind, whose fingers strayed again to the ribbon of her bonnet. The simple gesture made something shift within him, something that had weighed on him, maybe since he had gulped ale the previous day.

He had chosen to stop drinking. And he had chosen to stop kissing her. He was not sure how he had found the strength; maybe only because he thought stopping was right.

Yet they weren't the same sort of wrong. While ale—or wine or brandy or whatever he lay hands on—made him feel less himself, kissing Rosalind Agate made him feel…more.

And from the way she touched the ribbon, as though she could not believe it real, maybe she felt the same way.

❧

This far north of London, they met few travelers. Even so, Rosalind noticed that Nathaniel sent the outriders before and behind, ever watchful.

The party paused for a quick meal at midday, then continued southward at a steady pace. After their day's rest, the Thoroughbreds had recovered their spirits and were looking much like they'd never suffered from colic at all. Pale Marauder was like a child in leading strings, blundering off in every direction and always wanting to be first. If he didn't tire himself by making the trip to Epsom twice as long as it ought to be—weaving about the road, halting and backing, circling—his obstinacy would carry him to the front during the Derby.

Epigram was much better behaved, though also like a young child, there was nothing he wouldn't try to eat. Soon after the midday break, at which people and horses alike had eaten their fill, they passed a farmer traveling between farm and village. His low-sided wooden cart, painted green and pulled by a small donkey alongside which he walked, was heaped with the fragile good things of spring: spinach, cauliflower, lettuce, cucumber. Carrots, thin and small, their leaves a feathery riot of green. Stalks of rhubarb, early strawberries like bright gems. Even a few radishes, which made Rosalind think of the gelding Jake.

She fell behind the Thoroughbreds and Nathaniel, slowing Farfalla to watch the progress of the spring-bright cart. Thus she had a fine view as Epigram stretched out his sturdy neck. When the cart passed, he planted his feet, then wheeled and tried to follow. Lombard, holding his lead, coaxed him back around—but then the colt tugged, the folded rope slipped from Lombard's hand, and off went Epigram in a trot after the cart.

"Oh, no. No, no, no," muttered Rosalind. Lombard was shouting a far worse epithet, one that halted the outriders. He raced after Epigram, boots raising puffs of road dust, but no one could trot as fast as a horse except…well, a trotting horse. Rosalind drew Farfalla to a halt, but she was too unsteady in her sidesaddle to gallop, and the outriders were too far off…

But here came Nathaniel, nudging Bumblebee into an easy canter. Rosalind turned in her saddle, watching him pass Lombard and catch up with Epigram just before he reached the cart.

At once, Nathaniel halted the cob and leaned from his saddle to catch the colt's lead line. When Epigram tried to take another step, he found himself pulled up short, then had his head turned the way from which he'd come. Shaking his head, the bay colt took another step.

Rosalind could see Nathaniel's lips moving, a low, slow patter of calm speech. But Epigram, usually so placid, wanted to follow the farmer's cart as badly as Rosalind had ever wanted anything in her life. It was as though the colt wanted to make up for every mouthful of feed he'd left untouched during his colic.

She remembered the almonds in the pocket of her traveling dress. Pulling the paper twist forth, she rattled it and called Epigram's name. With one hand holding Farfalla's reins, she flipped open the folded paper. Could horses smell sugar? Surely they had a better sense of smell than people.

Aha. Apparently horses could. Farfalla's ears pricked up, and she turned her head to fix Rosalind with a reproachful brown eye. *You had a treat all this time, and you weren't going to share it with me?*

"Er—this really is not a good time, Farfalla," said Rosalind. "Please. I'll plait your mane if you help with this."

The dainty ears swiveled as though the mare was deciding. Again, Rosalind rattled the nuts and called Epigram's name. Nathaniel shot her a grateful look, and with a few more words in Epigram's ear, he turned the colt away from the cart. Puffing, Lombard pounded up to the wayward colt, took hold of his lead, and coaxed him back into line.

As they passed Rosalind, she extended a flat palm with the remaining few sugared almonds atop it. Epigram blinked at her with knowing dark eyes as he lipped up the treat.

"I wonder if you knew what you were about the whole time," Rosalind murmured. "Did you want these instead of something from the cart? I'd make the same choice. They are delicious, aren't they?"

As though annoyed that he had missed a chance to create a fuss, Pale Marauder stamped a foot and, as soon as Lombard drew near with the other colt, shouldered into Epigram. If Farfalla had possessed the power of speech, Rosalind imagined she would have rolled her eyes and muttered, "Boys. *Honestly*."

"You deserve that plait," Rosalind said, busying her fingers in the mare's coarse mane while Nathaniel clambered down from Bumblebee's back.

The farmer must have been hard of hearing to miss the agitation in the party he'd just passed. But he didn't miss Nathaniel riding up to him, hopping down alongside the donkey, and laying one gentle hand on the beast while the other pulled coins from his purse. Rosalind watched, curious, as he negotiated with the grizzled man, then came away with a handful of carrots.

As the cart trundled on, Bumblebee received the first treat. The bay crunched the thin young carrot from tip to leaf as Nathaniel remounted. Every other horse, from the sturdy quartet ridden by the outriders to the chestnuts that pulled the carriage, also received one. Even Pale Marauder, once he was pulled away from Epigram. And Farfalla, whose mane was now a tidy row of half-plaited, half-sprung sections.

And even Epigram, once he started walking alongside Lombard again.

When Nathaniel dropped Bumblebee into a rolling stride alongside Farfalla, Rosalind said, "I presume a milkmaid pulled the lead from Lombard's hand."

"Who else?" said Nathaniel. "And another encouraged the cart to roll by."

She felt shy about saying more, as though to speak would be to remind him of her superfluous presence. Nathaniel had handled this hiccup in their smooth travel swiftly and with goodwill. Rosalind hadn't been needed to ensure Sir William's wishes were respected. She really wasn't needed on this journey at all.

"You knew just what to do," she finally said. "To keep the horses calm."

"I've met milkmaids before." He darted a glance at her, sky-bright and loaded with wicked humor. "But what were you about, giving Epigram your almonds? If I'd known you hadn't eaten them all, I'd have shoved them in your mouth when you breakfasted this morning."

"How gentlemanly."

He chuckled. "I mean well, you know. I don't want you to give away any bit of that happiness you felt yesterday in getting what you wished."

While one hand held the rein, her other strayed to the broad silken ends of her new green ribbon. "I didn't give it away. I made it last longer."

"By rationing it out? Happiness is not such a scarcity as that, I hope."

"Whether it is or isn't, I like knowing I have a few almonds in my pocket in case of need."

He shook his head. As though feeling a change in the reins, Bumblebee shook his head too. "I can see I'm never going to convince you that you should gobble up treats when they come your way. So instead I'll thank you for your help. Without it, Epigram might have eaten half the fruit on that cart, and then we'd have had a new case of colic to treat."

"You wouldn't have let that happen." Yet his words brought a blush to her cheeks.

"I wouldn't have wanted it to. But no man can cope alone with the world's milkmaids." Though she watched the road, she thought he smiled. There was something different in the feel of the air. "I am glad you're here."

Now, what was she to say to that? She managed only a sort of squeak and a deepening of the blush.

Maybe she didn't have to ration out happiness at that. She might not have almonds in her pockets anymore, but as long as she traveled with Nathaniel Chandler, another joy would be coming her way.

∽❦∾

At the end of that day, they stopped at a posting house Nathaniel knew well near the town of Bishop's Stortford. The Blue Castle was an ancient wattle-and-daub structure with age-blackened timbers in a diamond pattern brightened by white plaster. The galleries around the central courtyard sagged slightly, rather like a traveler ready to set down a heavy load.

The innkeeper, Filbert, was used to wealthy travelers' custom of arriving with their own horses and carriages. In the entryway, he greeted Nathaniel with his usual simper and bow, revealing as he did a patch of thinning dark hair across which he had slicked desperate strands. Thus began anew the familiar process of arranging lodging for people and beasts, for setting watches in the stable.

When the grooms drifted off to join the ostlers in the stable, Filbert spotted Rosalind, and his smile fell. "We ca'er to polite folk, not to la'ybirds. She canno' stay here."

Nathaniel's head snapped back. He opened his mouth, ready to defend Rosalind's honor—but she spoke first.

"Mr. Filbert." She lifted her chin. "Do you honestly imagine that a *ladybird*"—she spread her plummy accent heavily over the word—"would appear dressed in a straw bonnet and riding habit? Or that I would travel in company with so many men if I were improper? A lady takes one groom to preserve her reputation. I travel with two of them, as well as five guards, a coachman, and—"

"Mr. Nathaniel Chandler," Nathaniel said helpfully. "Who is nothing but proper, Filbert, as you know."

The innkeeper wiped his hands on the clean white apron that overspread his linen shirt and breeches. "I haven' the room for her."

"Oh, that's all right. She can have my room, and I'll sleep in the stable." He smiled as though the entire exchange had been a delight. "Problem solved."

The innkeeper looked doubtful. "I haven' ever…"

"Mr. Filbert." Rosalind untied the bow of her bonnet strings, settling in. "If you know Mr. Nathaniel Chandler well enough to know how proper he is—"

Nathaniel coughed.

"—then surely you are familiar with his father. And with the baronet's exactitude. And with the amount of custom he sends southward from Newmarket."

A bob of the balding head. "I am, but—"

"I am his secretary since the marriage of his daughter, who is now Lady Crosby."

"But you're a woman." Poor Filbert. He didn't know when to keep silent.

"Through no doing of my own, yes. Fortunately Sir William is not concerned by the work of circumstance, but for the work of a person's own hands. He has entrusted me with the task of reporting to him on the conditions of our travel." Rosalind pulled off her bonnet, the better to look about the close, ancient entryway, all walls of the same aged black wood and plaster that made up the outside of the structure. "I wonder what report I shall make of you."

That ended the matter. Not only did Filbert recover his former simper, but he found a servant to bring Miss Agate's trunk up to her chamber. Nathaniel could not help but smile. It was rather fun, watching Rosalind wield this sort of secondhand influence as though she had been born to it.

"I meant wha' I said abou' no' having the room for one o' you," Filbert murmured apologetically to Nathaniel once Rosalind had ascended the stairs to her chamber.

He clapped the innkeeper on the shoulder. "And I meant what I said about being willing to sleep in the stable. It's quite all right."

The travelers partook of a simple but tasty meal wherever they happened to be: some in the stables, some in the kitchens making free with the maids, some in the courtyard enjoying a pipe with their food. Nathaniel was everywhere, settling his staff in, removing a scullery maid from the embrace of the roguish Noonan, and measuring out the feed of the horses.

He wondered if Rosalind would mention the forbidden treat of carrots in her letter that day. She probably wouldn't. Not that it would be so bad, really, if Sir William knew his strict methods were not the only way a horse could be kept in good health.

As twilight darkened the sky and servants lit lamps around the inn, Nathaniel searched for Rosalind. He found her just exiting the private parlor where she had taken her own dinner.

"I am sorry you had to give up your room." He thought she colored, but it was difficult to tell. The warm lamplight in the corridor made her all copper and gold.

"Don't let Filbert hear you say that," he teased. "There are times for stammering an apology and times for lifting one's chin. You did the latter, and beautifully."

Beautifully. She had, hadn't she? But how else could a beautiful woman do anything? She had taken on a glow of more than mere prettiness, and it had nothing to do with the lamplight. No, it was a feeling welling up from within. She looked happy. Proud, maybe. All sorts of good things that made him want to look, and look some more, and hope for a smile to flower over her features when she felt his gaze.

He cleared his throat, trying something—anything—to make himself stop staring. "Please don't worry about it. I had already planned to spend half the night in the stable. Now you've saved me the trouble of rousing myself during the night."

"It's kind of you to say so. It's not as though we could share the room."

"Um. No, I don't think that would be a wise idea."

And now which of them was looking more deeply? In whose cheeks was the color hotter? Because she had mentioned the idea, and he had admitted how unwise it would be, and now all he could think of was finding a place where they might be alone, and what they might do if they could let themselves be a little unwise.

Already he had kissed her lips, the lips that curved into a shy and secret smile. He had felt her pressed tightly against him, her fingers twining in his hair as though she could not pull him close enough. If they were alone—if they shared a room but for a while—he would kiss her again, and more. He wanted to see the curves he had felt dimly through clothing, to cup the softness of her breast. To tongue what he had touched and had only imagined touching.

"I hate being wise," he muttered. Since he was standing right next to the corridor wall, he rested his forehead against it and gave it a gentle thump.

Sense failed to return. His breeches remained tight. Wisdom laughed, flitting just out of reach.

"I have..." Rosalind's voice sounded thick. She cleared her throat, then tried again. "I have asked our host to send a letter for me tomorrow. I have told your father all is well, and that our progress is good."

He looked up from the blank whiteness of the wall. Her expression said more than these few sentences, but Nathaniel did not know how to read it.

Not wanting to say too much or something wrong, he settled on, "Thank you."

She nodded. Since she did not turn toward the stairs to leave him, he was clearly supposed to say something else. He groped about for a reply, but everything commonplace seemed to have fled. What could he say? *When you rode in silence today, were you thinking of me?* maybe, or *Why do you ration happiness?*

Are you standing here so I might kiss you again?

So tempting, this last question. "Are you…" He cut himself off, clutching desperately for that bit of wisdom. "I…like your new ribbon," he blurted out instead. "On your bonnet. It looks…nice."

"Oh." Her left hand drifted to her temple, though her head was not covered by the bonnet at present. When she dropped her hand, she used it to rub at the elbow that he assumed bore her old scars. "Thank you. It's not what I would have chosen for myself, but I'm glad to have it."

"Maybe we don't always choose best for ourselves." It was certainly true for him. He had chosen to pickle himself in drink, to hide the difficult things he did. The only thing he'd done well lately was to bribe Rosalind Agate to come along with him.

Which also hadn't been his choice, but his father's.

"Maybe not," she said quietly. "But sometimes I think we do." She rocked forward onto her toes, lifting herself. Closer, almost close enough that he could take her into his arms.

But before he could reach out, she sank back again. Her cheeks went pink—unmistakable this time, even in the lamplight—and her lips made the shape of another sound, unvoiced, as though she was about to say more.

Instead, she swallowed it back, only bidding him good night and mounting the stairs.

He watched her climb away, wondering whether she had been talking about more than a ribbon, and how much he had to do with any of it.

Twelve

THE FOLLOWING DAY BEGAN MUCH AS THE ONE before: with Nathaniel nudging his party into a tidy line and setting them southward on the road to Epsom in the early morning hours. The weather hinted at heat, a summery replacement to the rainy beginning of the week.

By late morning, the sun was bright and high in a cloudless white-blue. The road was pillowy with dust, flanked by fields of ripening crops on one side and sheep on the other, their neck bells jingling and their tentative *maa*'s like a hello. The world held a warm scent, all animal and turned earth and grassy young grains.

A trickle of perspiration had formed at the base of Nathaniel's neck and was currently trying to find a way down through his collar.

Eyeing a likely bunch of trees a small way from the road, he called a midday halt beneath their shade. Tidy and smooth as the workings of a clock, the grooms and outriders and guards unhitched and unpacked and watered and settled. They first took care of the horses, as always, removing tack and setting forth Sir William's prescribed amount of hay for the Thoroughbreds.

For once, Pale Marauder was docile and began eating from the pile.

Epigram swished his docked tail with impatience and bent his head to crop the grass about his hooves.

"I'll stop 'im." Lombard set aside the saddle he'd begun to rub dry, rolling to his feet. "Sir William won't like that none."

"Wait." Nathaniel reached out a quelling hand. What would be so bad about allowing the horse to eat grass? Horses were born to graze. Yes, Thoroughbreds were delicate beasts, but Epigram was a hardy specimen of the breed. He hadn't eaten himself into a colic; the other ill horses proved that. As long as the grass was clean and healthy, why should it not keep the horse the same way?

Nathaniel dropped to hands and knees, crawling around the horse—at a safe distance from careless hooves—to examine the ground. He spotted no insects or grit, no harmful plants. This was an equine feast of tender green blades, spring-tall and not yet dried by summer sun.

Rising to his feet, he patted Epigram on the withers. "Have a good luncheon, old boy. You can eat your fill."

Pale Marauder raised his head, eyeing Nathaniel with a baleful dark gaze.

"What? You're trying to look like the good son, aren't you, Roddy? No prodigals here. Eat grass if you like."

Horse to man, they stared. Pale Marauder's ears

swiveled, as though he was deciding what to do. Then he snorted, bent his head, and took another mouthful of hay. Then one of grass.

"You'll do it your own way, won't you? Fair enough." Nathaniel trailed a hand over the colt's back, petting the short, fine coat. "As long as you've thought about it, there's nothing wrong with doing something your own way."

God, he hoped that was true.

In for a penny, in for a pound. The outriders' horses and the steady chestnuts that pulled the carriage were turned loose on long lead ropes to roll and rest and graze near the road. A hamper packed by the Blue Castle was opened, its contents shared.

Thus they passed one or two of the hottest hours of the day. Somehow, the servants had heard of the marvelous way Rosalind had put innkeeper Filbert in his place the evening before, and Nathaniel watched as the men clustered around her with a laughing ease tied to respect. By claiming her own honor, she had given them a share too.

Peters offered to teach her to whittle. Egg and Love, the former boxers, feinted sparring at one another and showed Rosalind how to throw a punch. In one of her high-necked colorful gowns and with her bonnet ribbon untied, she looked every inch a lady and every bit a gleeful member of the party.

She hadn't wanted to join him on this trip. He was glad she had. He hoped that she was glad now too.

As they re-saddled the horses and rearranged themselves to travel onward, Nathaniel heard a bark. A somehow familiar bark.

"Damn," he muttered. They were near Sawbridgeworth, weren't they? Which meant these were Joe's fields.

Indeed, a sheepdog soon followed the sound of its barking, ducking under some fence and bounding up to Nathaniel, who stood next to Bumblebee. The leggy bay's ears flicked forward with curiosity as he eyed the dog.

Joe fell flat to his belly, the patient, waiting posture of a well-trained dog. He had long, shaggy white-and brown-and-black fur, eyes like little black currants, and a wet black nose he liked to poke into everything.

Rosalind walked to Nathaniel's side, one hand on Farfalla's bridle. "Nathaniel, you have made a new friend?"

"Met an old one again. Rosalind, meet Joe."

"Hello, Joe." She handed her mare's reins to Nathaniel and crouched before the dog. "You are a sheepdog, aren't you?"

"He is. Not that I know his real name. But every time I pass this way he comes to greet me, so I have to call him something."

Rosalind squinted up at Nathaniel. "You fed him once, didn't you." It was not a question.

He sighed. "I should have known better. But he was so *friendly*, running alongside me." Since that first encounter—complete with petting, playing, and a piece of beef sandwich—Joe seemed to have caught Nathaniel's scent. Now every time he passed these fields, the dog darted from its herd to greet Nathaniel with wagging plumed tail and pricked ears.

"He can come along with us for a little way today, can't he?"

"He probably will whether we like it or not." The dog was too well trained to run off entirely. But this time of year, the lambing ewes were in sheepcotes, so he must be bored and missing part of his flock.

The problem with Joe was that he treated everything as his flock. This was fine when Nathaniel was riding alone. But in a large group? Joe would be the canine equivalent of a milkmaid, causing delay on delay.

And yes, as soon as Dill and Button rode forward to take their usual positions ahead of the party, Joe trotted to their side. Weaving inward to nudge the pair of horses closer together and darting in front to halt their progress until the rest of the herd could catch up.

"Oy!" shouted Dill, reining in his black gelding to avoid trampling the dog. "Chandler, call off the creature! We ain't his sheep!"

Nathaniel boosted Rosalind into her saddle, noticing the spasm that crossed her features—that always crossed her features—when she moved her right side quickly.

But rather than comment on this, which he knew she wouldn't welcome, he asked, "Any ideas for convincing a sheepdog not to drive horses into a herd?"

She settled herself, taking up Farfalla's reins. "Even if I had almonds in my pocket, I don't think a sheepdog would be interested."

Nathaniel looked toward the outriders. Button had drawn his bay to one side of the road, and Joe trotted in quick circles around the pair of horses. White paws were a blur, as though the speed of his short strides would draw them closer together.

"He's going to spook the horses," muttered Nathaniel. "Or win himself a trampling." Already, the bay was beginning to bob his head and paw at the earth.

The drop of perspiration returned, tapping at Nathaniel's collar and threatening to slide between his shoulder blades and itch. Damn. One little dog, so eager to please, was keeping them from getting on their way.

To recall Nathaniel's notice, Rosalind tapped him on the shoulder. She grinned down at him from her saddle. "Why not give Joe some way to help in the way he wishes? Look, Pale Marauder is starting to wander again."

This was true. At the end of Lombard's lead, the cream-colored colt was pulling and winding as usual. He never traced a straight path when he could coil and backstep and yank with nervous energy.

"Rosalind, you are a genius." Nathaniel took a moment to admire her. Her worry of a few days ago had melted off, and she was every inch the tidy horsewoman from gloves to beribboned hat. "Where's that hamper?"

Without waiting for answer, he sorted through the packed-up belongings in the carriage with Noonan's help. Finding the leftover rind of a ham, he strode with it next to Lombard—currently grappling with Pale Marauder's lead line—and whistled.

Joe came lolloping back from the nervous pair of

horses, drawn by the whistle and the scent of meat. Nathaniel dangled the bit of ham before him, then let Joe snap it up with his panting doggy grin.

"All right, Roddy. Do your worst," he said to Pale Marauder.

"He thinks it's his best." Lombard rolled the straw he was chewing from one side of his mouth to the other, then spit. "C'mon, Rod. On we go."

Instead of stepping forward, Pale Marauder stepped sideways. Joe sprang into action, bounding to the grassy edge of the road and curving beside Pale Marauder's front hooves. The colt's next step was forward, and the next too, until he was walking in a neat line beside Epigram on Peters's lead.

Nathaniel chuckled, shaking his head, and swung up onto Bumblebee's back. Dill and Button rode forward, the Thoroughbreds walked, and he took his own preferred place at Rosalind's side as the carriage began to roll behind them.

"What a good dog," Rosalind commented with a nod toward Joe. With effortless energy, the sheepdog weaved to nudge Pale Marauder back into his place in the procession. "He so wanted to be useful. All we had to do was determine how he *could* be."

"Good old Joe," Nathaniel agreed. He couldn't fault the sheepdog for that. How often had he felt the same, figuratively running in circles for want of something to do?

Joe stayed with them until the rolling grassland at one side of the road was broken by a few houses, then changed to a tree-bounded village. As if recalling him to his post, a distant *baaa* sounded. Joe loped back to

Nathaniel, barked up at him—*Job done, thanks for the ham, have to go now*—and ran back along the road in the direction from which they'd come.

Within one minute, Pale Marauder was tugging and winding all over the road again. "Wouldn' mind having that dog join us all the way to Epsom," Lombard tossed over his shoulder. *Spit.*

Nathaniel laughed.

He liked being on the road, free and unfettered, matching his wits against the weather or circumstance. Or even a friendly sheepdog that adopted them as his own.

With Rosalind Agate at his side, everything seemed fresher and brighter. He didn't have to solve problems alone—and that meant, for now, there seemed to be no problem the travelers couldn't solve.

&ce;

The next day contained no sheepdogs, only the everyday milkmaids of carts and carriages for which to make way, heat and dust, water and grass to find. By agreement, the travelers again set off during the early-morning coolness, then spent the baking hours of midday resting in shade. They used the time to clean tack and tell stories.

Then, to Nathaniel's dismay, Lombard suggested a spitting contest. "Ever'one take part!"

"Mr. Nathaniel has a medal he could offer the winner," Rosalind mentioned. That rogue.

"I never had a medal before," Lombard said cheerfully.

And if the contest had been judged by volume, victory would surely have been his. But the contest favored distance—and Rosalind, who demanded a chance to try, proved to be the winner.

"Coo! She hit that tree," said Love. His craggy face bore an expression of great admiration.

"I have seven brothers," Rosalind explained. "Three older and four younger—plus one sister. Sometimes I think my whole childhood was spent spitting and learning boys' tricks."

"Never seen such a lady," commented Noonan in his gentle brogue. He began applauding, and Nathaniel had to join in, smiling.

"If you're all finished here," he said, "then we'd best get on the road again. But Miss Agate, you've won the medal fairly, and it's yours."

"Oh, I couldn't take it for *that*," she said. "I was only teasing about making you give it up. You received it when you helped someone. I spit on a tree. Really, you must keep it."

So he did. But he thought of it as hers after that, and the shining bit of metal felt warm in his coat pocket.

On that third day after the fete—the fifth since they had left Newmarket—when Nathaniel made to leave for the stables after the party had shared their evening meal, Rosalind informed him that her daily letter to Sir William included the phrase "no one could do better leading this company."

"Do you think so?" As they faced each other at the base of the inn's staircase, he wished they had stopped in full daylight so he could study every shading of her face.

"Of course I do. I wouldn't lie to your father." She sounded shocked, which amused him.

For a moment. "Thank you. But you'd better moderate your language or he'll assume you're being satirical."

"Secretaries," she began, and he knew what was coming next. He finished the sentence with her: "are never satirical."

He caught her grin, reflecting it back. "What about women with green ribbons? Or red flowers in their hair?"

She shook her uncovered head. "They might manage a bit of satire if something suitable comes to mind. But I am just a secretary for now, Nathaniel."

"You are never *just* a secretary," he replied.

"Right now I am." She caught the newel post in one hand and turned to mount the stairs. "But I think…I will not always be. Don't you?"

Today he didn't dare watch her walk away from him. After a comment like that, he just might try to follow her.

Thirteen

NATHANIEL WOULD HAVE LIKED TO AVOID LONDON entirely on the journey south, but the city was too large. To swing wide of it would add impossible days to their travel. From Newmarket to Epsom was a long arrow-shot through London's heart.

The following day, then, their quiet rural road began to change. London began long before one expected, the peaceful treed lanes and quiet roads giving way to wagon traffic, to inns and houses and shops, the blue skies smoke-smudged in inky thumb-prints. Soon enough the blue would become gray, and the buildings would cluster and press more tightly. The crowds would thicken; the noise would swell.

He kept his pistol always primed now, though he had never had any difficulty traveling during daylight hours. With Rosalind riding Farfalla next to him on Bumblebee, he chatted and knew all was well with her. And with the help of the outriders, there was no reason to fear for one's safety from criminals.

Nathaniel had not accounted for fashionable fools, though.

In late afternoon, when the sun was at its most insistent and Nathaniel began to drowse in the saddle and dream of iced wine, a burst of shouts split the air.

Then a panicked whinny. More shouting. The crack of a whip and a rumble of wheels—all so quick upon one another that almost before Nathaniel had taken in the first of these sounds, a phaeton barreled around a gentle curve in the road. It weaved and bumped over ruts, tilting and teetering on one of its great glossy wheels.

"Make way! Make way!" The driver's face was hardly visible between the fluttering capes of his greatcoat and the high crown of his silk hat. He lashed his lathered gray with a whip, and the horse jerked to one side. On his precarious perch, the driver was nearly unseated. He caught himself only by tugging hard at the reins. Pulled up short only feet from Dill and Button, the horse reared up, pawing the air, before returning to earth with a jolt that made his driver whoop.

Nathaniel held trembling Bumblebee still, quite still, until the fool driver and his poor lathered beast had passed by, their hubbub and panic receding. "You're all right, my good fellow." He rubbed the cob's withers. "I would never treat you thus."

It had been a near scrape. Had they been farther around the bend in the road, the reckless driver might have barreled right into them.

Wheeling Bumblebee, Nathaniel studied the party. Rosalind gave him a nod; both she and Farfalla had kept their heads. The others looked well too, though a few yards away Pale Marauder was making a temperamental nuisance of himself. Lombard had his hands full but managed a reply to Nathaniel. "He's all right. He just doesn't want to see another horse causing more trouble than he is."

"True enough." Nathaniel was about to call for them to proceed when he noticed the coachman clamber down from his seat in the carriage. "Come about," he called instead. Dill and Button cantered back to join the others, both cursing the phaeton driver.

In a knot of puzzlement, they made their way to the carriage that held the tack and baggage. The wiry coachman was crouching beside one of the front wheels, shaking his head.

"Felt a right jolt when I set them horses to walking again. Thought it might be a rut, but I hate to say it's more."

"More than a rut? Is the carriage stuck?" Nathaniel swung down from Bumblebee's back and handed the reins to Peters. The big redheaded groom also held Epigram's lead as the dark colt wandered to the side of the road to crop whatever grass he could reach.

"Someone is pleased by the stop," Nathaniel noted. He gave each of the stolid carriage horses a pat on the neck before crouching next to John Coachman.

He cursed. *More than a rut* was right. John Coachman must have taken a quick turn to remove the vehicle from the mad driver's path, and he had run over a rock. The formerly round wheel's wooden rim, its felloes, had split and was now as lopsided as a half-cracked egg.

"Damn. *Damn.*" This was the same wheel that had been damaged on his way up to Newmarket, and it was the same damage too. He'd had it repaired with a metal plate, but he should have had the felloes replaced entirely. Once broken, the wheel was never as sound as it had been before.

But he had not wanted to be late reaching Chandler Hall. He had hurried, had made the quick repair instead of the right one. And then he had forgotten about making any further repair once there were sick horses to care for. A trip to prepare for.

Not the time for a poem, he told himself.

John Coachman was apologizing, but Nathaniel halted him. "It's not your fault. It's mine. I was responsible for seeing to its repair." Pushing to his feet, he then helped up the older man. "I am relieved beyond measure that you and the horses weren't injured."

Lombard peered around Nathaniel, then spat into the dust. "Migh' be you could pop that plate back on to hold the felloes together. If ye'd somethin' to use as a hammer."

Nathaniel would have beaten his head against the side of the carriage if it would have helped. "A hammer... No, we've not got anything heavy enough. Do you remember if we passed a wheelwright recently?"

Spit. "Passed a smithy 'bout a quarter of a mile back. Saw the smoke from the forge. I could ride back an' borrow a hammer."

Nathaniel mulled this over. He felt responsible for making the repair, and at once—but riding toward an unknown smithy would eat time he ought to spend moving the carriage and caring for the horses. "Very well. Thank you, Lombard."

The groom took off on Bumblebee, and the rest of the party dismounted. Nathaniel and the other men put shoulder to the wounded carriage and rolled it to a stable portion of the road. They unhitched the carriage horses, and Nathaniel then pretended not to notice as the quartet of outriders and the roguish Noonan settled under a nearby shade tree with smoky pipes and surreptitious sips from flasks. John Coachman and Peters kept vigil over the horses.

And Nathaniel walked around to the far side of the carriage, worked open its door, then began tugging at the first trunk he could reach.

"What are you doing?" Rosalind's voice.

He didn't want her to look at him right now. Not when he had just failed them all. "If we can lighten the load, it will be easier to repair the wheel." In truth, he had no idea whether this made any difference to a wheelwright. A carriage weighed more than a half ton on its own. How much could the luggage weigh?

Still, he heaved forth the trunk. It felt better to be doing something more than blaming himself. Something to help.

She reached around him to grab a smaller bag. "You've the look of a man berating himself."

"And why should I not?" he grunted as he pulled at another trunk.

A light hand covered his, helping to support the weight of the heavy piece. "Because these things happen. Milkmaids exist. If anyone is to blame, it's the wild driver of the phaeton."

"A piece cannot break if it's not cracked to begin with."

"How does it get the crack, then? Doesn't that allow for accident and chance?"

She meant well. He knew she meant well. But he couldn't look at those green eyes, soft with *meaning well*. Not when this was why she was here: to make sure he, Nathaniel, did not bungle away his father's chance at a Derby victory. To make him trustworthy, but only secondhand. She was Sir William's secretary, Sir William's eyes along this journey. Though he had kissed her, though he had tried to persuade them both she was not a secretary, the truth was…she was.

Nathaniel had asked her time and again to trust him. He didn't want to see her stop, as his father had so many years ago.

Once he and Rosalind eased the heavy trunk to the ground beside the carriage, he moved to close its door. "You need not help me anymore. Please. Go rest beneath the tree like the others."

When she did not move, he said again: "Please." When he looked at her at last, her jaw was set.

"I hope," she finally answered, "you are not as unforgiving of others as you are of yourself."

He didn't know what she meant by that, but at least she left him. He had time to heave free one more trunk, cursing under his breath at its unwieldy weight, before hoofbeats alerted him to the arrival of a rider. Shoving back his hat, he wiped at his forehead and stepped around the carriage to see Lombard returning on Bumblebee with a soot-smudged man in his shirtsleeves mounted pillion behind.

Clearly the blacksmith, the stocky, balding man

dropped a kit of tools before swinging down from the large horse. "Wheel broken, your man here said?"

Nathaniel led him to the problem. The smith squinted at the metal plate. "Whoever forged this plate ought to be ashamed to call himself smith. Got cracks all through it, it does. Only a matter of time before it gives way."

"Even so, it's in better shape than the wood. Can you use it to splice the felloes?"

"Long enough to get you back to my shop, aye. M'brother's, to be truthful. He's the wheelwright, though we shares a space."

Nathaniel caught Lombard's eye. The wiry groom gave a nod, a shrug, and a spit, which Nathaniel interpreted as, *That's what it looked like to me. I think this plan might work. Also, I need to spit.*

He returned his attention to the smith, who had unrolled his tools from their heavy canvas. "And how long to complete the repair once your brother has the carriage?"

"If he has a felloes ready made to suit you, as fast as your coin allows. If he doesn't have one, he'll have to saw one bespoke-like. Could be a few days."

A few days. Yet the carriage had sat unused on Sir William's property for days on end, plated together piecemeal, when Nathaniel could have been repairing it.

Wasn't that just the way? Fate was a colicky horse; every burst of relief came paired with a heap of shit.

He pressed at his temples. "Then I'll hope he has a felloes ready-made."

Calling the lounging men back from their shady

respite, Nathaniel set them to following the smith's instructions for shifting baggage weight and bracing bits of the vehicle itself. As he too set shoulder to the wounded corner of the carriage, he considered how to dispense with this latest and very large milkmaid. As the crow flew, they weren't far from the Chandler family's town house. If they skirted London's roughest bits—no, then they would be caught in the privileged tangle of Mayfair. With a damaged wheel, he could not expect the carriage to survive hours of heavy London traffic.

They would have to go on without it, at least for tonight. They would have none of their baggage or tack, but for a night they could make do.

By the time the wheel had been clanged back into an approximately round shape and braced by the scorned metal plate, Nathaniel had concocted a plan. "I shall accompany the carriage and our belongings, and then I'll find you all at Sir William's town house. Egg? Love? You remember the way, I think? Good. You can see to Miss Agate's comfort and safety then, and that of the horses. If our repair is completed as quickly as I hope, I'll join you before nightfall."

Rosalind cleared her throat. "I have another suggestion that might serve the party. If you seek a closer place to lodge, we could be at the Eight Bells within the hour."

"Your parents' place?" At her nod, curiosity lifted his gray mood. "We are that close to your family, yet you'd have said nothing had the carriage not tried to disintegrate itself? Of course you've got to visit them. Would you like to leave at once? Let me see—maybe Button could go with you."

"We could all go. You'd be as welcome as I would." He could tell when she realized everyone clustered about was listening; her eyes grew wide, and she rubbed at her right elbow. "That is—all travelers are welcome. But you—as a fr—ah, employer. My employer's son. Your party would be well treated. As would all travelers."

"Beggin' pardon, Mr. Nathaniel," Lombard spoke up. "If Peters"—*spit*—"and I's to go with the carriage, you c'd stay with the horses. Take 'em to the maidy's inn instead of Sir William's house."

The redheaded groom seconded this with an eager nod. Ready to be off his feet for a bit, Nathaniel guessed.

Stay with the horses, yes; Nathaniel ought to. They were his responsibility. Well, the carriage was too, but he couldn't be in two places at once.

And if he stayed with the horses, he would stay with Rosalind.

And if he stayed with Rosalind, he would get to meet her family.

Interesting.

"Excellent suggestion," he decided. Another few minutes had sorted out the necessary money for Lombard, Peters, John Coachman, and one of the outriders to accompany the reloaded carriage and find food and lodging until it was repaired. Everyone else mounted up or took up a lead line and continued toward the sooty boundary of London.

Nathaniel drew up beside Rosalind, a lead in each hand as he walked the two Thoroughbreds. She was now walking Farfalla, saying she wished to stretch her legs.

He wondered. He wondered if she wanted to approach her family on her own two feet rather than on a sidesaddle. "How long since you have seen them?"

A vague question, but she did not pretend to misunderstand. "Ten years. But we write to each other often."

"You and your letters." He smiled. "Do you give them favorable reports of yourself?"

He could see only her straw bonnet; she kept her face rigidly forward. "I hope they like what I write about myself. But I think…I think I learn much more of them than I ever have to tell."

"Shocking," murmured Nathaniel.

"You have no idea." Amusement touched her tone. Then, her hand full of lead line, she rubbed at her right elbow. Quietly, almost too quietly for him to hear, she added, "But after ten years, neither do I."

Fourteen

ROSALIND HAD NOT BEEN EMBRACED BY HER MOTHER for ten years, but the sensation was instantly familiar. Her face pressed the pillow of Mrs. Agate's shoulder just as it had when she was a child—though her face was higher and the shoulder more pillowy than it had used to be. Each embrace came with the scents of flowery soap and lye and cooked meat, with the low hum that Rosalind and her siblings had once called "the mother song." Mrs. Agate had no kind of a singing voice, but when she hugged one of her many children, a note always burst forth.

"My dear Rosie, you've grown up so beautiful! Oh, but I knew it was you at once. You're the spit of me at your age."

Though Mrs. Agate's red-brown hair had faded to gray, her plumpness grown plumper, her features were strong and clean and familiar. Rosalind accepted this motherly effusiveness with a smile, then turned to her companion. "Mother, this is my—ah, my employer's son, Nathaniel Chandler."

What had she been about to say? *My friend? My*

fascination? Or worse, *my Nathaniel Chandler?* Thank goodness she had caught herself in time.

Nathaniel's greeting to her mother was just right. He didn't sweep over Mrs. Agate's hand like self-conscious charmers did; nor did he give her a chilly set of fingertips as some aristocrats were wont to. Tucking his hat beneath one arm, he made his bow, smiling that devastating Nathaniel smile, and told her how pleased he was to meet her.

"Though I wouldn't have wished our carriage to meet with an accident, I'm glad for the opportunity to stop here. Your daughter's love for this place was clear, and"——he tipped his head back to look up at the smoke-darkened beams of the ceiling, then back down across the wood-paneled public room where a scatter of people were eating and drinking—"I can see why."

If he'd still been smiling, Rosalind would have thought he was mocking her. But he almost looked surprised, his dark-gold brows furrowed and the twist of his mouth…wistful?

"You are a sweet lad." Mrs. Agate patted Nathaniel's cheek. "Oh, I know I oughtn't to do that to a grown man, but I've so many sons I can't seem to help myself. Now come in properly. Mr. Agate will see your servants and horses settled, then he'll join us. You're a bit late for the public dinner, but we'll find you something to fill your bellies."

Mrs. Agate looked around for something else to pat, then settled for crushing Rosalind into another hug. "Oh, Rosie, your brothers and sister will all be so glad to see you!"

When she released her hold, she added, for

Nathaniel's benefit, "Now of course my three oldest aren't here. Bert's got himself married to a grocer's daughter, and we can hardly get him away from work. Or his wife." She winked. "And the twins are at sea, and two bigger scamps the Royal Navy never had on its hands."

"I didn't know you had twin brothers!" Nathaniel looked at Rosalind with some surprise. To his hostess, he added, "I have twin siblings too. But they are male and female, and hardly inseparable. And neither has ever been particularly scampish."

"If not they, then someone else must be," decided Mrs. Agate. "Someone always fills the role of scamp in a family."

"I really can't say. I'm the soul of propriety myself."

Before lightning could strike him for this blatant falsehood, Rosalind spoke up. "You said you were still serving dinner, Mama? I want to help." Every one of those words was strange and wonderful. Like speaking one's native tongue after a long time in a foreign country.

"Nonsense. We're almost done, and you look run off your feet. Go on into the family parlor if you like, and we'll all settle around you when we're able."

The flapping of her hands could be gainsaid no more than her words. Even so, Rosalind didn't want to leave.

She rather thought Nathaniel understood this, because when he took her arm in his, his eyes were kind. "Only for a few minutes," he said, "and then you'll all be together. And in the meantime, you'll have the pleasure of my company. I'll try to entertain you, even if I *am* the soul of propriety."

"If *you* are the soul of propriety," Rosalind said as Mrs. Agate again waved them away before melting back into the crowd in the taproom, "I cannot imagine what impropriety looks like."

"That depends on the beholder," he said, falling into step behind her as she led the way to the kitchen near the back of the inn's ground floor. "Like beauty or wealth or good taste. You'll never get everyone to agree on what those mean."

"No, though you might get everyone to agree on what they are not."

The kitchen of the Eight Bells, she knew, was none of the three. Much used and well worn, the bricks of the hearth still bore the stains of smoke that bled into them in the years of cooking over an open fire. When Rosalind was a child, her parents installed a Rumford range, all boxy brick and solid cast iron, and its efficiency won the gratitude of every cook and kitchen maid. Perpendicular to the wall of hearth, oven, and stove stretched a long wooden table, burned and scarred by years of too-hot pots and kitchen maids too impatient to fetch a bread board.

For the moment, the bustle of cookery had ended; that of scullery in the back kitchen was now underway. Rosalind peeked in at the familiar clouds of steam, the piles of dishes, and the quick hands of the maids who washed them.

It was odd to be here with so much the same yet the stamp of time unmistakable. Had she changed, or had she not?

Nathaniel felt no such oddness, she could tell. Seating himself on the edge of the long worktable, he looked around with the same wonder he had displayed on entering the public room. "Do you know, I don't think I've ever entered the kitchens at Chandler Hall. Is that strange?"

"Not at all. Why should you enter them? You're a son of the house, and that's a room for servants."

"You're a daughter of this house."

"There's a great difference between a coaching inn and a stately home. Everyone goes everywhere in this building."

"Maybe." He ran a finger along the smooth edge of a bread paddle, on which a half-sliced loaf still sat. "How can a house be a home if there are rooms you never go into?"

"That's much what your father said about Chandler Hall, is it not? You mentioned he did not want attics built because he could not enter them."

"Yes, that's true." He tilted his head. "Yes, I suppose you're right." Hopping up from the long table, he peered into the hearth. The fire now banked, it glowered and put out a saucy tongue of flame. "The house in which I was raised had a kitchen much like this, except for the range. I can't tell you the number of times I sneaked into the kitchen. If I fixed the stove, I got a currant bun or whatever the cook happened to be working on."

Her imagination painted the picture to accompany his words: a gilt-headed boy, quick of speech and quick with his hands. How the cooks must have doted on him. "Was the stove often in need of fixing?"

"Constantly. It smoked. The chimney smoked. Everything had been pieced together out of old parts instead of built with purpose. I suppose it was better than cooking over an open fire, but not by much. How the cook was able to turn out such wonderful breads and buns, I can't imagine."

He paced the length of the range, trailing his fingers *hump-bump-bump* over the edge of its brick-and-mortar front. He liked to touch things, Rosalind had noticed. He wasn't a man of books; he was a man of stables and bricks, of determination and movement.

"You were lonely," Rosalind realized.

He turned back to face her, a neat pivot on one boot heel. "What? I tell you I fixed a stove, and you get that from it?"

"You fixed a stove for entertainment. Was there no one to play with? Your parents were busy seeing to the twins?"

"And my little sister. Do not forget Hannah." He gave a dramatic sigh. "Such is the tragedy of a middle child. No one had time for me, so I ran around stuffing myself with pastry."

Smiling, he added, "Sorry to take the excitement from my story, Rosalind, but I was really quite all right. I had friends nearby too. The old house wasn't off by itself like Chandler Hall, though the land it's on has always belonged to my father. Nothing changed when he was given a baronetcy except the house he decided to live in."

"Nothing at all?"

"Nothing at all. Everything else had already changed." He turned his back to the fire. "I wish the old place was still standing, but a fire got to it. Just as well. No one was caring for it. If I tried to go home again, I wouldn't be able to. Not like you. Here."

She was sure of no such thing. Everything seemed smaller and shabbier, but maybe she had only forgotten the size of utility. The shape of work. She was muddled by Chandler Hall, which no one could ever see in full, a house that felt like home to no one.

She was also not sure Nathaniel had not been lonely—or that he was not lonely now.

He rapped at the brick, the table, as he moved across the kitchen to again face Rosalind. "I am going to see to the horses and clean up as best I can. I don't want to look like a disgrace when I meet any more of your relatives."

"They won't mind." He looked dusty and tired, true, but that only proved that he had *done* things. That when something went wrong, he set his shoulder to the problem. That he would move heaven and earth—or a pile of trunks—to find a solution.

"Maybe not, but *I* would mind. Now that I know where the kitchens are, I'll be back in a short while." He paused, then took a step toward her. Close enough to touch, to lay a hand on her cheek. Close enough to lean forward and to kiss her forehead.

Her breath caught. The kiss lingered, surely longer than a quick gesture of parting ought to. When he pulled away, her skin tingled, warm where his lips had touched.

"I like seeing you here." He touched the tip of her nose. "Rosie."

"I…like seeing you here too." The words spilled awkwardly forth, bringing a blush. A woman who rationed happiness like a twist of sugared almonds was unused to speaking so boldly.

And then he was off, and she was alone.

For a moment. Not much more. Someone might come in at any second—a long unmet brother or sister, or even a maid escaping the steam of the scullery for a moment.

She pulled out a chair and sat at the long table before the bread board. The wheat-warm scent of the half-sliced loaf made her stomach pinch, eager for a meal. But she could wait for the others.

They would all call her Rosie, wouldn't they? She had not been called Rosie for years. Not since leaving her room at the Eight Bells as a half-healed, half-grown girl.

Cyfrinach, yes; she had been called that. Miss Any-Number-of-False-Names during her governess years. Jane before that, as a housemaid for a wealthy family who couldn't be bothered to tell servants apart.

But never had she been Rosie. Rosie was soft and flowery, a girl who had dreamed of riding a pony while wearing a wreath of flowers.

Cyfrinach and Miss Agate and Jane didn't dream. They did as they were told.

Now she was Rosalind. Rosalind rode a horse, and she did it damned well. And Rosalind bought her own flowers.

Rosalind knew what it was like to kiss and kiss and kiss. And that gave her something new to dream about.

She folded her arms atop the table, put her head down, and let her heavy eyelids fall closed.

❧

"Of *course* it's her, numbskull. Look, she has Mama's hair. Or hair like Mama used to have."

"But she doesn't look anything like Carys. How could she be our sister?"

"Because she said she was to Mama, and besides, she looks like Rosie. You don't remember Rosie? Nah, you were too little when she left."

A jumble of voices woke Rosalind from her drowse, and she snapped upright. "I'm awake." She shook her head, rubbing at sandy eyes. "Sorry. I just sat for a moment, and the warmth in here lulled me to sleep."

Four of her seven brothers stood around her, stair steps of ruddy brown hair and wide cheekbones so much like her own that she could have laughed and cried at once.

"'S'all right," said the tallest of the brothers. Severn, only a year younger than Rosalind. "Mama told us how tired you were and not to wake you. Except Elder"—he clapped the youngest brother on the shoulder—"couldn't believe it was you. As if we have a lot of women sneaking back into the kitchen to sleep."

"You have women sneaking all over, so how was I to know who she was?" protested the gangly youth. Elder had been a chubby toddler when Rosalind left home; now he was similar in age to the lanky youth who roasted food at the Kelting festival.

"Because I look like you." Pushing back her chair. "Like all four of you. God, how good it is to see you." One by one, she swept them into hugs. Severn, Alec,

Wilfred, Elder—they were all taller than her now. Elder's embrace was awkward, that of a boy hugging a relative he did not remember, with a fear that a hug might be followed by a pinch on the cheek or something similarly ruinous to his fragile dignity.

She did no such thing, only stepping back and looking up and down the row of them again. "My brothers. How long it's been."

"I thought you'd look fancier," said Elder.

Rosalind laughed. "Fancier than what? I'm fancier than I used to be." She smoothed her long skirts. They were dusty and the cut of her gown simple, but the green cloth and neat stitches were of good quality. "And so are the four of you. Waistcoats and cravats and fobs! You are young men of London."

"You used to be less fancy?" Elder drew back his chin. "I thought working for a baronet would turn you into a fine lady."

"Rosie, a fine lady? That's a good joke." Alec laughed. The only freckled one in the family, his hair was far more red than brown, and throughout childhood he had always had the readiest sense of humor. But then his smile disappeared, and he added, "Our Rosie has always been fine enough. Wish we'd known you were coming, Rose. I would have locked Elder in the larder."

"It's not too late," warned Severn.

Rosalind covered her smile. "No one needs to be locked anywhere, at least not on my account. But I'm wondering, has any of you seen my…" She colored, stumbling over the word again. "Ah, my employer's son? A Mr. Nathaniel Chandler? I traveled here with him and a party of servants."

"Have we seen them?" Alec rolled his eyes. "They're practically part of the household already. Chandler befriended Papa in the stable, and then his grooms befriended Papa, and Papa befriended the horses, and by now I think they're all half drunk."

"Not the horses," added quiet Wilfred.

"Not Chandler either," added Severn. "But Papa's pretty well lit. Never seen him laugh so much, and he hasn't even seen you again. Say, Rosie, is Chandler your—"

"Employer's son? Yes. That's what I said."

The brothers exchanged glances.

"All right, if you say so," Severn said in a tone of frank disbelief. "Now that you're awake, I suppose everyone can come in and eat dinner."

"Of course. I'm so sorry. I didn't mean to—"

"Don't apologize." Alec waved a hand. "You'll be needing to apologize to your Mr. Nathaniel Chandler after he survives dinner with this family." Screwing up his mouth, he added, "I suppose he *will* survive? Maybe I shouldn't presume too much."

"Did I say it was good to see you?" Rosalind mock-frowned. "I must have been addled."

"There's our Rosie." Severn rubbed a hand over her head, rumpling the plaited coils of her hair. "Every hug followed by a kick to the—"

"Why don't I go ahead," she interrupted, "and serve out the dinner?"

"If you like." Alec's grin was all mischief. "Only save room for roasted Chandler. I've a feeling your *employer's son* isn't prepared for the Agate family welcome."

Fifteen

"So, Mr. Nathaniel. You're the son of our Rosie's baronet, is that right?"

Nathaniel grinned. Mrs. Agate's question was the third time he had been asked the same thing.

The first time he had answered for himself; since then, Rosalind had been chiming in with her tone increasingly dry. "Yes, he is the son of Sir William, or so he has told me. But Sir William is not *my* baronet, Mama."

"I did. And Sir William told you so too. I hold many scandalous secrets, but my birth isn't one of them."

As he moved from kitchen to the family's sitting room with his second plate of mutton stew, various family members trailed after and around him like spectators at a menagerie watching some strange new beast.

"Is your last name really Chandler? Because a chandler's a job," Elder informed him.

"True, and an Agate's a stone," Nathaniel replied. "If you don't have to be a stone, I don't have to make candles for a living. How's that?"

The boy squinted, then nodded his agreement. "That sounds fair."

So far Elder was the only one of Rosalind's brothers Nathaniel had sorted out. How could one not remember when the family's youngest bore such a name? "It's for the sort of tree," the youth had explained to him when they were introduced in the stable earlier. "Mama and Papa said I was made under an elder, and—"

"Any more of that and you'll have our guest poking his ears out," the brother with the reddest hair had scolded.

"He's not the only one who's going to poke out his ears," a quieter brother had muttered. "No one wants to hear about that."

The exchange had made Nathaniel smile. He and Hannah teased one another like that, but Jonah—well, Nathaniel couldn't even remember the last time he'd seen his older brother joke or laugh. And he couldn't remember when he had last seen his sister Abigail, widowed young in Ireland, at all.

Balancing his plate of stew, he seated himself on one of the long sofas. The family's private sitting room was worn and comfortable, with dark paper in a busy pattern and horsehair furniture that might once have been fine. The sofa been sat upon so often that the sleek fabric and hard-tufted stuffing were molded to the human body. A large hearth backed onto the kitchen wall with the stove. In summer the heat must be unbearable, but on a chilly spring evening, the shared warmth was pleasant.

Small tables dotted the room, each with a lamp

and someone's plate and cup on it. The family would number eleven when everyone was at home, so Nathaniel guessed they were used to never eating all at once or in the same place. A few of the brothers sat on the floor, stretching out their legs across a carpet from which much of the nap was worn away.

Even so, it was a carpet. More pleasant underfoot than the costliest marble.

The food was plain and hearty—mutton stewed with vegetables, well spiced and warm. The brothers and Rosalind's sister, Carys, kept popping up to serve another plateful from the large pot in the adjacent kitchen. The door between kitchen and sitting room was never closed.

Nathaniel swallowed another bite of stew, then looked around. Every pair of eyes was fixed upon him. All—he did a quick count—eight pairs. Well, seven. As soon as Rosalind saw him looking, she ducked her head. With a slab of bread, she chased stew around her dish.

Setting aside his dish, Nathaniel settled against the back of the sofa, which was more unforgiving than it looked. "What else can I tell you all about myself? I can see you're curious about the sort of person who would turn up with your daughter in such a travel-worn state."

He had wiped off his face and washed his hands, but without a change of clothing, he still felt rumpled and rough.

"Are you married?" Rosalind's only sister, Carys, was a bold-eyed brunette. Had Nathaniel been a decade younger, he would have thought her fetching.

"No. Are you?"

She laughed, then drew forth a workbasket from beneath a table. "Not yet. I haven't met the right gentleman."

"I'd say not." The oldest of the brothers at home—Steven? Seven?—spoke up from his spot on the floor next to Elder. "You've met too many of the wrong ones. Every time you serve the customers, I have to keep an eye on the men to make sure they don't pinch you."

"Also, you're only sixteen," chided Mrs. Agate. Holding her hands out, she neatly caught a ball of knitting Carys tossed her way, then pulled forth the needles and set them to clicking through what looked like a long sock. "Plenty of time for you to find someone."

"Weren't you sixteen when you got married?" Carys pressed. She had set an embroidery hoop on her lap, then promptly ignored it. Nathaniel doubted whether any progress would be made on the…whatever it was. Some colorful blob.

"Sixteen is as sixteen does," said Mr. Agate, squinting across the room. He shared his wife's graying red-brown hair, though his was thin on top. Much taller than his plump little wife, and sturdy of form, he had enjoyed poking around the stable and chatting with the Chandler servants while Nathaniel finished seeing to the horses. From a manger, Mr. Agate had unearthed a bottle of something dark and spirituous. This had been shared with most of Nathaniel's company—though not by the first two men to keep watch, he had made sure. Mr. Agate himself had also enjoyed a drink or two or three, and he held his liquor with sleepy good humor.

"What does that mean, Papa?" Carys asked, still not picking up her needle.

"It means that not every opportunity is a good one," spoke up Rosalind from the other end of Nathaniel's sofa. "So mind you think about them carefully."

"I really don't think that's what he meant," said Carys.

"Look," shot the redheaded brother, "Chandler has all but told us to ask him questions. Are we really going to waste the evening by talking about how old Carys is?"

"Yes," said Rosalind.

"No," chorused everyone else.

Nathaniel hid a grin as he set his plate aside. "I'm the son of a baronet. I'm either half flash or half foolish, depending on who you ask. And I'm on my way to Epsom, at least once my carriage's wheel is repaired." He turned to Rosalind. "Have I forgot anything important?"

She took a bite of bread, chewed slowly, and swallowed. "You know how to physic a horse that has colic."

"True. I know how to do that."

"You know how to organize a party of travelers and to make sure everyone is safe and well-fed."

Her tone made him feel unsettled—in a good way. "All right. Thank you, Miss Agate. If we're to list everything I know, either your family will be bored by how long the list is, or I'll be ashamed of how short it is. Probably the latter."

"*Whisht.*" Mrs. Agate's needles clicked. "I don't think a modest young man has ever entered this room before."

"Nor has one yet," Nathaniel said. "The five things I know how to do, I'm the best in the world at."

"Only five?" This from Rosalind. She cut her eyes sideways at him—and licked her lip.

God. It was a good thing he was sitting, because otherwise his knees might have unpinned. Was she thinking of their kiss? She had to be, to lick her lip like that—or no, maybe she was still eating dinner and it was perfectly innocent. Maybe he was the only one thinking about how he had kissed her, and how that sunny spring morning with her had been one of the five best things, definitely, that had ever happened to him.

She was still watching him. And for that matter, so were most of the other Agates.

He hitched one leg over the other. "Five." He tried for nonchalance. "More or less."

"Carys, dear." Mrs. Agate's needles clicked. "Will you pop into the kitchen and put on a kettle?"

"All right." The dark girl tossed her embroidery back into the workbasket, then shot her mother a suspicious look. "But don't talk about anything interesting while I'm gone."

"I've got a boring question all prepared for him, so don't you worry a bit."

Once Carys had swanned away, Mrs. Agate peered over her knitting at Nathaniel. "You're headed to Epsom, you said. Is that where you live?"

He was still trying not to think about Rosalind kissing him; Rosalind, smiling under a crown of flowers; Rosalind, only an arm's length from him.

Rosalind, *in a room with seven of her relatives.*

Wrenching his mind away, he flailed for an answer.

"No, I don't live in Epsom. I'm merely traveling there for the Derby."

"Where do you live, then? In Newmarket with our Rosie's baronet?"

Surely everyone had heard Rosalind's muttered *not my baronet* protest, but no one paid it any heed. Nathaniel found the question more difficult to answer than it ought to be. Where *did* he live? He kept possessions in Chandler Hall and the London town house, but he found no more comfort laying his head in one than in the other. They were roofs and walls—that was all. Neither was a home.

So he dodged the question. "I travel England most of the time and go from Newmarket to London at least once a month. On family business. Horsey things."

"Do you have a town house or stay at an inn?" This from Elder.

"My father owns a town house in Queen Anne Street. When my carriage stays intact and gets me to my destination, that's where I stay in London."

"Coo-ee! You must be rich."

Mr. Agate laughed, while Mrs. Agate admonished her youngest for using such a low-class exclamation.

When both parents had quieted, Nathaniel added, "The money isn't mine, but my father's. And the house is not on an especially tonnish street. Why, the neighbors have been known to take their dinner when they feel hungry for it, even if the sun is still up."

"But you *are* the son of a baronet." Mrs. Agate looked not at Nathaniel but at Rosalind.

"Don't talk about anything interesting!" came the girlish call from the kitchen.

This gave the group the excuse to laugh, but Nathaniel wondered—what was Rosalind's mother on about? Was she trying to matchmake?

He wasn't against the idea. Though he would rather it had been Rosalind's.

But why should it be? He must remember that she was here for the promise of discharging her debt. She had not wanted to leave Newmarket; she would never have spent a moment with him if she didn't have to.

Though she *had* liked his kiss—or so she said.

And she *had* changed the ribbon on her bonnet.

"I am the son of a baronet," he repeated. This sentence made as little sense today, here, now, as the lessons in Latin he had once parroted from a tutor. *Romani ite domum.*

He tried again. "My father's a horse breeder. And trainer. He just happens to have been made a baronet too."

"And what is your part in the family business of—what'd you say? Horsey things?" Rising from his seat, Mr. Agate retrieved a decanter and glasses from another of the innumerable small tables about the room. "Are you a trainer?"

Another question that was more difficult to answer than it ought to be. Nathaniel didn't care what was in that decanter; he just wanted to upend the thing over his mouth. "Not exactly, no." He drummed his fingers on the seat of the sofa, the horsehair sleek and coarse beneath his fingertips. "I do whatever is needed away from Newmarket, since my father isn't able to travel."

"Your father must trust you," said the eldest. Of these brothers, that was. Nathaniel had to remind himself that Rosalind had an additional supply of brothers outside the household. "Mine would never allow me to buy and sell horses."

Mr. Agate looked up from pouring a garnet-dark liquid—port, it must be—into small glasses. "Severn, why should I want that when we've good beasts in our stable? You do well enough speaking with lodgers and diners, making sure they have what they need and behave as they ought. Though if you're keen for another post, only say so."

"He wouldn't be nearly so *keen* for another post, because then he couldn't be *friendly* with any *ladies* that visited," said the puckish redheaded brother. His elder sibling whipped a cushion at him, which, judging from the alarming embroidery upon it, was Carys's creation.

"You wouldn't understand, Alec, because ladies don't want anything to do with you." Severn, seated on the floor, stretched out his legs with a thump of boot heels.

"And the women who have anything to do with *you* aren't ladies." The redhead—Alec, apparently—whapped his brother on the head with the same cushion.

"Boys!" barked Mr. and Mrs. Agate at once. Though neither of them paused what they were doing—he measuring out tiny jewellike glasses of port, she now turning the heel of her sock—their admonition served to quiet their almost-grown sons.

Nathaniel hid a smile.

And then came the next question. "Do you know how to get a woman to like you, Mr. Nathaniel? Or a lady?" This from the quietest brother, a boy of about fifteen or sixteen who had begun to collect plates into a tall stack.

"Um." Nathaniel could feel the nearness of Rosalind at his side, almost within reach. Carefully, he did not look at her. "I have managed that feat on some occasions in the past, yes."

"What about now?"

Nathaniel coughed into his fist, hoping the question would go away. Of course it didn't; the gangly teen only stared at him hopefully.

Nathaniel would *not* look at Rosalind. "I have no idea. I suppose that depends on the lady, and the question would be better asked of her."

"What do you think, Rosie? You're a lady."

Oh, good. The brother's gimlet gaze turned to her. The boy shifted the stack of crockery in his hand and waited.

Rosalind set aside her own dish. "I think you need some help with the dishes, Wilfred."

Wilfred! That was his name. All right. Nathaniel had these four brothers sorted now.

"Rosie, Alec can do that. He's not doing anything useful. As usual," spoke up Severn. Naturally, he accompanied this with another cushion attack.

"Then I'll just...help Carys with the tea things." Rosalind hopped to her feet, then wove through the clutter of furniture.

For the first time, Nathaniel was relieved to see her gone. He didn't want her to answer her brother's question. He *certainly* didn't want to *hear* her answer. What could she say? If it wasn't to be a kindness, it would have to be a nothing. And leaving the room in such a hurry—that was a nothing.

With Rosalind slipping through the doorway back

to the kitchen, Nathaniel decided to ask a question of his own. To the room at large, he asked, "What was Miss Agate—Rosie—like as a child?"

Mr. Agate held out a glass of port to him, dark and lovely as a garnet. Nathaniel declined in the guise of leaning forward to await an answer.

"Noticed everything, but closemouthed as a clam." Severn accepted the same glass from his father with thanks, and Mr. Agate continued around the room with glasses. "Which was good, because she knew everyone's secrets."

"Was she? I wonder if that has changed." The noticing hadn't. Her eyes were curious; he'd been drawn to that about her at once.

"Probably not. Did she tell you about her, ah—" Severn waved his glass vaguely in the region of his torso.

"Her port? Her gown? Her fondness for gestures?" Alec snorted.

"Rosie was badly burned as a girl, Mr. Nathaniel," Mrs. Agate said placidly. "She's quite all right now. Elder, hold up your foot so I can see if this sock is large enough."

He hopped over and stuck a shod foot into his mother's lap. "Can I have some port?"

"When you quit being a pest," said Alec.

"How did you get a glass, then?"

To his credit, Alec gave a hearty laugh.

And that was that, the end of their list of Rosie's quirks. She was a great one for keeping secrets; she had been burned. And she was all right now.

Yet Rosalind had told Nathaniel about her burns and her debts. If she was still accustomed to holding information close, surely it was a mark of fondness that she had revealed so much to him.

He could only hope. And he wondered if she held any other secrets.

Did it matter if she did? Her family loved her. Despite her long absence, they welcomed her immediately. She was still a part of their circle.

If he had five siblings who laughed and smiled and called him *Nate*, he would never want to leave their home. Hell, if he had even *one* such sibling. But Hannah had her own home now, and Nathaniel could never be more than a visitor. Especially once Hannah delivered her baby in a few months.

How could Rosalind have stayed away from her family for ten years? And for that matter—"How could you let her go for so long?"

❧

Tucked next to the doorway, Rosalind listened, wishing for more ears. Her brother had asked a question she could not answer, all but wondering if Nathaniel had won her over, and if so, how he had managed it.

He had; oh, he had. Yet she was not sure how he had done it. She had not noticed him winning her until she was already won; until his lips were on hers and she was kissing him back as though he were her medal, her crown of flowers. Her beautiful unwonted triumph.

This worried her, because she couldn't afford not to notice how such things happened. She could not bear another lapse in attention, or another burn.

Thank goodness Carys had left the kitchen for a

moment. Rosalind was alone with a tray of tea things only half-assembled and her thoughts even less so.

Now Nathaniel asked a question she had never dared pose. *How could you let her go for so long?*

After a pause, Papa answered. "We wanted her alive, even if we couldn't be with her."

"She was thirteen," added Mama. The faint clicks of the knitting needles stopped. "That's an age when plenty of families send their girls off to service or their boys to the sea. It wasn't what we wanted to do, but— we had to make a choice between paying for a doctor's care or paying for a burial. We wanted her safe more than anything, but we hadn't the money. One of our neighbors, a saint among women, paid for Rosie's care. In exchange, Rose worked off the debt afterward."

Click, click. The knitting began again. "Rosie has done quite well for herself in all these years. Worked her way up through different households. And now she's secretary to a baronet." Her mother's voice held pride.

Rosalind hardly heard Nathaniel's reply. She had hardly heard anything after the frank words: *It wasn't what we wanted to do.* Some choices were between bad and worse. She hadn't been able to make the choice, so her parents made it for her.

Love could do no less, could it? Love made the bad choice instead of the worse one. Love sent letters for ten years. Love welcomed her back in an instant.

How simple it sounded. Ten years and so many agonies in a few sentences, all ending with pride.

Aunt Annie described as *a saint among women*.

Her parents didn't know what it had been like for Rosalind, leaving them to work for Aunt Annie. The loneliness of snipped-off friendships. The gut-turning worry as she searched desks in the stealth of night for the papers Aunt Annie needed. Tranc like a shadow following them both. Cold, strained, fearful.

They didn't know any of that. And because she loved them, she would never tell them. She didn't have to. Once she reached Epsom, she would pay that old debt, and those days would be over.

Leaning against the wall, so warm she let it soak through her, she shut her eyes. A deep emotion seized her, so hard it almost hurt her heart, but it was not pain. It was too sweet for pain and too strong for fear. Too solid for all the filmy worries that had layered on her.

It was contentment. Joy. Happiness. It was a blessing with a bladed edge, one she knew she could hold for only one evening, one night. A bit of the morning, then another good-bye.

If she had not accompanied Nathaniel Chandler on this trip, she wouldn't be here at the Eight Bells. If he hadn't known so well how to deal with all the difficulties of travel, she wouldn't be here.

What was his part in the family business, her father had asked. Nathaniel had avoided the answer. Rosalind knew those quite well, the dances around the real answer. The dodge about words one couldn't bear to say.

But what was there not to bear? He sold things; he fixed things. He led groups of people with dogged patience and cheer. She would have followed him across Europe for the way he laughed with her and watched over her.

She had brought him home to meet her family, after all. The family he had given back to her without a moment's hesitation. *Of course you must go.*

Opening her eyes, Rosalind smiled.

"Let's all have some more port, shall we?" said Papa from the sitting room.

"You've finished the bottle, Mr. Agate." Mama sounded amused. Papa had always liked his drink, but Rosalind never remembered him showing signs of intoxication. He became a little sleepy, that was all. But who didn't at the end of the day?

"Then let's get another," Rosalind heard Papa reply. "Our Rosie's return is worth celebrating, isn't it?"

"There's always something worth celebrating," said Mama. "Elder, let me see your foot again—oh, this will never fit…"

Rosalind rubbed at her right elbow, where the scarred skin pulled tight. If there were always something to celebrate, what a wonderful way that would be to live.

For tonight, it *was* true, wasn't it? For one single night, for a sliver of a morning.

And once the evening passed, she knew exactly with whom she wanted to celebrate.

Sixteen

ROSALIND TUCKED THE FOLDED CLOTHING BENEATH her right arm, then knocked at Nathaniel's door.

"Come," he called. When she eased open the door, he added, "Is that Severn? You'll have to excuse me; I'm still bathing."

The privacy screen had been shifted to hide the large copper tub made available to guests who wished a hot bath. Rosalind had just made use of another such, and her unpinned hair still hung damp and drying down her back. With her belongings in a trunk in the traveling carriage, she wore a print muslin gown belonging to Carys that, though pretty, fit her tightly and loosely in all the wrong places.

"It is Rosalind," she said. "I brought clothing from Severn. There's a shirt and cravat for tomorrow, and a nightshirt for tonight."

A splash from behind the privacy screen. "Rosalind. I—ah, didn't expect you to bring the clothing yourself."

"This is the sort of household where one does what one can to help," she said lightly.

Severn had been only too glad to deliver this small

errand into her hands, though not without a wink. And then he was off, his eye on the comely lady's maid that had arrived with another party of travelers that evening.

"Well—don't look behind the screen. I'm not dressed."

"The bath would be less effective if you were." She shut and secured the door, then sat at the end of the bed, the neatly folded clothing beside her.

It was a small but high-ceilinged chamber, one of a spread of rooms that had been carved from the family apartments of the former manor house. The wooden floor was laid over with a knotted rug, pleasant underfoot. The room was furnished with a small writing table and a painted privacy screen of three panels behind which resided the chamber pot and, for now, the copper tub. Nathaniel had angled the screen to invite the warmth from the fire.

And there was a bed, of course. This one was covered with a quilt Rosalind had first smoothed as soon as she had been old enough to change sheets and coverlets. It was a piecework mosaic of golds and browns and reds. She had once thought of it as shapes, tiny interlocking hexagons. Now it looked like medals, which could be won for any number of ridiculous things.

Another splash. "Rosalind? Are you still there?"

"Yes. I'm sitting at the end of the bed. I can't see behind the screen, if that's what you're wondering."

"In truth, I'm wondering why you are here." Nathaniel's tentative tone stripped the words of any harshness.

Because I don't want to go. Perhaps the words would

come more easily when she and Nathaniel were face-to-face. When she could see his warm blue eyes, the strong line of his jaw, the thoughtful curve of his mouth.

She gave him a different reply instead. "My family asked questions they'd no right to. I'm sorry."

"Your family is delightful. Their questions mean they are interested in the sort of person who might bring you for a visit all in a scruff. If I didn't want to answer, I just said something else." *Splash.* "A trick I learned from you. And yes, I noticed you just used it again."

What was he doing when he splashed? Was he stretching out his limbs in the tub? It was too small, surely. Rosalind had to fold her legs when she sat in it, and his body was much larger than hers.

Knowing he was in the bath, naked, made the whole room seem smaller.

She traced the old lines of stitches on the coverlet, not knowing what to say next or what to do. "Shall I feed the fire?" she fumbled. "You must be cold."

"Not yet, but once I get out of the water I will be. Did you mean it, by the way, when you said you were staying at the end of the bed? Because I have finished bathing, and I can't stay behind this privacy screen forever."

She traced another line of stitches, a pattern spiraling and repeating on itself. "I would like to stay. A little longer. If that is all right with you."

More splashing, and then he peered over the top of the privacy screen. Rumpled wet hair, sharp brows, curious blue eyes, all licked golden by firelight. "You know. I can never resist. Your short sentences. Here,

I'll wrap up in a bath sheet"—the eyes disappeared, and the tone became somewhat muffled behind the screen—"and if you could just kick that chair over, I'll sit behind the screen by the fire and dry out my wetter bits. Stay as long as you wish. I like your company."

Again, he peered over the screen. "Tell me about whatever you wish, too."

Standing, she dragged the chair over from the desk to the edge of the privacy screen. A bare forearm—well muscled, its hairs faintly gilded—stretched forth to pull the chair behind the screen. "All right, Miss Agate. Rosalind. Rosie. What's brought you in here with a stack of Severn's clothes and a verbal trunk full of short sentences?"

Rather than retreating to the bed, she sat on the floor beside the screen. "Thank you for bringing the traveling party to the Eight Bells."

"You're welcome. It was your own excellent suggestion." He sounded so close, just a thin panel between them. His voice rained down like the warm water of a bath.

"I should have answered my brother's question about whether you know how to get a lady to like you. The truth is that you do."

"I would have been shocked beyond reason if you had said so before such a crowd." A faint thump, as if he had put his palm against the screen on the other side. "How did I manage such a feat?"

"Fishing for a compliment?"

"Ah…let's call it 'searching for evidence.'" He must have stretched out his legs; she saw a bare foot slide from behind the screen toward the brazen coal fire. "I am wondering what I did to make you like me, because I want to keep doing it. And I am also wondering whether you liking me has anything to do with you being in this room, or if you are just tormenting me."

"Can liking and tormenting go together?" she wondered.

"Anyone with relatives knows the answer is yes."

She laughed. "I did not seek to torment you." Her booted foot was inches from his bare toes. Heat was pooling, soft and slippery, through her whole body. "And I do not know how I have come to like you. It came upon me gradually."

"Like an illness?"

"If an illness can be thought good." She had thought words would flow more easily under his gaze, but this was better. The screen made it simple to speak phrases that would otherwise have been impossible. "I cannot think of any reason not to like you."

"Oh, is that all?" His tone was dry. "If you simply need a bit of persuasion in the other direction, you'll find plenty of reasons in Chandler Hall. Not that I'm fool enough to remind you of that. In fact, forget I said anything."

"But I remember the things you say." If she tipped her left foot just so, she could almost touch one of his toes. "You told me once that you don't play the suitor. So I wonder why you kissed me."

"Ah, now *you* are doing the wondering." He cleared his throat, but his voice still sounded tight. "I did it because I wanted to, and because I thought—I hoped—you would like it. It had nothing to do with having drunk some ale."

"Ale?" She searched her memory. "That's right, I had offered you ale. You didn't want it, but you drank it all the same."

"I don't drink ale anymore. Or port or brandy or—"

"—any sort of intoxicating spirits?"

"Exactly."

"Ah." She rubbed at her elbow, wondering how they had quickly swung from kissing to drink. "And why is that? If you'd like to tell me."

"*Like* to? Not really." He chuckled. "Ought to, maybe. When I drink wine or spirits or anything like that, I feel I'm not myself anymore. For a long time I liked that. Now I don't."

So simple, not to do something one didn't like. As simple as buying sugared almonds if one liked sweets. Or so he made it sound.

"I didn't know," she said.

"Of course you didn't. I hadn't told you. I don't usually want people to know, because then they feel awkward."

"But if you don't tell them, then you feel awkward."

"Better me than someone else."

A low rasp, as if he had slid his palm down the panel. Were there nothing dividing them, where would his hand be? Would it rest upon her hair? On her shoulder? Would he stroke the line of her neck?

Here was yet another reason to like him: for protecting the world from any small awkwardness. For wanting something but choosing not to have it.

She wondered if he wanted her. If he did, would he think of a reason he should choose not to have her?

These were questions she could not answer. She

only knew this room was where she wanted to be, and that she wanted him to claim her as no one ever had. She had few choices, but she had retained this one.

"There is one question I didn't yet answer." She drew up her legs again and began to unlace her boots. "Why I am here in this room. I heard you ask my family how they could have let me go away from them for so long."

"Ah." His own bare foot drew back behind the screen. The small chair creaked as he stood. "Well, that's the sort of thing a man wonders once he gets to know you. I hope you heard their answer too."

"I did." Her wet hair dripped onto the laces as she leaned forward, fumbling with the knots. "The answer was a gift."

"They would keep you on any terms, even bad ones, rather than lose you completely."

"And what do you think?" Was he looking over the top of the screen? She tipped her face up and met deep blue eyes.

"I would keep you on any terms too. But it's not for me to ask."

She tugged off her boots, one after another, then stood. "You could ask."

His brows lifted. "May I come around the screen?"

She managed a small nod. "No one has ever—seen me. Bare."

He stepped around the privacy screen, a bath sheet wrapped about his waist. His chest was broad and strong and unscarred, all flame and shadow from the lamp and the fire. Its hairs were gold. His skin was gold. He was a medal she had never thought to win.

"You've seen yourself. And anything you have seen, I want to see too."

His words made her eyes prickle. *This is why I like you*, she thought. "I meant it, Nathaniel. No one has ever seen me as you do. Not even myself."

"That has always been true." He tucked the fabric about his waist more tightly, then took her shoulders in gentle hands. "For you see yourself as a secretary above all, and it took me very little time to notice the woman beneath the role."

He had no idea how much of a role it truly was. *I will not lie to you*, she said. But she did not promise never to leave out the essential.

She swallowed that thought. There was no room here for the past, for worries about Spain in 1805, or whatever Aunt Annie would ask of her next. There was not even room here for the trip to Epsom and the promise of freedom at its end. He chose her now, and she chose him.

She only wondered if he would ever choose her again, or if once would be enough. She already knew it would not suffice for her, not when he looked at her as though she were a wreath of red blooms or a half inch of brandy. A long-wished-for treasure, an essential part of the day.

His hands slid from her shoulders to the cap of one long sleeve. "This is different from your usual sort of gown."

"I have my own gowns made with buttons up the front, so I can dress myself without a maid's help. This dress is borrowed."

"You cannot do the buttons yourself?" His hand was gentle, tracing the line of her collarbone.

She shook her head. "They march down my back."

"You can't undo them either, then. Let me help you."

Still facing her, his hands slipped around her. It was like an embrace, but better, as the tiny circles of horn slipped free from their buttonholes. Beneath his fingers, teasing free each button down to the high waist of the gown, she shivered.

When the bodice parted and loosened, she hesitated. "My right arm…"

"Do you want to tell me about it? Do you want me to touch it?"

"There is nothing to tell that you don't already know. It was burned, and it healed with scars." She looked toward the fire, then back at Nathaniel. "There are scars on my right side too. And on my hip and back."

"Do you want me to see them, or do you want to keep them covered?"

She swallowed. "What do you want?"

"What I don't want"—he tipped her chin up with one strong finger—"is to be an arse by doing the wrong thing when I think I'm doing the right thing."

"If you don't know how to do the right thing in the bedchamber, then we're in a bit of trouble. Because I've never done this before."

He raised his eyes to heaven, though a plaster-and-timber ceiling was in the way. "I am not referring to the mechanics of the act. I don't want to hurt you."

"I don't think you will."

Finally, she touched him. There was stubble on his chin, rough as other parts of his face were smooth. She explored them all with curious fingers: the hollow behind his jaw, the back of his earlobe, the arch beneath his brow, the crease of his lid. "There are so many places to touch," she murmured.

"You haven't found nearly all of them. And neither have I." He wrapped his arms around her, the loosened bodice bunching in his embrace. "If you were a proper Rosalind, you'd be as high as my heart. But look, you fit so nicely beneath my chin."

And when she stood on her toes to catch his lips with her own, the fit was nicer still. She kissed him as he slipped her bodice down her arms, letting the gown pool about her waist. In her shift and front-lacing stays, her arms were uncovered. She opened her eyes, prepared to see him staring with disgust.

He wasn't, though. He was only staring. Not with disgust, but with what instead?

She folded her arms across her breasts. The scars over her right elbow tugged. "Not what you expected?"

"I never know what to expect where you are concerned." He smiled. "But if you refer to your scars, they saved your life. I can only be grateful to them."

He took her within his arms again, kissing his way down from her smooth shoulder to the puckered web over her arm.

She felt little on the scarred areas of her body—less heat and cold, and hardly a gentle touch at all. Sometimes she felt her skin was too tight. Sometimes it itched.

Never had it been kissed like this, sweet and slow and gentle. Down the arm that had protected her face and neck, the arm that had beat back and rolled over the flames. It was a good arm; it had saved her life as much as Aunt Annie's treatments had. After all it had been through, it still held reins and wrote. It could unfold to stop protecting her body, her heart. Its fingers could twine in the still-damp silk of Nathaniel's hair.

And it could still feel pleasure, a prickling dance of sensation down its length. Here the skin was thickened, her own armor that she always carried about. It bumped and puckered; it was darker and redder and paler in spots. Her scars did not match the rest of her. Her scars were a part of her.

Tears welled up, filling her eyes, but they were not from sadness. "They did save my life," she said. "You're right."

She would still have traded them in an instant for smooth unmarked skin that had never known fire. But that wasn't a choice. The only choice was to be grateful or not to be. For her life being saved. For her body, still strong and healthy.

For the firelight that warmed without hurting, and for this man who lifted his head to look at her with desire.

There was only one choice, when she thought of it like that, and the choice was to pull closer, to take his hand in hers and trail it over her scarred arm, then over to her breast. The nipple went tight, begging for his notice even through shift and stays—and ah, he noticed. First with gentle fingertips, then with a cradling palm as he kissed his way down the side of her neck and over her shoulder. Sensation ebbed and flowed, then came in a deep tide of pleasure that made her arch her back.

"Will you take me to bed?" she gasped.

Almost before the words had left her lips, he swept her up in his arms. "It would be my pleasure. And I shall do my utmost to make it yours."

Seventeen

ROSALIND PULLED BACK THE COVERLET AND LAY on the bed, then helped Nathaniel strip her bare with hands grown tentative. Together they rolled her stockings down, unlaced her stays and tossed them aside.

When Nathaniel lifted the hem of Rosalind's shift, she pulled in a bracing breath, knowing what he would see. Here were more scars, covering her side, her hip, stretching over her back. But she would be lying about what she wanted if she clutched at her shift instead of clutching at him. Or instead of yanking the bath sheet from about his narrow hips to bare him as he had bared her. To see where the indentation of muscle at his hip bone led.

Now it was her turn to stare. His shaft was big, jutting forth, easy to reach, to touch. The skin was hot, and when she stroked it lightly, he moaned. His was so different from hers, this blatant desire. This ease with which he stripped and showed his skin.

He showed her more than that. The rough and smooth bits of her—he kissed and stroked them all until she was wet within, eager for him to touch every part of her. On her back, she twisted to escape the startling sweetness of his touch, to press herself more closely into his hands. She caught his arm and rubbed up its firm line as he braced himself above her.

This was the best view of all: his face above hers, the light of lamp and fire throwing his features into shadowy intimacy. Shaping his mouth into a curve just for her, deepening his eyes to onyx.

Would she ever tire of touching him? Of looking at the fine shape of him with the strength of planes and angles? The awe on his features when he touched her? Of noticing the way he breathed deeply when he kissed her, as though pulling her scent deep within himself?

She wondered, but she had no answer. Except for what she wanted next.

His breath was slow and shuddering as he lowered his head to the curve of her shoulder. He smelled of soap and the smoke of the fire. "Do you want me to stop now?"

"No."

"Soon, then?"

"No."

His hand drifted to cup her breast; his knees parted her thighs. "At…all?"

"No, not at all." She covered his hand with her own, lacing her fingers with his.

"Ah, thank God." Settling himself on his forearms, he covered her in a blanket of sensation. The fine hairs of his belly and chest, the hard muscles of his legs rubbed against her softness and made her slick with wanting. He made her feel beautiful. Valuable. Powerful.

His hot length pressed her thigh, then her private area. "Don't stop," she said. So on he pressed.

He joined with her in a shallow thrust, holding himself steady above her. The closeness was a shock, a wonder. But the fullness—she bit back discomfort. It was too much, like the scarred tightness she knew so well. As each thrust took him a bit deeper, she tensed.

He must have felt the change, cradling her between his forearms. "Let me try something different." He pulled out, leaving her cold but relieved.

And then came a touch of his fingertips, gentle and teasing, where he had left her. At the same instant, he bent his head to nuzzle at her breast. Closing his lips on the hard tip, he drew on her until she relaxed, melting into sensation.

With fingers below and kisses above, he worked her in slow strokes, each wetter and hotter and slicker than the one before. He claimed her, drawing her tight, and this time the tightness was nothing like scars, with not a bit of pain. It was winding up, up in a spiral of delicious anticipation. Each touch drew her onward, like a gold wire pulled infinitely long and fine and strong. Higher, tighter, she was wound and pulled, until at last she sprang free with shudders of pleasure. They shocked her, drawing a moan from her and making her limbs tremble.

At once, he came into position above her again. "May I?"

"You can try," she gasped. Her voice hadn't quite returned to earth yet.

He joined with her slowly, the new slickness easing his path, the shocks of pleasure opening her to him,

further and further. She widened her legs until her
scarred hip protested; let it protest. Nathaniel was with
her, in her, and just as he had made her shake with
pleasure, now he shut his eyes, neck corded and shoulders and arms taut. The same joy spiraled in him too.

She would make sure that he felt the same spring
into infinity. He liked to touch; maybe he would like
to *be* touched too. With a firm palm, she ran her hands
up his sides. The ribs were solid, the muscles shifting.

He pulled back; when he pushed in again, grind-
ing his hip bone against hers, the pressure made her
arch into him, locking them closer. On his back, her
exploring fingers splayed hard, pulling him deeper
within her.

The sounds they made were incoherent; all breaths
and moans, then *yeses* and *mores*. Her hands slid down
to clutch the taut muscles of his arse. He poised himself above her, breathing hard. Perspiration dampened
his skin. In the firelight, the coarse hairs on his chest
glinted red and gold. "I wish we could stay like this
forever," he said, and then he pulled free of her body
and clambered from the bed.

His hand did something—she couldn't see what
before she propped up on her good elbow—and
he groaned. Hand over the head of his erection, he
disappeared behind the privacy screen, and she heard
a splash. Washing off.

She understood then: he had finished himself rather
than spill seed within her. The wise choice.

She collapsed onto the sheets again, aching for him.
Knees loosening, she hesitated—then found the spot
he had touched to bring her to the peak.

"That is beautiful."

She pulled her hand away so quickly she almost swatted him. "I didn't hear—I thought you were behind the screen."

"Only for a moment. I would have been sorry to miss this."

"You didn't miss anything," she blurted out. After everything he had seen, after all they had done, it seemed odd that anything would make her blush. It seemed greedy, though, to seek her own finish a second time. She had been more used to rationing pleasures than taking what she wanted.

"Good. May I join you?"

She managed a nod. "But don't look at me. Please?"

"I've already seen enough to remember it forever." He eased back onto the bed, hitching one leg atop hers. His erection had sunk, and the coarse hair and weight of his male parts against her thigh were different, a new sort of enticing. "I'm still seeing it in my mind, the way you touched your—"

She silenced him with a kiss.

Though he closed his eyes, the wretch must have been peeking. How else could he have found her fingers so unerringly, covering them with his own? With his hand on hers, she found the slick bud, then teased and stroked it.

Together they rubbed at her to the point of delight, then beyond. They found a spot at which thought and worry vanished, and she quaked and cried out at the pleasure they had brought on together.

He rolled her onto her side, tucking himself in behind her like a nested spoon. Boneless as she felt, she fit neatly against him. Warmth and satiation made her drowsy; the arm about her felt secure.

She had taken Nathaniel Chandler as a lover. And it felt…right.

Which was new and different. When had she ever done something simply because of the way it felt?

"Hmmmhnm," she mumbled, wiggling closer to him.

"A Houyhnhnm sound." He untucked his arm from about her, but only to pull the coverlet over them. "You must be thinking about something profound. A stake in a wager of one hundred fifty pounds for your thoughts?"

She chuckled. "They're not so profound." If it was not profound for one to think—*this man. If only things were different, this man would be the one.*

She wanted the freedom of paying her debts, of working where she wished, of being honest. But she'd never had such freedom, and if she won it now, she did not know where it would carry her—or whether it would crush her.

"Rosalind." He rested his chin on the crown of her head. "I would like to be your suitor."

You would not want that if you knew how I spied on your father. Or that I work for someone else instead. But she couldn't say that, so she fumbled for another reply. "Secretaries don't have suitors."

"Secretaries…" Nathaniel was silent for a long moment, taking a half dozen deep breaths with his arm secure about her body. "Rosalind, you are more than a secretary. You have a right to a suitor if you wish."

No, she didn't. She didn't have a right to anything.

Nothing had been her own, not even her life, for a decade.

She couldn't admit that either.

"Maybe," she demurred. "But neither of us has a home. How can we speak of such things?"

But what she really wanted to tell him—what she really saw—was that he was half gentry, half nose to the grindstone. He would have made a marvelous country squire. He would have made a marvelous…anything.

He could build a home anywhere, and people would be happy to follow him to it.

She swallowed the words, hard.

"'I pray you, do not fall in love with me, for I am falser than vows made in wine.'" So said Rosalind in *As You Like It*. She had never expected to live out these words.

"I'm not asking anything of you, Rosalind. I know better than to ask for things I cannot have. Stating what I want is risk enough." His arm slid over her belly, her waist, then up her ribs. Just touching; he liked to touch things. Maybe they seemed more real when he did, an anchor to the world.

When his hand settled, he sighed. "You push back every time I come close, but not so hard that I think you want to break me. Just hard enough that I think you want to see if I'll stay." He lifted his head to press a kiss to her temple. "I'll stay."

That pain lanced her heart again, that joy that hurt with the knowledge it must end. "For now."

"For now. In the morning we'll both have to leave. But *for now* is good, is it not?"

"It has to be good enough, if it is all we have." She

turned onto her back, then the other side, so she lay face-to-face with him. The stretch and tug of her scars made armor once more. They had saved her life; they reminded her what was hers or not hers to give. "Will you kiss me again?"

This much she could ask. For now.

And as their lips met, as his hands again found her breasts, she tried to forget everything except the now.

To pretend that now would be enough. That paying her debts would be enough. That the escape she had wanted for ten years would be enough to make her happy, even if *now* was the only time she ever had with Nathaniel.

❧

They slept apart. Nathaniel had not wanted to let Rosalind go, but he knew it was only wise for her to return to her own chamber. "Just as though I were a guest," she said lightly.

She was more than a guest to her own family, of course. And to Nathaniel, she was far more than a woman for a night.

Their parting ought to be bearable, if it were only for now. But there was no promise of a different sort of now on the other side. She'd been right: he had no home. He had no notion what the future held for him.

Somehow, he hoped, he would find the answers in Epsom.

In the pale light of early morning, he tugged on Severn's clean shirt and knotted a fresh borrowed cravat. His own waistcoat would do, and his own breeches. A maid had cleaned his boots and brushed his coat.

When he opened the door to his chamber, he found Rosalind leaning against the wall next to it. She was wearing the borrowed gown from the night before, her long hair now pinned up and tidy. Her smile was shy. "Good morning."

"Good morning." His heart thumped a hearty greeting. "Are you all right this morning?"

Color stained her cheeks. "I am very much all right. Yes. And if you'll note, I was ready to proceed downstairs before you this morning."

"What a shame that no one receives a medal for that sort of thing." Rosalind's angular sentences made him smile. When she smiled back, he took her hand. Just for a moment—then he released it so they might proceed downstairs in a proper line.

At the bottom of the stairs, Mrs. Agate bustled by. Glancing at them, she called over her shoulder, "Rosie! Aunt Annie's here to see you. She's waiting for you in the family parlor."

Rosalind caught the newel post in one hand. "She is?"

"Oh yes! She just returned from—where was it? That foundling home somewhere near Wales where she spends so much time." Mrs. Agate waved at Nathaniel. "A saint on earth, I tell you! Well, go on, Rosie, and give her your good morning."

"All right," Rosalind said, but Mrs. Agate was already off to the common room, from which the sound of clattering plates issued.

"Your aunt wishes to see you? That must be a... nice surprise," Nathaniel finished in some doubt, noticing that Rosalind's face had drained of color.

"Yes. Yes—of course." She fumbled for words. Surprised, maybe, at the quick shift from the silent corridor of early morning to a caller before breakfast. "She—she is no relation, though we have all called her Aunt Annie as long as I can remember."

"She must be fond of your family," he ventured.

"Yes. She is a widow with no children. She used to travel a great deal with the army when her husband was alive, but she was a near neighbor of my parents before that time and has been ever since."

Maybe he had imagined the odd cast of her complexion. She looked like her usual self now, features as tidy as her braided coronet of hair.

"I don't wonder she wanted to call on you," Nathaniel said. "You haven't seen her for ten years?"

"No, though we—correspond. As my family and I do."

Pieces of conversations old and new locked together, and he realized: "She's the neighbor to whom you are in debt. The one who paid for your treatment after you were burned."

Rosalind nodded.

"She's your benefactress, then. May I meet her?"

"She's not the sort of person you're probably imagining, Nathaniel. She's not going to joke with you and befriend you like my brothers did."

"Was that friendship? I'm glad I didn't get on their bad side," he teased.

Still she hesitated.

He touched her chin, bringing her gaze up to his. "If she's important to you, then I want to know her. That's all."

Wide green eyes searched his, and then she gave another quick nod. "All right. But please do not refer to my debt. To her. I should—not like to discuss it."

Back came the short sentences. The pride. The armor. Now, why was that? Shouldn't she be thrilled to see the person who had provided her with lifesaving balms and care?

Maybe not. No gift came without strings of obligation; this one had taken her from her family when she was little more than a girl.

"I promise to greet her as I would any new acquaintance," he said. "With my usual charm and winning personality. You'll love having me there."

She smiled as he hoped she would, though the expression was fragile.

Well, he would just have to make good on his word. He'd win over the benefactress, and that would help convince Rosalind that he was more than the sort of home-lacking, wheel-repair-forgetting, late-for-dinner flutter wit she must think him.

The family's sitting room appeared shabbier in daylight than it had the evening before. On the worn horsehair furniture, the caller sat like a jet brooch, glossy and black-clad. Rosalind accepted a polite embrace from the older woman, then introduced Nathaniel to Mrs. Bowen Jones.

"Pleased to meet you," he replied with perfect correctness as he bowed.

Mystified to meet you might have been more accurate, though. Where was the effusive cheer from one who was, as Rosalind had described, practically a family member? Instead, the Widow Jones was almost impossibly serene. A small, neat woman of about forty years of age, she had raven-dark hair and a pale face that must once have been stunningly beautiful.

"Chandler, did Miss Agate say?" Her voice was low, with an accent Nathaniel took a moment to place as Welsh. "You must be related to Sir William."

"Yes, he's my father."

"And what is that like?"

"Having Sir William as a father?" An unusual question. "It is a never-ending delight, madam," he said drily.

"In what way?" Her black brows were lifted, her expression as cloudless and tight as a porcelain doll's.

Huh. No smile at all. "In every way imaginable. For example"—he grinned at Rosalind—"I was able to make up part of the group traveling to Epsom, which meant I had the privilege of meeting the Agate family along the way."

Aha, this won a tight smile. Even saints had feelings. "It is a privilege indeed to know them." She turned her back on him then, giving her attention to Rosalind. "I have much to discuss with you. Do you need breakfast first?"

Rosalind made some quiet reply, catching Nathaniel's eye over Mrs. Jones's shoulder for just a second before she returned her attention to the widow. There were so many things in that look of hers. Embarrassment? Shyness? She hadn't wanted him to meet Mrs. Jones, and he'd blundered by insisting. Now he was an intruder in their first hello after a long good-bye.

It was a relief a minute or two later when a knock sounded at the door, giving him something to look at besides the pattern on the papered wall.

One of the grooms peered in, hat in hand. "Mr. Nathaniel, the wheelwright sent over a messenger. The carriage will be ready in an hour."

And this a Sunday. He wondered how much Lombard had promised to pay the wheelwright. Whatever the amount, it was worth it to get on their way again.

Nathaniel thanked the servants, then stood to bid the women farewell. "That's a piece of good news. I'd better see to the rest of the party. I need to visit the family's town house to collect a few items, then I'll fetch the carriage with Lombard and return for you, Miss Agate. Will you be prepared to leave in, say, two hours?"

"Certainly." At his side, she folded her arms and rubbed at her right elbow. He had seen that elbow, had kissed it along with so many other parts of her body. Now he must call her *Miss Agate* again.

Mrs. Jones's delicate brows lifted. "Your carriage met with some mishap, I take it?"

"Yes," he answered. "Such things happen on the road."

"Indeed they do. If that is all that befell you, you must consider yourself fortunate." She looked thoughtful. "Please tell your father hello for me."

He blinked. "I'd be glad to. I wasn't aware that you knew him."

"I did once, yes." Again, that tight smile. "It was—how did you put the matter?—a never-ending delight."

❧

Queen Anne Street, where Sir William owned a house, was a few miles from the Eight Bells. As Bumblebee cut placidly through the morning traffic of London, all clopping hooves and carriage wheels and calling voices and coal smoke, Nathaniel hummed at the memory of Rosalind admitting there was something she wanted. Rosalind, baring herself. Rosalind, with him.

It was precious to be sought by someone not used to wanting things. If only she could have pulled him closer instead of pushing him away when he mentioned the word *suitor*. She wanted him, yes; she liked him.

But she still didn't trust him. Not enough to allow him a piece of her future.

He was used to not being trusted. That didn't mean it didn't hurt, though. Especially by someone he wanted to pursue.

Someone he could fall in love with. If he allowed it. If she did.

The house in Marylebone was damp and cold, with a fashionable address but little living space. It was shut up almost entirely between Nathaniel's visits, with only a few servants to keep it in repair.

When he arrived then, he would not bother approaching the front door. He'd simply ride around to the mews, leave Bumblebee with a groom, and dart inside.

From the safe where he kept a store of his own ready money, he would take…oh, say, one hundred pounds. For Rosalind, to stake her wager once the party reached Epsom in safety. Maybe he'd place a bet himself.

Such a withdrawal would nearly beggar him for the quarter, but if he could have, he would have paid twice as much. More. Any amount to give her the peace of knowing her debts would be paid.

Soon enough, he reached Queen Anne Street and drew near the townhouse. And halted.

Because in front of the redbrick house was a carriage with a familiar crest. A *Chandler* crest.

"Impossible," he murmured. Someone must have borrowed the vehicle.

Spurring Bumblebee into a trot, he threaded through the passage to the mews and handed off the horse as he'd planned.

As he pounded up the rear steps and entered the house, he peered into each room. No signs of activity, even from the few servants who ought to be present. And the curtains were still closed as though the house were deserted.

But the *carriage*. Why was the carriage here?

On the ground floor, he crossed the tiled entryway. Before he made for the stairs, he ought to check the back parlor. "Hello?" he called.

Before he reached the room, he heard something familiar. Expensive wooden wheels over costly marble, a low, luxuriant rolling sound.

And a second later, Sir William Chandler emerged through the doorway.

Eighteen

As soon as the sitting-room door had closed behind Nathaniel, Aunt Annie pulled Rosalind to a seat beside her. Her familiar scent of lemon verbena had once seemed sweet; now it tugged Rosalind back to the sickroom.

"You have neglected your letters since leaving Newmarket," said the low voice.

"I'm sorry. The days of travel were long."

At once, she regretted offering an excuse. Aunt Annie was sure to poke holes in it, revealing it for its own emptiness.

"Oh? Yet I saw a notice in a village broadsheet about your traveling party's participation in a fete. There was time enough for that."

Rosalind sat silent.

"I am not angry with you," Aunt Annie added. "Only disappointed. I rely on you, you know."

"I know. I couldn't stay in Newmarket. Sir William would have become suspicious if I refused to travel."

"Quite all right." She took up Rosalind's unresisting

hand and patted it. "You shall return soon and continue the search through his papers."

"There's no need." She pulled her hand free, spirits lifting. "I have good news. Excellent news. I've bartered my presence on this trip for a stake to wager on the Derby. The amount of my choice, the horse of my choice. If I lose, I'll lose nothing of my own. I intend to bet enough so that if I win, I'll be able to pay every debt. One hundred fifty pounds."

Aunt Annie's expression did not alter.

Perhaps Rosalind had not been clear. She tried again. "The money I win, I'll give to you. Then you may give it to Tranc to pay my debt and yours. We will be free."

Her voice was almost pleading by the end of this speech, but Aunt Annie remained as carved-pearl as ever. Then, with a sigh, the widow sank back against the hard cushion of the sofa. "You have made this bargain with young Nathaniel Chandler, I suppose. And you take him at his word?"

"Well—yes. He needed me to accompany him to Epsom, or his father would not have entrusted the traveling party to him."

"And what has he taken from you, along with your time and so trustworthy presence?"

"Nothing."

Aunt Annie twisted the heavy gold rings on her fingers. "You are a terrible liar, Cyfrinach. Remember what I taught you."

"'Don't lie,'" recited Rosalind. "'Lies are messy and sure to be found out. Just leave out parts of the truth.'"

She didn't want to leave out parts of the truth about

Nathaniel. She didn't want to discuss him at all. He was hers, untouched by Aunt Annie and Tranc.

"Very good. I am pleased that you remember." The widow's smile was like a blade. "By your own admission, Nathaniel Chandler has agreed to defraud his father. How can you be sure he won't lie to you as well?"

"Defraud—no! It's not like that at all. Neither of us is lying to Sir William." Not exactly. They were only…well, leaving out parts of the truth. "And I know he would not lie to me."

She knew because of the way he had traced her scars so tenderly. The way he had taken her, leaving no inch untouched, unkissed.

Aunt Annie tutted. "How long have you trusted me, and how long have you known him? What do you owe me, and what do you owe him?"

So it was to be this as always.

"There can be no comparison." Rosalind felt dull as a stone. Too dull by far to be an agate, with all its varied layers and bright stripes. "I owe you my life."

Yet she wondered how much she would choose to give were it not wrung from her endlessly.

"Aunt Annie. If I do get the money, will it suffice? Will it be enough to clear my debts and for us both to be free?"

"Ah, Cyfrinach." Aunt Annie shut her dark eyes. When she opened them, her gaze was gentle and sad. "It will never be enough. The information is what we need. The proof to trade with the knowledge Tranc holds."

"I don't understand. What knowledge could he

hold? I have done nothing—" Rosalind cut herself off. She had done nothing for which the law could touch her, but she had done much she knew was wrong. Taking papers from locked desk drawers, copying them over and sending them off to Aunt Annie. Listening at keyholes. Stealing secrets that could never be unknown again. All for Tranc, who owned her debt.

She wished, not for the first time or even the hundredth, that Aunt Annie had never done business with such a creature.

"He does not hold over us knowledge of your doings," Aunt Annie broke in, "but of mine."

And finally, in the cramped sitting room of the Eight Bells, in a voice as quiet as rain, she told Rosalind what had happened in Spain in 1805, thirteen years before.

There had been a baby. Sir William's baby.

"Though at the time," Aunt Annie said, "he was not yet a baronet, only a mister. He was a widower, and I was a new widow. The affair was not so wrong, surely, except for its result."

She twisted a ring off entirely. Beneath it, her finger was marked tight and pale. "Tranc helped me find a safe place to deliver the child once I returned to England, then found a family with which to place her. He has used this information against me ever since. My secret, my shame, could lose me my place in respectable society."

A saint on earth. Mrs. Agate wasn't the only one who thought of Anne Jones thus. Benefactress not only of Rosalind Agate, but of foundling homes in Wales and East London. Yes, her tidy place in the welcoming, vivid Holloway neighborhood would be erased if her secret was known.

Of course, Rosalind had lost many places in the service of Aunt Annie's secret. Her place amid her family had been the first.

She shook her head. "The money must satisfy Tranc, Aunt Annie. That has always been the understanding. I worked to pay off my debt."

"The money will pay your debt, yes, but it will not absolve me."

Rosalind slid away, wishing the sofa permitted more distance between them. "I am sorry for that, but once my debt is paid, my dealings with him will be completed."

"But that is impossible, Rosie. Cyfrinach. You must see that. You've used forged references. Everywhere you have worked, something has been damaged. Papers stolen, outbuildings burned, horses made ill. It wouldn't take much of a hint for someone to notice the pattern."

The voice was calm as ever, but there was steel in Aunt Annie's dark eyes. *You're in it as long as I am*, they said.

Aunt Annie had used her, just like Tranc was using Aunt Annie. For a long while, Rosalind had thought this.

But she had never known about the child, and that changed matters. That softened the stone about her heart. Some things were far too difficult to bear alone, and giving up a loved one was one of them.

"Why did you have me hold so many posts?" she asked. "If what you needed to learn was at Chandler

Hall, why did you not approach Sir William at once, years ago?"

"Tranc." Aunt Annie jammed the ring back onto her finger. "I had always to do his bidding before my own. He collects secrets as your mother collects spoons. Only recently did I get a step ahead of his demands, enough to send you to Sir William to look for evidence of our affair in Spain."

But it was Rosalind, not Aunt Annie, who had done his bidding. Only Rosalind had taken the risk of searching desks, copying notes. Rosalind left friends as soon as they were made.

Only Rosalind had been fool enough to think one hundred fifty pounds would save her life.

"Do you ever see the child now?" she asked.

"No. Never in thirteen years. It is for the best, though. She does not know the people who have raised her are not her parents." When Aunt Annie looked away, Rosalind noticed threads of gray in her neatly pinned dark hair. "I send money every year. As much as I can."

Rosalind put her arm around Aunt Annie, easing the older woman's head onto her shoulder. It was a bony substitute for Mrs. Agate's pillowy hugs and the low hum of her mother song. But it was better than nothing, better than solitude.

After a moment, Anne Jones, mother of a lost girl, relaxed onto Rosalind's shoulder and drew the sort of shuddery breath that meant one was trying not to weep.

"Thank you for saving my life," Rosalind said. And she began to hum, smoothing back Aunt Annie's hair with a gentle hand.

She thought of Nathaniel. Again. Always. Her scars had saved her life, he said. If she had not scarred, she would not have healed.

But there were so many ways to be scarred, and one could not buy healing with the transfer of coin. Not even one hundred fifty of them, silver sovereigns in towering stacks.

No, Rosalind didn't want to be part of these old, old secrets and rivalries anymore. But someone had to be. Tranc would exact whatever he thought his due from whomever came his way. As long as he got what he required, he'd have no reason to turn his gaze to those who were more vulnerable. To Carys, as Aunt Annie feared, or to the child Sir William did not know he had.

Better me than someone else.

Nathaniel had said that too.

If Rosalind had been free to choose her own path, she might have chosen to love him. Just for that.

Nathaniel shook his head, but the vision in the townhouse's entryway did not disappear. Here was Sir William, who ought to have been in Newmarket receiving Rosalind's glowing letters of Nathaniel's progress. Sir William, unmistakably real, heavy hands gripping the rims of his chair wheels as he rolled across marble tiles to face Nathaniel.

"Father. How did you get here?"

"Surely you remarked the carriage before the house. I have traveled day and night to meet you, only to find you—not here."

Nathaniel's week of careful planning began to unspool under his father's scrutiny. "True. Yes. I was not here, but now I am."

"And the rest of the party, and the horses?"

"At an inn called the Eight Bells, belonging to Ros—ah, Miss Agate's family. It's not far." Sir William looked skeptical, and Nathaniel added, "It's a respectable neighborhood. And I have had the horses under watch day and night since leaving Newmarket."

"I do not know the Eight Bells. I haven't approved it as a place to lodge."

This was the sort of situation in which Rosalind would turn the subject to one she preferred. So he did the same. "If you planned to travel to London, or even to Epsom, why did you send me?"

"I didn't send you. You forced my hand. And I didn't plan to come, but you forced my hand there too."

"How is that?" Trailing toward the stairs, he plumped down on the third one and faced his father at eye level.

"I received a copy of the *Kelting Monitor* with an enlightening article about my groom's participation in a village fete. Two days out of Newmarket, you stopped on the road for a fete." Sir William's voice held all the weary calm of one who had learned a harsh truth he'd been expecting for some time. "I saw how you were treating my trust and that of our respected neighbor, Sir Jubal. You used your time for carousing."

Damn. Damn. Damn. "Not carousing—no, it wasn't like that. It was a day of rest, since our progress on the first day of travel was excellent. As I mentioned, the horses have always been under guard. Their safety was my first concern."

"A day of rest. I see." Sir William's steely brows lifted. "So you work a day, then rest a day. Is that how it goes?"

Nathaniel set his jaw.

"And I arrive in London to aid you, after traveling day and night, only to find the house smelling of neglect."

"It always smells like that. The roof leaks, as I mentioned in a letter a month or so ago."

Not that Sir William was listening. Though his eyes were gray-shadowed with fatigue, he seemed buoyed by the conviction that he was always, above all, right.

Certainly he looked like himself, crisply attired and clean and groomed. Not like a man who had been through the hell of overnight travel on bumpy moonlit roads.

"Who has seen to you?" Nathaniel asked. "Where are the servants? The house should not be empty like this."

"I sent them out to comb the city for you. For all I knew, you had been set upon by thieves. You were entrusted with valuable horses."

"Who are safe and healthy." Despite not following the baronet's stringent guidelines as to feed—not that he was going to mention that at the moment. "How are the other horses that fell ill? The ones that stayed behind?"

The topic of horses softened the edge of Sir William's voice. "Sheltie is recovering slowly, but I've hopes she'll be all right in time. Jake, that old rogue, made a fine recovery. When I left, he was collecting ear scratches and radishes from every groom and stable boy."

"Such coddling," Nathaniel said drily. "And here I thought you expected your horses to be all business."

Sir William hands traced his chair rims. "It's good business to have healthy horses," he said by way of excuse, looking away as though embarrassed by this hint of softness. "It's clear the horses were fed something noxious, though I've been unable to find out what or by whom without a secretary to aid me."

"And because you've been away from Chandler Hall for several days yourself." Nathaniel braced his elbows atop his knees, settling his face in his hands. So the horses were well, but no one knew why they'd sickened. Everyone was in the wrong building this morning. Sir William was in the wrong *city*.

Damn.

Nathaniel looked up, chin on steepled hands. "How did you come by that article in the *Kelting Monitor*? Did you decide to travel based on that?"

"Yes. An old acquaintance sent me the article," Sir William said. "One Anne Jones."

Nathaniel sat up straight. "She mentioned she knew you. I was to greet you for her."

"You've met her?" Sir William's brow creased.

"Just before coming here. She is an old friend of the Agate family." Anne Jones. Well, well. The sainted Aunt Annie had sent Sir William the article. If Nathaniel had the chance to meet her again, his *Pleased to meet you* would become *What the devil?*

"What is Mrs. Jones to you, Father?"

Sir William shrugged the question off, impatient. "Nothing, nothing. I had not seen nor heard from her in years."

"So you didn't think it odd she sent you an article?"

"No more than I thought it was odd my son should have stopped for a day at a *fete*. When he was supposed to be on his way to *Epsom*."

So they were back to that.

"What now, Father? Do you intend to come to Epsom, or to stay here now that you know the horses haven't been slaughtered along the road?"

"I'm joining the party to Epsom, of course."

"Of course. I should have guessed." Nathaniel stood, then looked up the stairs. "I just need to fetch one thing, and then I'll… What is it?"

Sir William had rolled forward to catch his coat sleeve. "First I…" The baronet trailed off. "I need some assistance."

"All right," Nathaniel said again, this time cautiously. Remembering Rosalind's advice—it seemed like ages ago when they spoke as tentative allies in the stable—he asked before reaching for the baronet's wheeled chair. "What do you require?"

The words were almost ground out. "A chamber pot."

"Oh—*oh*. Yes. One moment."

Nathaniel pounded up the stairs to grab a chamber pot from the first bedroom he passed. He moved toward his own room, thinking of the money he needed to fetch from the safe, then decided against it. Sir William spoke as though he were uncomfortable, and he was without aid to mount the stairs. Away from the wonder of his modern piped-water bathing room, too.

Thundering back down the stairs, he set the pot down before Sir William. "Do you want a privacy screen?"

The baronet's lowered chin and glare were speaking.

Nathaniel managed not to roll his eyes. "I'll be back in a moment."

There was a large japanned screen against one wall of the back parlor. To reach it, he had to weave through a clutter of chairs and around a sofa. Then he collapsed the great paneled piece. Good Lord, it was taller than he was, and as long as a man laid out flat. Lugging it *bump-bump-bump* back over the carpet and around furniture, he wondered how Sir William had managed to squeeze his wheelchair into the room. He must have been halted right inside the doorway.

With a screech and scrape of old lacquered wood over marble, Nathaniel tilted the heavy screen on one corner and dragged it near his father.

"One more moment." Nathaniel was beginning to feel a bit winded as he wrestled with the tall panels.

"Please. Take your time." Sir William folded his arms.

Again, Nathaniel did not roll his eyes. Or sigh. There was nothing good about this: a grown man unable to piss in private in his own house.

He arranged the six folding panels in a crooked semicircle about Sir William. "Is there anything else you require?"

"No."

"Then I'll leave you in private."

"Why?" came the voice from behind the screen.

"Afraid you might catch sight of my legs? Need a drink or two?"

Now he did sigh. "I don't do that anymore." Over the front of the screen, intricate gilded beasts chased one another. Frozen, poor beasts. Never getting anywhere or catching what they wanted.

Leaving the entryway, he descended to the kitchen, where he found a pitcher and a bucket of clean water. By the time he returned to the japanned screen, Sir William had emerged from behind it. "Water to wash your hands, if you wish." Nathaniel explained.

Sir William raised a brow. "So that's it?"

"What?"

He took the bucket, dunking and splashing one hand after another. "You don't drink spirits anymore. Not ever."

"Rarely." He fixed his eyes on his father's. Those told the truth of the man, not the powerful arms or the unresponsive legs.

Surely it was worth something that as many times as Nathaniel had been tested and tempted, he had never fallen back into his old way. Until Rosalind Agate gave him her ale and the chance to put his lips where hers had been.

Oh, who was he trying to persuade? It wasn't worth anything. Refusing a glass of wine—or a bottle of brandy—wasn't the sort of thing a man received a medal for, any more than arriving on time for dinner. He chose not to drink for his own sake. He knew he didn't like the results if he did. Knew it was too difficult to stop after a bit, and so it was better never to start.

But he did like the feeling of going away for a

while. Especially when someone looked at him like this—with disbelief and a hint of disappointment.

"Good, if you mean it. You've already drunk enough for a lifetime." Sir William set the bucket on the floor. "I'll return with you now to the Eight Bells."

Nathaniel arranged the unneeded pitcher beside the bucket. "I arrived on horseback."

"Then we'll take my carriage."

"We could. But your horses looked tired. They could do with a feed bag and a bit of rest." Privately, Nathaniel thought his father could use a feed bag and a rest too, but Sir William was far more likely to be concerned with his horses' health than his own.

Indeed, the baronet's heavy brows drew together, considering.

"I can return for you within an hour, Father," Nathaniel suggested. "Or perhaps two. With the rest of the traveling party."

Sir William looked around, and now Nathaniel could guess what he saw: the otherwise empty entryway, dominated by a formal screen hiding a chamber pot. A parlor he couldn't navigate, stairs up which he could scoot only with great effort. And no servants to help.

"This really is a horrible house, isn't it?" Sir William's voice sounded resigned. "Come back for me, then, and we'll all go on to Epsom together."

Nathaniel's jaw went slack. When was the last time Sir William had asked anything of him besides a chamber pot and screen? When had he suggested they do something together?

This was a road he had not expected to travel to Epsom. Or at all.

"I'll return soon," he said, already moving toward the back stairs that would lead him outside. "I think you'll be pleased with the party's progress."

"I'd rather be pleased on Derby Day."

"It's just possible," Nathaniel called back, looking over his shoulder, "that you can be both."

Sir William's reply was an unintelligible mutter, then a wave of his hand. "Shoo, now."

Which, considering the source, was almost like a benediction.

Nineteen

WHEN THE TRAVELING COMPANY CAME TO A HALT IN Queen Anne Street, Rosalind followed Nathaniel up the steps of the town house with both curiosity and apprehension.

Curiosity because this part of London was unfamiliar to her. As a governess to an earl, she had remained in the country with his ignored children, seeing fashion only secondhand. Marylebone was a world of cravats and lace, of bespoke gowns that buttoned up the back. Of lady's maids and valets, and servants who fetched tea and left the daughters of the house to sit in idleness.

She felt apprehension too, because this was the home of Sir William, who had given Aunt Annie a daughter of whom he knew nothing. This was the largest secret with which Rosalind had ever been entrusted. Would it sneak through to show on her face? Nathaniel had suspected nothing, but then he was distracted by his father's unexpected arrival and would probably not have noticed anything less than a missing member of the party.

The Chandler town house ought to have been

elegant. It was tall and slim, with white-framed bay windows set into red brick. But heavy draperies hung within like closed eyelids, and when Nathaniel rapped at the wood of the door, she realized the brass knocker had been removed. No one was supposed to be in residence.

A servant opened the door, his expression changing from suspicion to relief as soon as he saw Nathaniel. As he and Rosalind stepped over the threshold, a brief conversation ensued with the man about the whereabouts of the household's few other servants— they had returned from searching for something, apparently—and Sir William.

"I cleared a path through the back parlor, Mr. Nathaniel, and he's made himself comfortable," explained the servant. "And I've seen the screen replaced and had what was behind it taken away."

"Thank you, Sutton." Nathaniel looked at Rosalind. "Miss Agate, let us retrieve Sir William so we can continue on to Epsom. Or do you care for tea now that we're here?"

"This isn't a social call, Mr. Nathaniel. I am quite all right. I breakfasted while you were gone."

"Breakfast," he murmured. "I think I remember hearing of such a thing."

Before they had taken more than a few steps through the narrow entry hall, Sir William emerged through a doorway. Stern and solid, hands on the wheels of his chair, he seemed only to need to wish himself from one of his houses to appear in a blink in the other.

"Miss Agate. I need some private speech with you."

He sounded clipped, but then he so often did. She looked up at Nathaniel, who shrugged. "Father, the traveling carriage and horses are waiting in front of the house. Will this take long? Should I have them brought 'round to the mews?"

"No need. We'll speak for only a minute or two." Sir William backed into the parlor.

Rosalind followed him in, then looked about uncertainly for a place to sit. The room contained enough furniture for a space twice its size, but every chair and table and desk had been shoved together, leaving the other half completely bare except for a deep-piled carpet dotted all over with the dents made by furniture resting on it.

"Close the door behind you."

Rosalind obeyed, then stood, folding her hands neatly behind her back. She wished she had changed into one of her own familiar gowns instead of wearing this flowered nonsense from Carys that tugged and bagged and added to her discomfort.

When Sir William spoke, it was with a slight tilt of his head, as if he wished to study her from the corner of his eye. "Nathaniel mentioned that you have known Anne Jones for a long while."

Rosalind's mouth opened, but it took an extra moment for the word "yes" to issue forth. And then she closed her lips. Hard. Best to say no more than she had to.

"What is she to you?" asked the baronet.

"A friend of the family."

"More than that, surely. She called on you personally this morning."

"A natural curiosity to meet with one whom she had not seen for years."

"Hmm." Sir William gave his wooden rims a gentle push, the familiar back and forth of his moments of consideration. The sleek chair wheels hardly moved on the carpet. "Why do you think she contacted me, then? What sort ·of curiosity was that?"

"She contacted you—" Rosalind's fingers knotted together behind her back. "I was not aware you were a present correspondent of Mrs. Jones."

"I had not been for some years. But it seems she wanted me to rejoin this party of travelers. Why would that be, do you think?"

"I don't know, Sir William." This much was quite true.

"Could it be because she was concerned that my son would debauch one she sees as a daughter?"

A startled laugh popped from Rosalind. "I doubt that was her concern."

Sir William's brows lifted.

Rosalind hunted for words. *Leave out parts of the truth.* "If she is interested in my doings, it must be because she paid for the treatment to save my life. After I was burned."

"You owe her a great debt, then."

"Yes. I intend to pay it."

This was the wrong thing to say. Why had she not stopped at *Yes*? Her employer's deep-set hazel eyes, so unlike his son's, kindled with interest. "Can such a debt ever be paid?"

She considered her reply carefully. "What is your

own opinion? Surely there were physicians who saved your life."

"I saved my own life. Now, how are you to pay this debt? Did you place a wager?"

"No."

"You're getting the money from my son, aren't you? Is that why Anne Jones contacted me?"

"I doubt that is why she contacted you, Sir William."

He sighed. "That is only part of an answer, Miss Agate. Which in this case is answer enough. How much is my son paying you?"

Damn. She swallowed, unsure how to parry this question. "He intends no money for me, Sir William."

"So I should trust everything you've told me? The first few letters I received from the road—those were perfectly accurate?"

"Everything good I told you about your son was perfectly accurate."

He shook his head. Reaching into his coat pocket, he pulled forth a sealed paper. "I had time to prepare this while Nathaniel was fetching you. Just in case this conversation went as I suspected it might."

Rosalind took it with cold fingers. "Ought I to read it right now?"

"There is no need. It is not for your eyes, but for those of a prospective employer. It is a qualified letter of reference."

Her fingers clenched, crackling the paper.

"If I cannot trust you to represent my interests, Miss Agate, I have no further need of your services as my secretary."

"Because I accepted help when it was offered?"

In for a penny, in for one hundred fifty pounds. "I wish to understand for what it is you fault me, sir. Is it that Anne Jones paid my medical expenses when I was a child, or that your son offered to stake me in a wager in the hopes my winnings would cover my debt? Or is it that neither transaction involved you?"

"As my secretary, you should have no transactions save those that involve me."

"You expect that one should have no outside life." This served her right for all the times she had used *Secretaries don't...* as an excuse.

"When you accept money in exchange for letters you write me, we are not speaking of an outside life."

She fumbled for words. The plan for her to write letters all the way to Epsom had seemed a victory for both her and Nathaniel. Now Sir William made it sound sordid.

"I should have discussed my debt with you," she ventured.

But that was not the answer either; he was not interested in her private affairs. And until the trip to Epsom severed her from his household, she would have continued to search his papers, trusting in secrets rather than coin to pay her debt. The money she had asked of Nathaniel was only so she need not spy further for Aunt Annie.

When she thought of it that way, Sir William underestimated how sordid the whole matter was.

The folded corners of the letter in her hand pressed sharply into her skin. An introduction to someone unknown, supposedly, but it was really a good-bye.

She had not realized how much it would hurt to be thought well of and then…not.

His lack of faith in her was justified, and that hurt too.

She had abandoned the habit of looking in the glass when she was scarred. How long since she had seen herself clearly?

Sir William's broad hands played on the sleek rims of his chair. "We cannot afford to be weak, Miss Agate. When one is hurt, the jackals come sniffing. They smell blood and they want a taste."

"The jackals have been sniffing about me for a decade, Sir William. Your son offered to help me escape them." Her throat felt tight, and her scars ached no more than her heart. "He helped me find my family again."

"Then you have a place to go once you leave my employment." His voice was not unkind. In fact, his eyes were sad under his heavy brows. "I do not wish you ill, Miss Agate. But I have no use for someone I cannot trust."

She smoothed out the folded letter she had creased in tight-clenched fingers. "I understand, Sir William."

"I shall have your things sent to you."

"Do not trouble yourself. I left behind nothing that I want back." How lightly she had stepped through the world, owning little, knowing few. In Newmarket, she had thought to grow a few roots, but it was not to be. Her life was not truly her own, and she could be plucked from her setting at any time. A weed.

She had to try to plant one last seed first. "Your son is a good man, Sir William, and a good leader. I told you nothing but the truth where he was concerned. I do not know what has come between you, but I know he wishes it gone."

"He has always been better at wishing than at taking action."

"I have not found that to be the case." With a curtsy, she excused herself and left the parlor. The door shut behind her with an oily click.

How easy it was to find oneself on the other side of a closed door.

❧

She waited dully in the entryway for a long moment. What was she to do now? Sir William was probably giving her a chance to compose herself, but he would emerge at any second. And she could not bring herself to step out the front door in view of the grooms. Not when she would not be traveling on with them.

Just when she had decided to exit through the kitchen and walk home, Nathaniel thundered down the stairs with a fistful of papers. "Ah, good. Done speaking? Are you ready to leave?"

"I have been let go," she said.

He leaped down the final two steps in one stride. "How do you mean, 'let go'?"

"I mean it in the usual way. Your father does not wish to keep me in his employment anymore. He—he gave me a letter of reference."

Nathaniel lost his hold on the papers. As one piece fluttered to the floor, Rosalind recognized it as a banknote.

"This was why he wanted to speak to you?" He smacked the heel of his free hand against the green-painted wall. "Damn it. Damn him, damn me. I am so sorry. That is detestable."

Had his anger flared at her, she would have stepped back from its burn. But he lashed himself instead. He blamed everyone but her.

Even though it had been *her* idea to exchange money for travel and a few positive words. *Her* Aunt Annie who had combed the newspapers between Epsom and Newmarket once Rosalind failed to send a few letters.

Of the two of them, she was the only one who had done wrong and lost something. He could carry on.

"You'll be all right," she said. "You don't need me to finish the journey now."

He leaned forward, peering from end to end of the entryway. Then seizing her arm, he pulled her up the stairs after him until they rounded the first bend and were shielded from view.

"Here," he whispered. "This is a hundred pounds. It was going to be our stake—but you need it now. Put it in your pocket."

"No." She made fists of her hands, letting the money rain over them and fall to the stairs. "No. I didn't get to Epsom. My letters didn't help you. They *hurt* you."

She stared at the colorful notes on the worn tread of the stairs. "Your father made everything sound so dirty." As though she were a whore. A liar. A cheat.

When in truth she was only the last two.

Nathaniel sighed. "I want you to have the money. It's my fault you lost your post." He looked angry and wretched at once.

"That's just not true. You got this far on your own." She matched his quiet tone. "I lost my post on my own."

He leaned against the wall and let his head fall against it. *Thud. Thud.* "You don't want to allow any connection, do you?" Blue eyes pierced her. "Take the damned money, Rosalind. Please. Think of it as thirty pieces of silver if you must, but just take it. I always meant you to have it, whether we arrived at Epsom or not. Ever since you asked for it, I thought of it as yours."

He wasn't only talking about the money. She knew that. And she wasn't used to this: to wanting something and being entrusted with it simply because of her desire.

She shook her head. "As though asking is enough to get what one wants, whether one deserves it or not? That might be acceptable for almonds. Not this. Not…" *Not you.*

She could not ask for anything more from him. Not when there were so many things she could not tell him.

I never truly worked for your father.

I came to Epsom as an alternative to prying through your family's papers.

You have a sister about whom you never knew. She is just the age of my youngest brother, Elder.

The words unspoken were like stones. They caught in her throat, choking her.

"It's not my money," she said. "It cannot be mine."

He looked at the discarded banknotes, then slid down the wall to sit on a stair. "I want to help. I just…I just want to be of some use to you, Rosalind."

"You are not mine to use, Nathaniel."

"Am I not? What *is* yours?" His tone went harsh, all the fiercer because of its near-whispered intensity. "I'm not yours. The money isn't yours. What is?"

Nothing. Not even my own self.

There was just space enough to sit down beside him on the stair. Even so, she felt too much distance between them to even take his hand. "Asking isn't enough to get what one wants."

"Of course it's not." He leaned back on his elbows, letting the stairs hold him up. "If it were, I would have been on the way to Epsom without having to bribe you into chaperoning me. And my father would have remained in Newmarket, trusting me to do well."

Looking tired, he fixed her with eyes devoid of their usual spark. "And if you chose to come along after all, you would have been proud to introduce me to your family and their friend. You would have said, 'Yes, be my suitor. Even though you have no real home and your work is tenuous, court me.'"

There was not enough air in this tiny box of stairs and walls. Rosalind shuddered in her thin gown, eyes sandy and throat dry.

Oh, so many reasons he hadn't even thought of. *Even though you don't know all my secrets, court me. Even though I'll never be able to look at your father without wondering where your sister is, court me. Even though I won't be able to tell you why or what's bothering me, court me. Even though he doesn't trust me and eventually you won't either, court me.*

"I wish you could have those things." She forced herself to stand. "I should go."

"Why? No one is expecting you."

"Because if I don't go right now, I'll beg you to stuff me into a trunk and take me to Epsom with you."

"I'll go get an empty trunk." He made as if to get up, but she caught his hand.

"No, Nathaniel. I can't see you again."

"Is this that ridiculous notion you have that secretaries don't have suitors? Because it's not true. And you're even not a secretary anymore."

She dropped his hand and walked down a few stairs. Bending awkwardly at the waist—Carys's gown was tight about her ribs—she gathered and smoothed the banknotes. Even the first one that had fallen. All of them.

Once they were in a neat stack, she folded them and extended the handful to Nathaniel. Politeness should have brought him to his feet when she stood; politeness dictated that he would take what a lady sought to offer him.

He only watched her face, ignoring her outstretched hand. It seemed they would wait in silence forever, the seated statue and the standing one. As she stood on a lower stair, their faces were at the same height.

And he began to smile. "You could be, though. You could be a secretary. You could come to Epsom, and I needn't even stuff you into a trunk."

She set the money down beside him, not breaking his gaze as she bent. "I can tell you are having a diabolical idea. What is it?"

"I find myself"—he folded the banknotes and tucked them into his waistcoat pocket—"in need of a secretary."

Her mouth fell open.

"Shocking, is it? But you see, I am on an important journey and must keep careful account of racehorses and servants alike. How am I to do that without the help of a secretary?"

Her feet shifted and fumbled on the steps, finding the next riser down. "That's silly. You haven't needed a secretary thus far."

He dropped the hearty mien for a moment, his expression softening. "But I have, Rosalind. I didn't come a step of the way without you." His smile was sweet and a little sad. "Not that I ever thought of you as anything but a Rosalind. Still, if I have to call you secretary, I will. I'll say what I must, do what you wish, so that you can finish the journey."

Extending one hand, he added softly, "If you want to, that is. Only if you want to."

That hand had touched her, loved her, brought her to pleasure. And then it had become part of an embrace, tucking her to his heart as long as they dared.

What had he said to her? *You push back to see if I'll stay.* Something like that. And he had kissed her again and said he'd stay.

And he had.

"I'll stay," she said.

By those two short words, she meant far more.

Maybe he understood, for the smile that crossed his features made her heart reel, dizzy with delight. For a moment, his fingers closed over hers.

And then he released her, all business—though that smile kept tugging at the corners of his mouth. "Then you're hired, Miss Agate. The wages are terrible and the hours are worse. Your employer is prodigal and presumptuous and—"

"Passionate? Perplexing? Plays the piccolo?" She turned to lead the way down the stairs. "Whatever he is, I am sure I can handle it."

"Very true, for you've worked for Sir William Chandler. Come along, then, Miss Agate. We have a new city to visit and a Derby to win."

Twenty

As Sir William navigated the steps of his crested carriage with the help of his arm strength and two servants, Nathaniel descended the town house steps at Rosalind's side.

As always, he helped her to settle into Farfalla's saddle. Then, with her nod of approval, he led the mare before the open door of the lacquered carriage.

The wheelchair was jammed between the carriage squabs. His father was seated with feet flat and knees canted out. Between his legs was a walking stick on which his broad hands were clenched. "What's this?" grunted Sir William, settling back onto the squabs. "Are we taking Miss Agate back to the Eight Bells?"

"Why should we take her there?" Nathaniel feigned surprise. "No, Father, my secretary is traveling to Epsom with us."

The baronet's gray head tilted to one side. "Your secretary?"

"Indeed. You gave her a letter of reference. How could I help but hire her?"

Snort. "Nonsense. You don't need a secretary."

"Nonsense. You all but told me I did by sending one along on this journey." It was pleasant to echo the baronet's own words, but with a twist into something positive. "And now I've found I can't do without her."

At his side, Nathaniel felt rather than saw the startled movement of Rosalind's shoulders. "No need for a waltz in the saddle, Miss Agate. It's quite true."

She fidgeted again. "As a dutiful secretary, I should never gainsay my employer's opinion."

Sir William craned his neck, his deep-set eyes searching the pair of them. "So that's the way it is."

"That," Nathaniel said with some relish, "is the way it is."

"And what do you think about this, Miss Agate?"

She hesitated before replying, her pause so long that Nathaniel looked up at her. Chin lifted, she finally said, "I think it's only right that I should finish what I started."

"And so he has hired her as his secretary," muttered the baronet. "Good Christ almighty."

Nathaniel smiled. "Did you hear that, Miss Agate? He is inspired to pray. I haven't heard him pray for thirteen years."

"It *is* a Sunday," she said mildly. "Maybe it's the influence of the date rather than our own sterling characters."

Sir William shook the cane. "Off! Off with the two of you."

Nathaniel arched a brow. "'Off with the two of you' as in 'off to Epsom'? Or as in 'off to a faraway location'? Because I'm quite willing to honor the former request, but not the latter."

Sir William sat back, his face dropping into the

shadow of the carriage's deep velvet interior. "To Epsom, of course. We've already dawdled far too long. Let us get back on the road."

Nathaniel bowed. "Very well. Your wish, my command, et cetera."

As he closed the carriage door, he thought he saw grudging respect cross his father's features. The contrary old scoundrel.

❦

Rosalind had snapped up the opportunity to travel onward with Nathaniel and the servants with whom she'd come to feel so comfortable. Yet as the procession set off, familiar yet a little different this time, she felt awkward about the journey.

Was it Sir William's presence that changed matters? Another carriage was added to their company. And though the baronet couldn't see them from its plush interior, his nearness was like a weight. Lombard held Pale Marauder on a shorter line; the outriders hung closer and kept their hands on their weapons. Nathaniel didn't whistle.

Maybe it wasn't Sir William's presence at that. Maybe it was London itself. Used to traveling at a drifting pace alongside Nathaniel and Bumblebee, Rosalind now had to keep her head and her seat as she guided Farfalla through the congestion at London's heart. Farmers' carts were replaced by hackneys and drays that squeezed into spaces far too small for safe passage, reins in a tangle and horses in a lather. The bark of a friendly sheepdog had seemed loud a few days ago; now she wouldn't even hear a dog over the

sound of carriages on cobbles, of shouts and whin-
nies as everyone tried to go every direction at once.
Buildings walled in the streets on both sides, and a roil
of foot traffic covered the pavement.

Had it always been like this? Were her parents used
to such clamor? Was Nathaniel? For the first time
since leaving Newmarket, Rosalind kept her balance
by thinking of *next* instead of savoring the *now*.

After hours, the traffic gradually began to thin. The
stone under Farfalla's hooves gave way once again
to earth. The noise about them softened and fell as
the walls of buildings were cleaved by the welcome
sunlight of late afternoon.

Rosalind's hands loosened on Farfalla's reins. Only
now did she realize her hands had been clenched so
tight as to ache.

Nathaniel and Bumblebee fell into stride beside
them. "Glad to be through the thick of it?" At her
nod, he added, "In another week, carriages and carts
will fill the road all the way to Epsom."

"That many people want to see the Derby?"

"Nearly everyone in England wants to see the
Derby. Only a fraction have the time and coin to
make the journey."

Her brow creased. "You did tell me once that horse
racing was a world of its own. I had no idea it was such
a large world."

"Not such a large world as all that. The people
involved in the race are few compared to the people
who only want to celebrate. Derby Day is…" He
trailed off, studying the Thoroughbreds on their lead
lines. "It's rather like a fete for all of England."

"I like fetes," she said simply.

I like your kisses. I like when you tell me, 'I shall have a man at my feet'—as long as there is a hope that maybe someday he will be you.

He shot a glance at her, smiling. "I like fetes too."

The familiar calm settled between them. Rosalind was about to comment on it when Nathaniel added, "I'm sorry we couldn't stop at midday today. There's no good place to halt a large company within the city, and I wanted to press on. We'll stop soon for the night. At that point, Sir William will probably want to take charge of everything."

Indeed, he was right about this. They halted for the day at the Queen's Noggin, a tidy inn with enormous brick chimneys proclaiming its great age but a fresh white coat of stucco over the exterior. Almost before the crested carriage could halt, Sir William had worked the door open and was calling for the innkeeper.

Nathaniel dismounted, then walked Bumblebee over to his father's carriage. Rosalind watched as some quiet conversation ensued—first between the two of them, then in a trio with the innkeeper, a bowlegged elderly man with bright, dark eyes and short-cropped white hair.

"The hay is all the horses need," Sir William said. "We only require stalls; no ostlers and feed."

"I've been allowing them other feed," said Nathaniel. "They wanted it. And they've thrived on it."

"Those weren't my instructions."

"What's more important? Your instructions or the health of the horses?"

Excellent questions, and Sir William let them pass.

With the help of a few servants, he descended the carriage steps, sitting on the bottom one until his wheelchair was worked free through the other set of carriage doors.

Once settled into his accustomed seat, he rolled to the doorway of the inn. And from there, he issued order after order: for the unloading of the carriages, the scheduling of watches over the horses. The parceling out of rooms. The dressing of a family parlor on the ground floor for Sir William's accommodation.

Rosalind leaned against the white front of the inn, only feet away from the tumult of unpacking. It had been so easy to know what to do before, but now Sir William had supplanted her. When the baronet turned his gaze to her, she straightened up. "How can I help, Sir William?"

He made a dismissive gesture. "You can't. You needn't."

Her shoulders hunched.

The baronet looked up at her, then sighed. "Nathaniel is busy in the stables. He doesn't really need a secretary. I've hired you a nice chamber on the second floor. If you'd like a bath, of course you're welcome to it. And you must ring for dinner whenever you feel hungry."

So that was that. She was to be placed properly within the inn, just like the traveling trunks.

Sir William turned his chair, calling for one of the outriders, then issuing some instruction for the following day's travel.

"Thank you," she murmured unheard, then stepped inside the inn. Step by step, as she mounted the stairs, she was carried along by the promise of a fete the size of a city.

The evening passed slowly, because every time she left her chamber, there was a servant to trundle her back inside. "Just ask for whatever you want, miss, and we'll fetch it," said her benevolent jailers. A meal and a bath only passed part of the time, and then there was nothing for her to do. No letters to write to Sir William or Aunt Annie.

As Nathaniel's secretary, maybe she could have arranged to visit his room. But it could not be the same sort of visit they had delighted in only a day before. Even if he employed her in name only, she couldn't let their passion become a transaction. And in her mind, it would be.

Secretaries don't…

He was worth far too much to her to sully the memory of the night before. It already seemed so much longer since she had been with him.

She could not be sorry for the spell of pleasure under which he'd laid her. But she wondered whether she should have stayed in London and not been greedy for more, only to watch the spell be broken. She didn't have a reason to be here, other than this false job Nathaniel had given her. And whether it was to spite his father or to keep her close—well, it didn't matter, did it? She'd lived for ten years going where she was told, with the reasons opaque.

Every reason, every wisdom she'd collected over the past decade, said she should keep her distance. That she should have taken Sir William's letter of reference and turned on her heel.

Every reason but one: she wanted to be close to Nathaniel far more than she wanted to be wise.

Heart troubled, she fell into an uneasy sleep.

∽

The morning brought her better cheer, and the group's arrival in Epsom shortly after midday even more so. Rosalind had decided to pretend she was on holiday, happy to help when needed, but otherwise enjoying the air and the sights that were utterly new to her.

Epsom was a town dressed as a city, its main streets wide and buildings of neat brick quoined with stone. Chimneys poked up like curious heads, and trees sighed in the light sultry breeze. There were ten days until the Derby, and the promised throngs had not yet arrived, but everyone seemed to be preparing. To one side of the street, a servant was painting an inn's door a fresh bright red; to the other, a maid was scrubbing the front steps of a shop.

"I've arranged rooms for us here at the King's Waggon," said Nathaniel, halting the party before that edifice. "It's an easy distance to the Downs."

Rosalind skimmed the pleasant Georgian facade, smiling at the pale green-blue color the shade of a starling's egg. With a slate roof atop and wide windows on the ground floor, its bright brass sign proclaiming it a Royal Mail stop, it was a cheerful, neat structure. And for now, there was space before and around it. Over the next ten days, as England's population shook up and settled southward, that would change.

Nathaniel knocked on the door of the crested

carriage, then popped it open. "Father, do you intend to stay here too? The ground floor is all taproom."

"We'll see about that," said the baronet. "They were sure at the Queen's Noggin that the ground floor was all public and family rooms."

"But you convinced them otherwise. Well done, you. You deserve a medal." Nathaniel sounded tired all of a sudden. Maybe he hadn't slept any better than Rosalind had.

She ventured through the doorway of the inn, finding herself in the taproom to which Nathaniel had referred. It was dark brick with dark wood paneling and a smoke-darkened pictures on the walls. A few scattered customers sat at the tables, each with something dark in his glass. The space would be soothing to pounding heads.

Behind a bar, a slim woman was laughing with an older woman in a mobcap. "...wasted all that money on an express! I took it, of course, since postage was paid, and the rider seemed right glad to head home again. But I never heard of this woman. She in't staying here."

"What was her name again?" the older woman asked. "Maybe she's in town. You han't been here long enough to know everyone, Flora."

"Rosalind Agate," said Flora.

Rosalind tripped over a chair, catching herself on the edge of a table with a bone-jarring thump.

"Funny sort of name, in't?" Flora added, oblivious.

"Never heard of 'er," added Mobcap. "Keep it a while, I s'pose. Maybe she'll turn up for the Derby."

Rosalind untangled her feet, kicking the chair back into place, and almost flung herself across the room. "Excuse me! Mrs.—Miss—I overheard—that is, I'm Rosalind Agate. You've an express for me."

"Oh, aye?" Flora, a pretty blond, set her hands on her hips. "Why should I believe you?"

Rosalind frowned. "Why should you not?"

"Now, Flora," said Mobcap. She turned to Rosalind, a cunning smile on her plump features. "And glad to see you, we are, Miss Agate. I'm not saying we *dis*believe you and all. But I think Flora means a shilling would go a fair way to convincing her."

"Aye, and a half crown'd be even better."

Rosalind's pockets were empty and had been ever since the Kelting fete. "You said the letter had been paid for, so you weren't put to any expense. Please, give it to me."

Flora's hand wandered to her apron pocket, but then she paused. "I'd take that ribbon off your bonnet instead of a coin," she decided. "That's right pretty."

Rosalind gritted her teeth. Considered. "No," she decided. "I don't think so. And if this is how the King's Waggon treats its customers, I'll tell Sir William Chandler's party to find other lodging. Ah, here is Mr. Nathaniel Chandler now."

With a sour look, Flora produced the letter from her pocket before flouncing off. Mobcap at least had the grace to curtsy and mumble an apology before cleaning a glass that already sparkled.

"What was all that about?" Nathaniel asked, brows raised. "I come in to find you intimidating the servants out of secret letters."

The paper crackled in her hand. "It's an express. It arrived for me just a short while ago."

She turned it over. The handwriting was familiar, and a sick swell of dread caught her. "Aunt Annie. She—something must be wrong at the Eight Bells."

"Here, let's find you a private room." Nathaniel took her arm. With a quick word to Mobcap, he escorted Rosalind through the taproom into a private parlor and shut the door behind them.

This is where Sir William will sleep, she thought dimly, hardly looking around. She cracked the seal and stared at the brief lines.

> *You are needed at home to protect Carys. Return at once.*
>
> *Anweledig*

Under her breath, she cursed.

"Bad news?" Nathaniel asked.

"I don't know. Yes, maybe. I–I think I must return to the Eight Bells. Right away."

"What is it? May I see?" When she handed over the paper, he skimmed it, then shook his head. "This doesn't mean anything. Who is Ann-well-a…"

Damn. She'd forgotten about the signature. "That's Aunt Annie's real name," she blurted out. "It's—it—something must have happened that she didn't want to write in a letter."

Something to do with Tranc, no doubt. No sooner could Rosalind leave than Aunt Annie could jerk on the strings knotting them. And Rosalind would be pulled back. She had to be, to save her sister—or whomever Tranc turned an eye to next—from the life she herself had lived.

Her throat was tight, so tight she could hardly speak. Secrets clutched at her like iron-banded scars. And they weren't even her secrets, so she could never be free of them.

Sliding the paper from Nathaniel's hands, she said, "I have to leave. Can you arrange a hack for me? I'll have payment sent to you once I arrive."

"Surely you needn't go at once. Your sister has two parents and four brothers at home to see to her safety. You could reply—stay a few days, then go..." He looked puzzled, as though he couldn't understand his own sentences.

"Nathaniel, it was an express. It can't be put off."

"Ah. An *express*. So if I pay a few shillings, I can get you to do whatever I want?" He smacked the plaster wall with the flat of his hand. "Damnation, Rosalind. I can do that. You work for me. I have an ungodly amount of money in my pocket, because you wouldn't take any before. Take it now, and stay in Epsom."

How tempting. How tempting it all was; every inch of him, from the flat of his hand now bracing him to the boots that had guided her somewhere private.

"Others have a claim on me too," she said. "Do you really want to be nothing more than an employer who orders me about?"

He turned to the wall, his palm sliding down, flat. "No," he said. "No, of course not. Not as an employer, then. As a...someone who wants you to stay. Let your Aunt Annie send her worries to someone else for a few days."

"It's not only a few days." The words almost choked her. "I cannot come back."

"To Epsom, you mean."

She shook her head. Just a sliver, as though any greater movement would break her.

He was turned away still, but her silence was answer enough. "To me?"

"Yes." Thin as a spiderweb, she sounded. But spiderwebs were strong too, and she steeled herself. "This must be the end. I—owe much loyalty to others, Nathaniel, and I've let myself forget that. I should not have…"

It would be too cruel to them both to finish the sentence.

Come to you. Kissed you. Allowed myself to fall for you. I should not have permitted myself to love, because someone will be hurt. And it's better it be me than someone else.

How terrible that at the moment she realized she could not have him, she came into the full understanding of her love. It was knife sharp and gleaming, a bladed pleasure like the throb of joy she had felt at being home. It cut at her heart.

Balling her right hand into a fist, she covered her mouth and permitted herself a silent sob.

And then her scars tugged, reminding her that her life was not her own.

Quietly, Nathaniel said, "Rosalind. Please. You could stay if you wanted to. You stayed the last time I asked you. Couldn't you do the same again?"

"I can't do the things I want to, Nathaniel. You know that."

He whirled, rounding on her. "I know nothing of the sort. You could stay now if you wanted to. You could look me in the eye." He jerked her chin up, blue eyes hard. "You could answer my questions."

He swallowed heavily, dropping his hand from her chin. "You…you could kiss me again, Rosalind. Or agree that I might court you. You could fall in love if you wanted to." The muscles of his jaw went hard. "So I can only assume you don't want to."

She was a terrible liar, Aunt Annie had told her. And so Rosalind could not feign agreement with him. She could not bear to disagree either, to tell him all the things she wanted and had no means of having. At this moment, even sugared almonds and a crown of flowers were beyond her reach. A life with Nathaniel? She might as well wish to fly.

Already the fruitless wanting was painful, like being burned all over again.

"I could kiss you again," she said. "If that would be enough."

"Of course it won't be enough." He almost growled. "But I'll take it."

Closing the distance between them with a swoop, he fisted his hands in her hair, tumbling it and sending pins flying. She had expected a sweet good-bye kiss, a gentle farewell, but he pulled her into his arms like a starving man seeking a feast.

His lips covered hers; his tongue brushed against her own. One kiss became many, more—or maybe they were all the same because he never let go of her—and then her hands were on his shoulders, pulling him closer as her thighs clenched, belly heated.

Love is merely a madness, she tried to remind herself. So said Rosalind from *As You Like It*. She was mad for him; this was mad, to kiss him in a private parlor while an express lay crumpled on the floor. Knowing she must leave. Any minute, she would have to leave. She should not let herself—let him—ah—

With every fall of her hair, every pin that dropped, she felt herself weakening. It would be so easy to beg him to take care of her. To become another of the milkmaids he handled with such grace and good humor.

But they were obstacles. She would not become that sort of thing. She had spent enough time flat on her belly as she healed. She deserved more—and so did he—than for her now to spend her life on her back, her mouth closed against every truth.

Once more wasn't a lifetime, though. She was desperate not to leave him just yet. To have him touch her roughly as though he could not resist.

He ground her against him, pushing a knee between her legs. She was wet for him, wanting him.

"Take me," she gasped, helpless against the pressure. A moment to forget herself now, a flood of passion to remember later.

"A kiss is all you offered me," he said. "So that's that. That's good-bye." He helped her to regain her feet as coolly as though a flame had been extinguished, though his nostrils flared with deep unsettled breaths.

"You think that was only a kiss?" She was reeling, ready to fall upon him again.

"Well." His smile was bitter. "Close enough. Did you really trust me to do exactly as I said?"

"I always have."

He shook his head.

This could not be the end, not quite yet. She seized for something to say. "My wager," she blurted out. "Will you still stake my wager? I want to bet on Epigram. Whatever amount you think right."

"None of this is right," he said. "But I'll place your bet. Come now, I'll arrange a hack and servant to take you home."

And so she might go. But her heart, she knew, would remain in his keeping.

She wouldn't have need of it anymore.

Twenty-one

"ROSIE? DID YOU FORGET SOMETHING?"

Mrs. Agate had bustled into the vestibule, an expression of welcome on her features. When she spotted Rosalind standing by the door, that expression altered into one of surprise.

For the first time, Rosalind disliked the jingling of the eight little bells that greeted everyone who passed through the doorway of her parents' inn. Could she have slipped upstairs unseen and unheard, she would have done so.

Not that she had passed through the doorway quite yet. She struggled with her trunk, which bumped and threatened to topple as the contents shifted. A cold May drizzle had spattered the worn leather as she heaved it—with the help of her chaperone, the burly outrider Button—up the steps of the Eight Bells.

She'd sent him on his way before opening the door. Once he'd sworn to her that "Mr. Nathaniel said Sir William owed you wages, and those'd cover this journey."

Thank God for that. She had spent all her ready

coins days ago on a wreath of red flowers and on a lace fichu she'd never yet worn.

"Is everyone all right, Mama?"

"Yes, of course. We'd have written at once if that wasn't so."

Her mother's smooth, confused expression proved to Rosalind exactly what she'd suspected: there was no emergency here. Only Aunt Annie, yanking on a lead line when Rosalind began to wander.

Or Aunt Annie, worried about Tranc. Not wanting to face him alone.

"You've brought your trunk with you, Rosie?" Mrs. Agate's forehead furrowed.

Rosalind gave the simplest explanation for her return that she could think up. Thumping the end of her trunk to the floor, she said, "I've been let go."

Every innkeeper, especially one who kept a well-frequented taproom, had spoken the phrase so often to lazy maids and dishonest grooms that there was no misunderstanding it. Mrs. Agate's pleasant features changed yet again. Her eyes widened, and her mouth drooped. "Oh, Rosie. By your baronet?"

"Certainly not 'my baronet' now."

"Did you—" Motherly delicacy and faith kept her from finishing the sentence.

"I was to receive some money from Nathaniel Chandler once we reached Epsom safely. Sir William disliked this private arrangement. He found it to be untrustworthy." That was not the whole truth. But it wasn't a lie either.

That had been the whole cursed problem from the start: Rosalind had sworn she wouldn't lie. Not to Sir

William and—she thought—not to anyone else. But she had, especially to herself. *You can tell Nathaniel about yourself without giving too much away. Especially not your heart. Why, secretaries don't even have hearts.*

You can take what you need and then leave.

Saying good-bye won't hurt. You're used to it.

But she wasn't used to it. She was used to slipping away in secret, not to leaving after a kiss that rocked her senseless.

And she was certainly not used to falling in love.

"How much money, Rosie?" Mrs. Agate ventured.

To her mother, the money to pay off her debt would seem a fortune. Just as it had to her. "No money, Mama. I received nothing."

"Then surely you did nothing wrong. Not if you were still doing your work properly. If you just explained to your baronet, maybe he—"

"The more I explained, the less good came of it." The letter of reference, still sealed, was sharp in her bodice within her stays. The same place she had always stuffed her letters from or for Anwelcdig.

She'd had plenty of time on the way back from Epsom to work out the words that would convince her parents to let her stay. But they still cut, too sharply true to be easily spoken.

And it cut too to excise Nathaniel from her explanation. *I wanted to stay with him so badly, Mama, that I almost risked Carys's safety.*

Her mother knew nothing of Tranc. Of the debt held by Rosalind and the sainted Aunt Annie. And Mrs. Agate didn't need to know about that. The top layer of honesty was enough. Bad enough. "I no longer work for a baronet. I am sorry, Mama. I know you were proud of that."

"Oh, Rosie." Mrs. Agate collected herself, drawing her plump little form up straight. "Did he give you a character at all?"

The reference, she meant. "Yes. Of sorts."

"Then you'll find a new post soon enough." Her mother enfolded Rosalind in a quick embrace. One of transition rather than comfort, with no mother song. "Until you do, you must stay here."

A shout came from the public room, and Mrs. Agate looked over her shoulder. "That Mr. Elton. Drunk off his feet every time he comes in. I'd best go see him out, since your father's still out in the stables. You take your things on up to Carys's room, all right? You can carry your own trunk up?"

These sounded like questions, but they weren't really. Mrs. Agate was trundling away without waiting for an answer.

Rosalind heaved her trunk onto one end and dragged it. First toward the stairs, then up. *Bump. Shove. Thud. Bump. Shove. Thud.*

Maybe if she made enough noise, one of her brothers would come help her.

But Mrs. Agate reappeared first. "Rosie!" She called from the edge of the public room, peering up at the stairs. "Carys isn't in the same room you might remember. She uses the chamber you once did. So that'll be nice, won't it? Familiar?" Again, she was off before Rosalind could reply.

Familiar indeed. This had been the way of her childhood: a parent or older brother swooping in with quick words about something that needed doing or correcting. And then off again; there was always more work than time or hands to do it.

Bump. Shove. Thud. She made her way up the remaining stairs to the first floor, then dragged her trunk to the back stairs and bumped it up to the top story of the Eight Bells. The family chambers were the least desirable in the building, small and plain and high up. Rosalind's brothers had crammed themselves three and four to a room. Rosalind had always shared a chamber with a maid or two, while the younger children like Carys slept in little bunks in a room not much larger than a pantry.

Now three of her brothers had grown away from the inn. There were no more small children. The sleeping pantry was locked, probably used now to store bedding.

Carys had left her chamber not only unlocked, but also untidy. The bed in which Rosalind had slept a decade before was unmade, its sheets and coverlet tumbled. The wardrobe door hung open, as did two of the drawers of a tallboy between the room's two beds.

Across the top of the plain wooden tallboy were scattered glass vials of scent, all nearly empty. Jars of cosmetics that were—Rosalind checked—yes, also almost used up. Necklaces with broken clasps. A brooch missing its pin and one of its paste gems. Carys must persuade the lady's maids of the Eight Bells to give up their mistress's exhausted trinkets. An eager, pretty face was difficult to deny.

Sharing a room with Carys, Rosalind could make

sure that nothing happened to her carefree sister. *Better me than someone else.*

Rosalind smoothed the unmade bed's sheets and coverlet into place, then shifted her trunk to the end of the second bed. She wished she could change into one of her own gowns, now that she had her things with her. But she couldn't reach the buttons of this one. Even trying would enrage the tight skin of her right arm and back and set up an uncomfortable ache in her elbow.

That was that, then. She was settled back at the Eight Bells.

For now.

The room now neatened, she shut the door behind her and descended the stairs. First, she needed to find Aunt Annie. And then, until and if she found another post, she needed to find something of use to do.

Some task that would help her forget all she'd left behind—not only in Epsom, but year after year. If such a task existed in the world.

❧

Ten days until the Derby, and Nathaniel took Dill's place on watch that night so the servant could pursue the arrogant barmaid at the King's Waggon.

It didn't help. All Nathaniel did was stare into darkness, remembering how Rosalind hadn't even looked back over her shoulder when she climbed into the hackney in Button's company.

He wanted her to stay with him of her own accord. But he just wasn't that important to her. And so he did the thing he was good at, which in this case was saying good-bye with a smile and pretending like it was fine, completely fine, to see the person to whom he'd hoped to prove himself worthwhile cast him aside.

If Sheltie had been here in the cozy brick stables of the King's Waggon, he'd have settled into straw beside her and leaned against her warm swayback. Instead, he kept a hand on his pistol and listened for other sounds besides the shifting of animals and Lombard's snoring.

Nine days until the Derby, and their jockeys arrived in Epsom to exercise the horses. Nathaniel spent the day on a training course, eyes bleary as he watched horses move over the long sweep of green. He glanced at his pocket watch, about which a second hand swept, but was unable to keep numbers in his mind to time the fast-moving animals.

Eight days. Another night watch.

Seven, and more exercising. Button returned from his journey to the Eight Bells with a shrug and an assurance that Miss Agate had arrived safely. No, he bore no note from her.

Nathaniel's throat felt dry—the sort of dry that only a sharp, biting liquor could ease. He gritted his teeth and went back to work.

Six days until the Derby; again, the training course. Five, again. And four, and three. Keeping watch on the jockeys, Daley and Pring, as well as over the horses. Pale Marauder and Epigram looked stronger and fitter every day.

Nathaniel supposed he ought to be pleased. He'd manage it someday when he allowed himself to have feelings again.

The city was beginning to fill now, the wide streets

cluttered by everything from shining carriages and new-fangled velocipedes to rough-wheeled boards on which lamed former soldiers rolled along. Innkeepers were shoving in guests four and six to a room. Many of Epsom's homes let rooms to race-day visitors. Some people slept on the pavement or in the street. Tents popped up like wild mushrooms all over the green sweep of the Downs.

Sir William's private parlor-turned-bedchamber remained inviolate. Graciously, the baronet offered to let Nathaniel share his space.

"I'll sleep in the stable," was Nathaniel's reply. Though he left his trunk in Sir William's room under the baronet's lock and key.

There was little else for Nathaniel to do besides keep watch at night or walk to the track during the day. Ordering the servants? Done by Sir William. Arranging care for the carriage horses? Ditto, ditto. All the milkmaids of travel were shackled and sent away, and Nathaniel had too little to do.

Why had he been foolish enough to think a trip to Epsom would accomplish something? It was an ending. An end, probably, to Sir Jubal's hopes of a double champion; an end to this stolen time with Rosalind. An end to Nathaniel's hope of regaining Sir William's trust.

Even if a horse ran his heart out, anything could keep him from winning. A careless jockey, a false stride, a collision. Victory was unlikely at the best of times.

Potential was so sweet compared to reality.

And on every corner, in every inn, were bottles. Tankards. Flasks. Wine and gin and ale and brandy and

God only knew what else. Buoying the raucousness of the ever-growing crowd. Tempting him with their jewellike wink.

The day before the Derby, he could bear it no more. He fumbled through the taproom of the King's Waggon, squinting to hide the sight of the bottles and glasses that held forgetting. Probably he looked drunk, but drunkenness was common enough today, and it raised no notice. A shoulder slammed into the door of the private parlor, and he reached for the handle.

Unlocked. Oh glorious day.

Of course, the reason it was unlocked was because Sir William was inside it. Nathaniel's eyelids sprung open as soon as he realized. "Beg pardon, Father."

"Not at all. Join me." Sir William's brief surprise had vanished in a flicker.

He had transformed the parlor into a tolerable bedchamber. Sofa and table were pushed to one side, and a pallet of mattress and sheets had been made up on the floor. His trunk and Nathaniel's were tucked into the corners. Through the middle of the room, the wood floor was smooth and clear. The inevitable path for the wheeled chair.

"I was just about to have brandy." The baronet sounded doubtful. The small bottle on the room's table was still sealed and the tumbler empty.

One sealed bottle. That was fine. Nathaniel was used to the ritual of brandy. "One-half inch," he said. "Do you want me to pour it out?"

"No, no. I will." The wooden wheels made a sleek ticking sound as they rolled over the floor. Sir William eased himself into place before the table. His hand reached for the bottle—then stopped. "Did you know, Nathaniel, that I don't like brandy?"

"Ah…no. Why do you drink it every day?"

Cheering and shouting leaked beneath the door. Edged around the lace-edged draperies hung at the window. Racegoers, happy as drunken lords.

Sir William's voice cut low beneath those sounds. "Because I cannot do without any drink at all. And it is too easy to take more than one ought. The brandy reminds me of that."

Nathaniel's chin drew back. For a moment he could only stare. "You…you have it too. This craving for drink."

"I have it too. I wish you had inherited anything else from me." Sir William's palms were flat on the table, ready to push himself away.

The brandy was a daily test, not a daily reward. "How long do you have to test yourself with it?"

"Every day. Forever. Until I know without question I would pass."

"Huh."

As usual, there was no place to sit in the chamber. The cut-velvet sofa was almost hidden beneath the decorative detritus of the room, plus an unrolled shaving kit.

So Nathaniel perched on the edge of the table, one boot braced on the floor, half expecting his father to say *Off. Off the table* as he always did in his study.

Instead, he was the one to speak. "I hated you for leaving us."

Sir William's hands spasmed, but he said nothing.

So Nathaniel explained. "We were no more than

half-grown when Mother died. We were sick with the loss of her. We needed you to tell us everything would be all right, that there was still someone who cared for us."

Instead, Sir William was gone more than ever. As if with his wife dead, there was no reason to stay in Newmarket. As if his children were nothing.

Jonah had turned inward. Abigail married horribly young. Hannah, sweet of heart, had latched on to Nathaniel and Sheltie and the grooms. Out of such inadequate substitutes had she made partial parents. "I was the only one who told you the truth, Father: that you had abandoned us. I know you only came home because you were ill. You would never have come back if you'd had legs to walk away from us."

The words flowed so calmly, so readily, that Nathaniel realized he'd been waiting to speak them for quite some time. They had lined up and marched forth, presenting themselves like soldiers for inspection.

Pushing to his feet, he paced across the room. Two steps before he was halted by the pallet. "I was horrid to you. I know that. And I'm sorry for the way I acted. It was wrong of me. But after all this time, I wanted you to know why I'd done it."

He turned his steps toward the doorway, but Sir William held up a hand. "Wait, Nathaniel." Back and forth, he rolled the empty tumbler between flat palms. When he spoke, the words seemed unearthed with great effort. "I had no idea how to be a father without a mother. But I knew how to travel and connect. I could turn conversations into contracts, and contracts into coin. I was fooling myself, I know, to think that piling up money would be enough for you all."

He sounded bitter, so Nathaniel said, "It was certainly better to have it than not, if those were the two choices."

"I hated you too," added the baronet mildly. "At least I hated that you spent your days in a bottle. Not even old enough for Oxford, and you were pickling your healthy body. No help when I tried to learn to walk again, or when I realized I never would."

Nathaniel leaned against the door frame. He felt time like a distance, as though they were talking about people so far away they could not be seen clearly anymore. "Did you want my company? Or did you only think I owed you?"

Smack. The tumbler slipped and skidded across the tabletop. "Both, if I'm honest. Both of those things. Even before your mother died, I made a comfortable home for all of you. Traveling about to the races and the sales, earning money. So often absent that I was never able to be a part of my own family."

Nathaniel had never considered that before, that his father had felt pushed to the side in his own home. Taken for granted. Pressured to provide.

"You were a good provider," he said. "We never doubted that. I should have told you."

Sir William waved this off. "Your mother told me. She told me she missed me, and she wrote me letters about what you children were doing, and…" His hazel eyes seemed to be looking at those faraway figures. "In truth, I wanted to be that person she made me feel I was. I wanted to be indispensable."

Nathaniel had to smile at this. "You never really wanted my help, did you?"

"I have never wanted any help. From anyone. But sometimes I have needed it. And when I came back from Spain you made clear to me, with your drinking and scorn, that I would not get it from you."

This was so deep a wound, Nathaniel realized, that it had never truly healed. It had scarred, closing with a tight wariness that made Sir William tense every time something approached that tender spot.

"I am sorry, Father. I wish I could undo that old selfishness and give you the help you needed."

Sir William shook his head.

And Nathaniel knew that this apology could never be adequate. Nothing could make up for the years of hurt on both sides. Of wanting the other to say, *Be there for me*, and of wanting the other to have been present.

But an apology was all he could give.

And then his father pushed back from the table to face him and smiled, an expression so halting that Nathaniel hardly recognized it for what it was. "You gave it now. That's enough."

Nathaniel slid down the door frame about a foot before his knees remembered to hold him up. "What?"

"I asked Lombard about the... What do you call them? Milkmaids? Yes, right. All the milkmaids you've encountered since leaving Newmarket. You handled them well."

"Milkmaids love being handled," Nathaniel mumbled.

"You hid from me all the good you could do. Have done all these years to help the family. Or maybe

I didn't want to see it." The hazel eyes, so unlike Nathaniel's in shape or color, held an expression he understood well. "I'm not sorry I came along to Epsom. I'm only sorry I didn't come on a journey with you long ago."

They would have fallen into silence, but a round of drunken cheers erupted from the taproom, making them both smile. "Are you going to place a bet?" Sir William asked. "Only one more day to enter your wager."

"I don't know. The turf has never seemed the sort of place I might find victory."

What form would his own victory take? He had once thought he would find it in Epsom. But now a future without a bronze-haired, wry woman at his side seemed incomplete.

And he remembered—yes, he needed to place a bet for Rosalind. "Father. Yes, I do want to wager on the race. Do you know the odds on Epigram?"

The baronet scratched his head. "Fifteen to one at noon today. Prince Paul is the favorite, going off at eleven to five."

"As though I'd bet on a prince when I've seen how good a knight and a baronet's horses can be," Nathaniel scoffed. "Have you a bookmaker you trust? Oh, that's good. Will you place a wager for me?"

He pulled notes from his waistcoat pocket. Day after day, he'd kept them with him like some sort of talisman of Rosalind. "Place it all on Epigram. One hundred pounds."

Sir William took the money slowly, smoothing the notes out flat. "Is some of this for her?"

Nathaniel did not pretend to misunderstand. "Miss Agate left that up to me. She trusted me to decide."

"Good for her. She's a bright girl. I put money on Epigram myself." Sir William rolled forward, aiming for the doorway. "Oh, I put a bit on Pale Marauder too, since he's my own horse. Didn't want him to feel neglected. But Epigram—he's the sort of horse that does what he sets out to do. He's a good horse."

He looked up at Nathaniel. "Good horse," he repeated quietly. "Thank you for bringing him—all of them—as far as you did. I...have been pleased with their progress."

And then, with a press at the door handle, he was gone with a steady *tick, tick, tick* of chair wheels before the door closed behind him and left Nathaniel alone.

Well, not quite alone. There was a full bottle of brandy here.

For the first time in thirteen years, its golden wink did not appeal to him not at all.

Twenty-two

AFTER SEVERAL DAYS AT THE EIGHT BELLS, ROSALIND remembered why she had fallen into the habit of silence as a child. With the building always bustling with relatives and lodgers and those who stopped in for a pint or meal after a day's toil, one had no privacy save the thoughts one kept inside one's head.

Perhaps because of this, she was entrusted with many secrets by others who couldn't help but let the words out. Peg the kitchen maid disliked Polly, who worked in the scullery, supposedly because Polly was lazy but in truth because Peg's man had flirted with her. Carys and Elder were battling over some Spanish trinket from Aunt Annie—given to their oldest brother, Bert, but left behind when he married. And so on, daily.

You've got the sort of face people want to talk to, Nathaniel had once told her. The world tipped its troubles into her ear until she was full of them and could not let them out. Why could not all life be changing bedding in guest rooms or currying a horse in need of soothing? Straightforward work, honest work. To fit within a web of people made Rosalind feel tugged about.

But though uncomfortable, it was not unpleasant. The unpleasant bits were inside her, remembering the night in Nathaniel's simple room here—and not only when she passed by the chamber door or smoothed the coverlet after making up the bed anew. And then there were the stairs, over and over, so different from Chandler Hall. Reminding her of the parlor in Epsom, a room she had hardly seen for begging, and where the desires of her heart and flesh were denied.

She could not regret these memories entirely. Not as tied up as they were with Nathaniel, who would always be the taste of sugared almonds, the scent of soap, the warmth of a body over hers.

After some discussion of where best to put Rosalind to help, her parents had agreed to let her work in the scullery. This was Rosalind's own request. Though the scullery was the lowest of the low, a position so ill paid and dull that other maids looked down upon it, there was really nowhere else help was needed. And Rosalind would do any job to feel useful.

So she spent her days beside the heat of the kitchen, testing her limits with hot water and soap. It seemed to soften her tight parts and steam away her sentimental bits. She stacked up clean dishes, knowing she had done something to help.

Aunt Annie seemed to be avoiding her, as though she knew she had pushed too far. When a line was tugged sharply, the animal might bite. Rosalind was not as well trained as Anweledig had long assumed.

When the week finished its turn and the next one

had marched along, Rosalind realized it was Thursday. Derby Day. Scrubbing at a pot, she wondered whether Nathaniel had placed a wager for her. The favor now seemed as pointless as the price she had once thought to put on her freedom.

Still, if he had placed a wager for her, that would mean he thought of her. One shining thought to lay next to the great pile of thoughts she had about him.

She hoped Epigram won. It was impossible not to like the steadiness of the horse and his determination to get what he wanted, whether a mouthful of grass or a victory against blue-blooded colts. He'd no idea that asking and trying were not enough to get what one wanted. To a horse, ignorance was both bliss and success.

That afternoon, Aunt Annie poked her head into the scullery. "Come speak with me in the sitting room."

"Ah, so you've made an appearance at last," Rosalind replied without looking up from the plate she was scraping into a slop bucket. "You waited long enough to tell me what was on your mind. By now, you could have sent an express ten times over."

"Of course, my Cyfrinach. You have every right to be puzzled." Aunt Annie stepped into the scullery. "We can speak in here just as easily."

Puzzled? Ha.

"If you want to talk, help me dry these." Rosalind flung out an elbow to indicate a stack of plates. "They'll be needed again soon. They haven't time to dry in their racks." She didn't bother to try to sound other than she felt: like an automaton.

"Where is the other scullery maid? Polly?"

Rosalind shrugged. Polly was probably out with Peg's man somewhere, not that Rosalind cared to investigate. Her head already held more than enough secrets.

A long pause succeeded, during which Rosalind kept her hands busy and her eyes down. She never looked at anything now but soap and plates. Slops and hot water.

And sometimes the back garden, which was springing into life outside the scullery's sole window.

But she did not look at it often.

"Your mother told me you lost your position." Aunt Annie crossed the few feet between the doorway and the worktable on which Rosalind had stacked dishes. From the corner of her eye, she saw the older woman pick up a cloth and a dish, then begin to dry. "I am sorry for that. I did it for the best."

"You did it. For the best." Rosalind pumped water over the plate, then rubbed it with soap. "So there was no reason for that express? There's no danger?"

"There is always danger—but this time, it was to you. I sent the express for the same reason I sent the article to Sir William. It is unwise to grow too close to one's target. You were beginning to grow fond of the Chandlers, were you not?"

More than beginning. Far, far more.

Aunt Annie was still speaking. "Your jobs were to find the information we needed to meet your debt. To keep Tranc satisfied so he would not turn his gaze to your sister instead."

Rosalind clenched her jaw so tightly her teeth ground against each other. *Better me than someone else.* She knew that, but it was not as easy to say as

it had been before she lost hope that her situation
would change.

Maybe it was the soap or the hot water or the
lack of fogging optimism, but she finally calculated
that Aunt Annie's daughter had been born in 1805.
Rosalind had been burned in 1808. "Was it my debt
or yours? You turned over my debt to Tranc only
because he held your own secret."

"I *had* to, my Cyfrinach. I had no power to decline."

"So you sold me. My burns were an opportunity
for you." A pawn which, if saved, could be sent out
to battle for and protect the queen.

"Not *sold*. I needed your help. That was all. You
were willing enough to give it at first."

"I was a *child*. You should have protected me."

"Protected you? I paid for the care that saved your
life. What has made you so ungrateful now? *Wfft*.
Spending time with Chandlers. It's best you're away
from them."

Rosalind could hardly disagree more if she painted
the words on her forehead. She shook her head and
scrubbed harder.

The silence was broken by the tidy sound of
crockery set onto a tabletop. Then one dish set within
another. Then another.

"However," Aunt Annie spoke up, "your associa-
tion with that family might not have been entirely bad.
After all this time, I believe I have found what I need."

She crossed to Rosalind's side and extended a letter
before her lowered head.

"My letter of reference from Sir William Chandler."
She couldn't even touch it; her hands were soapy and

sopping. "How—Why do you have it? Why did you open it?"

"You and Carys never lock your chamber. I couldn't have taught you to search so well if I didn't know a bit about it myself."

"Why were you searching my things?" As though the answer mattered. No answer would be acceptable.

"To see if there was anything I could use."

Rosalind dropped the plate into the sink, where it bubbled down into murky dishwater. Wheeling to face Aunt Annie, she said, "I am not yours to use. And I own little enough in this world that I should think I could go unmolested."

The widow shook this off. "But you see, you *were* useful. I have this same writing on a—a personal letter from 1805. It's signed Gwilym, which is what I called Sir William in—personal moments. But until now I had no paper to connect my Gwilym to Sir William Chandler."

"Surely signed papers from Sir William Chandler are not hard to locate." Rosalind wiped her wet hands on her apron. "You don't need that one. Give it back. It's mine, and I haven't even read it."

A serene smile crossed Anne Jones's features. "You'd never have it, were it not for me."

"I could say that about a great many things. Good and bad."

"Well, then." As though this were an answer and they were in complete accord, Anne slid the letter into the bodice of her black crepe gown.

"What does it say? Why couldn't you lay hold of any other letter over all these years?" Rosalind's voice was rising. Her voice *never* rose. "Why must you take from me one of the few things I have?"

With each question, the older woman's expression became more bemused. "Have you finished?"

"No!"

"My Cyfrinach, the letter says very little. That he found you as efficient in certain tasks as he had his own daughter. For a character, it was not likely to do you much good."

Rosalind plunged her hands into the dishwater and retrieved the plate. "Was it the reference to a daughter? Was that why you took it?"

Anne Jones did not reply but turned to trail about the room, peering into pots and drawing fingertips across furniture.

Searching.

Grimly, Rosalind returned to her scrubbing. Questions were no use. Words were weapons, and Anne Jones was marvelous at wielding them. She twisted them, creating them anew. Why, she had a forger at her beck and call to create characters and references for Rosalind's every post.

A forger at her beck and call...

Rosalind dropped the plate into the water again. Forcing her tired back upright, she looked the other woman in the eye. "You have given me forged papers time and again. If you needed a paper from Sir William, why did you not forge it?"

The widow dipped her head demurely. "If you must know, the personal letter was a love letter while we were in Spain. He promised me marriage." She looked up with liquid dark eyes. "But then he became ill—with palsy, you know—and he was taken back to England. I never heard from him again. I didn't dare write."

"You dared write to him last week to summon him to London."

"But that was for *your* sake, my Cyfrinach. I needed to get you out of that household."

"Why? As far as you knew, I hadn't found anything useful yet."

Anne Jones glided back to the worktable and resumed drying dishes. "Do you know what my name really is? It's not Anne."

"And mine is not Cyfrinach."

"It's Annwyl. It means 'beloved' in the Welsh tongue." She set down a dry bowl, then picked up a dripping one. "It's not so difficult to turn from someone's *annwyl* into a dirty, dark secret. A *cyfrinach*. An *anweledig* that must remain invisible ever after. I didn't know it had happened to me until it was done. Almost like you with your burns. Do you remember that time?"

"No." Rosalind rubbed at her right elbow with her damp hands. Her memories were morphine-fogged until the blisters healed and were popped. Then agony, raw agony, and she lay on her belly for weeks as her own skin turned into a vise about her.

She released her elbow, then picked up a second cloth and began drying a different stack of dishes. "You have answered none of my questions."

"What more could you possibly want to know? If I'm satisfied with this letter, then the debt is paid. You shall not have to go into service again. Isn't that good?"

"But I didn't pay the debt. And I want to know—"

"Oh, of course. I should have said that at once. Tranc will have no reason to come for Carys if your service has been satisfactory."

"But you said he wanted information, not money."

Not everything people tell you is true. Nathaniel had spoken the words to her a few days before, a pebble tossed against the wall of secrets between them.

Maybe more than a pebble.

Rosalind set a plate down unsteadily. It rolled on its base in a slow circle before clattering flat. Just so spun her thoughts.

She looked at Aunt Annie, so familiar that her presence—her goodwill—was taken for granted.

Now she looked again. Really looked. *Looked.* This was Annwyl Jones. Mrs. Bowen Jones. The proper widow, once a beauty, whose hair was threaded with the gray of loss and sorrow. A saint on earth who moved benevolently through Holloway. Who traveled about visiting foundling homes.

Or did she?

Why had she befriended the Agates? Had she always hoped to gather an indentured servant from the plentiful ranks of their children? For less than one hundred pounds in physicians' fees, she had won ten years of service from Rosalind.

Rosalind had once regarded Anne Jones with the trusting eyes of the wounded child, salved and grateful. Now she looked at her with the skeptical gaze of the adult.

The other woman seemed to feel the weight of this gaze. When she looked up, her dark eyes were all sympathy. "I should have known it was the money you were concerned about. Do not worry, my Cyfrinach. You gave me this letter. And now we will get all the payment we want."

"You have answered none of my questions," Rosalind said for the second time. It was easy to become distracted from this fact when one was bombarded with irrelevant replies. "I'm not interested in money. I want to know who Sir William is to you, and who Tranc is, and how you think he is to be satisfied. I want to be certain my sister is safe."

She wanted to be done with Anne Jones.

"Do not worry, my Cyfrinach. Let me take care of everything." The widow sighed and smoothed her drying cloth onto the table. "I must be going now. I know you are busy. You see? You don't need a new post. You already have one."

Before Rosalind could protest, Anne Jones trailed from the scullery, leaving behind more questions than ever.

And the determination on Rosalind's part to find the answers at last.

Twenty-three

THE MORNING OF THE DERBY WAS FINE—BUT THEN Sir William Chandler had always found the morning of a race to be fine. Whether the rain fell in sheets or the sun baked, the thunder of hooves over turf was the weather he most cared about. Especially since he hadn't seen a Derby run for more than thirteen years.

He had missed this like he missed walking. The world never seemed more alive than on the day of a great race, the rolling green about the track crammed with carriages and people on foot. Nobles with picnic baskets sat atop gleaming equipages; whores and pickpockets slipped through the crowd looking for custom. Gypsies told fortunes; hawkers in stalls sold everything from fried fish to lucky talismans. Their calls wafted above the throng along with scents of oil and hot food, the odor of perspiring humans packed shoulder to shoulder, the smell of the turf and the horses bred for this day.

Nathaniel walked at his father's side, helping to clear a path. Sir William didn't mind rolling his chair over an unwary foot, but progress was certainly quicker with a companion who broke through the crowd.

His younger son bent with a question. "From where do you want to watch? The starting line?"

This was almost the first word Nathaniel had uttered that day.

When Sir William had returned to his chamber the day before with Nathaniel's betting slip, the bottle of brandy had still been sealed. His son's thanks had been absent, as though his thoughts were somewhere other than the paper that represented his allowance for a full quarter.

They were either in the past or with Rosalind Agate. Maybe a bit of both.

If it hadn't been Derby Day, Sir William might have done a bit of dwelling in the past himself.

"Watch from the start if you like," he said, shaking his head at a seller of rabbits' feet who approached with a hopeful expression. "I intend to be near the judges' box to see the finish. That's all that matters."

"Not how the race is run?" That mischievous smile seemed so *Nathaniel*. Sir William had used to smile like that himself once, hadn't he?

"If you're trying to be metaphorical, it won't work," Sir William grunted. "Just try telling a bookmaker that such-and-such horse ran a courteous race and see whether you'll be paid."

"All right. We can split up. Do you want me to go with you to find a good vantage point at the finish?"

"No need for that. A member of the Jockey Club can always find a good vantage point." More accurately, a man with a full purse and a close eye on it could. Sir William would throw his weight about—perhaps figuratively, perhaps literally—to reach the spot he wanted.

Why not? It was what he had always done before palsy confined him to the wheeled chair. He traveled about differently now, but he was still the same man. Maybe he was not as confined as he had grown used to thinking.

"I should have done this years ago," he murmured.

"What's that?" Nathaniel tipped his head.

"Nothing, nothing." Sir William waved him off. "Go find a place by the start. We'll meet up later at the King's Waggon to toast our victory. With water."

"We're to win, then? I'm glad that's decided."

"I am too," murmured the baronet as his son tipped his hat and threaded off through the crowd. At once, the crush seemed heavier, people looming head and shoulders above him. All around him.

But if he tipped his head back, he could see the flags above the judges' stand. They snapped in the warm breeze as though summoning him.

And so he rolled forward, an inch and a foot and a yard at a time, and found his way to where the race would finish.

At the judges' stand, a neat wooden box from which the winning colors would be thrown, the white rails of the course ended. The globe-topped starting pole was at the other end of a curving horseshoe a mile and a half away. Not that anyone could see both start and finish. The inner field was just as crowded as the outer boundary of the track, and the Prince's Stand—the only permanent spot from which to clamber up and watch the race—was so full that the spectators were crushed in shoulder to shoulder.

Sir William edged his chair into place beside the judges' stand, waving at the lucky few chosen to determine the outcome. He recognized one of them, a local landowner named Martinet. The younger man squinted, gaped, then grinned and gave a hearty greeting. "Happy to see you back on the turf, Sir William."

"I am too."

A ripple of silence spread through the crowd: the horses must be lining up. Somewhere, Pale Marauder's jockey wore the Chandler silks of black and gold. Epigram's jockey wore the same, but with the crimson hat of Sir Jubal Thompson. They'd be straight in the saddle, their lean faces set. Waiting for the shot that would fire them into a gallop.

Then came a groan, a clamor of protest.

"False start," guessed Martinet.

He didn't have to guess the second time or the third—or any time after that. Word filtered around the curve of the track: two of the colts, Prince Paul and Pale Marauder, kept stepping out of line.

"Damn you, Roddy." Sir William shook his head, not entirely surprised.

And then, after ten false starts, came the starting shot. With a whoop and a scream, the crowd cheered on the horses. Sir William craned his neck, as though the extra inch or two gained could show him the fast-flung bodies, the pounding hooves. Which would be the first to round the bend? A bay? A chestnut? Whose strides would be the first to cover the smooth green turf?

At last, after an eternal minute, the Thoroughbreds rounded the curve of the track and came into view. Their silken galloping was a joy to watch, as first one then another lowered his fine head and nudged forward. From Sir William's angle, he could not see who led the pack, but in the thick of it he spotted a cream-colored coat and a flash of gold and black.

"Come on, Roddy! You've got it!" he shouted again and again until he was almost hoarse. So loud was the cheering around him that he couldn't hear himself. The noise of the crowd seemed to lift the horses on a wave of sound, washing them down the slight slope toward the finish in a burst of fresh speed.

The judges yelled. Waved. Called to each other, nodding.

And then came the winning colors, flung forth over the stand.

Black and gold.

A roar of victory ripped from Sir William's throat.

Martinet looked about, puzzled, then shook his head and snatched down the scarlet flag over the stand and tossed that across the silks.

The roar cut off—and then Sir William began to laugh. Not his horse, but Sir Jubal's. Epigram. Epigram had done it.

Martinet climbed down from the stand to speak to Sir William. "Sorry about that. Epigram's jockey lost his hat somewhere along the course. Didn't mean to give you the wrong impression there."

The laugh still lingered on Sir William's lips. "Martinet, Epigram is a great horse. It feels like my own victory to have brought him along."

A double champion. Well, well. Sir Jubal would be delighted by how the Chandlers had served him. Trust was a lasting victory, maybe worth more than having a Derby winner in his own stable.

"You always could turn anything into a triumph," said Martinet.

"Do you know, I really can," said Sir William. He patted his pocket, where his and Nathaniel's betting slips lay safe. "Especially when I bet on a winning horse. If you'll excuse me, Martinet? I need to see to my horses now."

"Of course, of course. Hope to see you again next year."

Sir William doffed his hat to the judge. "Plan on it."

❧

Pockets full of banknotes, Nathaniel unlocked the private parlor of the King's Waggon.

Epigram had won. A good result to the weeks of good work.

And now the journey and the race and the waiting and the preparation were all over.

All Epsom was a fete, still shouting and raucous. The sound rang through the walls like the notes of a brass band. Yet Nathaniel had the same flat feeling he experienced every time he ended a journey with the sight of Chandler Hall. That deflated sense of not knowing what to do next.

One tiny next awaited him: he'd stash his winnings in his traveling trunk. Fifteen hundred pounds. A fortune.

And how much of that was Rosalind's? One

hundred fifty was what she'd wanted to pay her debt. She ought to have that. At least that.

She ought to have been here to see the race. She'd been a part of every step of the journey from the horses' first illness to Epsom itself, and it seemed utterly wrong that she wasn't here for the final triumph.

But she had chosen not to be. Hadn't she? She'd chosen worry about her family over her own wish to stay.

He couldn't fault her for that. Maybe he'd have done the same. Maybe she was right, and she hadn't really had a choice to make. Maybe she could never have chosen him at all.

Sliding to the floor, he leaned against a leg of the table. Knobbly and uncomfortable, it pressed at his head and his spine.

How he wished he could become someone else for a while. Someone who knew where he belonged. Someone who knew how to get people to love him. Not just respect him; not merely follow him down the road.

To *love* him.

The brandy was still there on the table, the bottle unsealed now. At some point yesterday Sir William must have drunk his customary half inch.

Nathaniel wasn't interested in the brandy. No matter how one wished, there was no purpose to trying to forget or become someone else. Memory would return; he would return. And both would be a little duller and sadder for the departure.

But enough of that. There was his trunk, with its lid open and box full of neatly folded items. He slid across the floor and sat in front of it, shifting aside the clothing. Beneath it was a secret compartment, and in there he could stash his winnings.

Damn. Where was the latch of the thing? He'd have to unpack to find it.

Rising to his knees, he lifted free the trappings of gentlemanly life. Neat cravats and linen shirts, waistcoats and breeches. He reached into the trunk again for the last of it. This time his fingertips brushed not fabric, but a book.

When he pulled it forth, he recognized it at once. It was one of the set of Shakespeare's plays, leatherbound and gilded and banded. There were four plays in this volume: *A Midsummer Night's Dream. The Merchant of Venice. As You Like It. The Taming of the Shrew.* So many romances, so many dreams. A pound of flesh and the quality of mercy.

A Rosalind who would not and should not be tamed.

He wanted to look at her name on the page.

As he flipped through the heavy laid paper to the beginning of *As You Like It*, something slipped from the pages. He lost sight of it among the folded stacks of clothing—then spotted a dried flower on the floor.

Picking it up, he clambered to his feet and held it up before the window. Though faded and flat, it was unmistakably a red carnation.

"Rosalind." A blossom from the day of the fete and the first time he had kissed her. When had she slipped this into his book? When there was still the hope of more kisses, or no longer a prayer for anything but a memory?

With hands that shook, he held it by the fragile stem until his eyes blurred from gazing at it.

It would be easy to drop it. Stomp it. Crush it to nothing but a deep red powder. For a moment he considered this.

Sighing, he again seated himself on the floor, took up the book, and slipped the flower between its pages. Packing it away.

He turned a page, then another. Not reading. Just feeling the paper, fibrous and rich. Seeing the name *Rosalind* like a blur, again and again.

And then one line leaped out at him.

Yet your mistrust cannot make me a traitor, said Shakespeare's heroine. She had been blamed for being the child of an enemy. Blamed simply for being herself.

Exiled and mistrusted, she had protected herself with a disguise. But she remained herself within, always. Sure that she was worthy.

No matter what anyone thought of her, she did what she thought best.

He sat upright with a *clunk* of head against wall, but he hardly felt it.

For so long, he had tried to live up to his father's expectations. But Rosalind...she just *was*. She was used to having no one but herself, and so it was for herself that she sought respect. Liking. Love.

She thought she couldn't have the things she wanted—and maybe she couldn't, not all of them. But the things she possessed? Those were precious to her.

And for a night, she had owned him.

No, she would own him forever. Whether she

wanted him or not, he was hers. As surely as this petal had been a piece of her wreath, he had given her a piece of himself.

Now that he thought about it, he wasn't rudderless. From here, he knew *exactly* where he wanted to go next.

Twenty-four

"DID YOU NOTICE HIM TODAY WHEN WE SET OFF? Fresh as a daisy. Strong as an ox. Sleek as a—"

"Father, please. You've been spouting similes about Epigram for an entire day. Surely we could pause for a moment."

The baronet laughed.

Nathaniel would have preferred to ride Bumblebee northward, but at his father's request, he instead sat in the carriage with Sir William. For the day and a half since they'd left Epsom, the baronet had mulled over the race—aloud, always aloud, as though a tap had been opened and thirteen years' worth of wishful planning had been allowed to flow. He'd asked Nathaniel to recount all he could remember of the ten false starts, dissecting each one. In turn, he had described the finish, speculated on the middle, and told Nathaniel about every detail of the bookmaker's reluctance when he paid out for the wagers on Epigram.

"But you love similes," the baronet replied. "Something else on your mind?" He leaned forward, bracing himself with the walking cane he enjoyed holding onto in the carriage. "Something you love more?"

At Nathaniel's startled glance, the baronet angled his head toward the carriage window. Outside, the heart of London had fallen away, and he realized the road would soon lead them past the Eight Bells.

Devious Sir William. He must have asked the servants for its location.

"As a matter of fact"—Nathaniel tried to sound casual—"I need to stop when we reach the Agates' inn. There's something I must return."

"Something you need to return. Hmm. Should I suggest that you send it through the mail?"

Ha. Hilarious. "You absolutely should not." Adopting an expression as mild as Sir William's, Nathaniel teased him back in kind. "It will only take a moment. If you're embarrassed because you don't want to face Miss Agate's family after dismissing their daughter, you may of course wait in the carriage."

"It's *my carriage*. I don't need permission to stay in it."

"Then you won't mind me leaving it for a few minutes, will you?" Craning his neck again, Nathaniel watched for the white-painted brick structure to appear. "Ah, here we are. I knew we had to be close." He rapped on the ceiling of the carriage, and the coachman obediently drew to a halt.

As Sir William grumbled about *good deeds* and *nothing going unpunished*, Nathaniel sprang from the carriage and strode back to the rougher traveling carriage. Walking, riding, and driving, the whole party had come to a halt. "Ever'thing all ri', Mr. Nathaniel?" called Lombard.

"Perfectly all right." He waved. "Just need to get something out of my trunk."

The nearest outrider, Button, rode up to Nathaniel's side. "We surely have missed the maidy since she left us. You'll tell her hello, will you?"

Nathaniel paused in the act of shifting trunks. "I... Yes, of course. If I see Miss Agate, I will tell her hello."

Of course, he couldn't halt here only to call upon Rosalind, even if the hope of seeing her was ninety-nine percent of why he wanted to stop here. As it happened, he had thought of a different excuse. "Aha." From his trunk, he pulled Severn Agate's shirt and cravat.

And a fistful of banknotes.

He closed up the trunk, then the carriage. With another wave, he tucked the items under his arm and strode to the front entrance of the inn.

When he entered, eight silvery chimes greeted him. The next greeting came from Mrs. Agate, who scurried by to see what was needed. On recognizing Nathaniel, she enfolded him in the sort of embrace one generally only got when returning from battle. "Oh, Mr. Nathaniel, what a lovely surprise! I'll get Rosie at once. You must have come to call on her?"

He should have taken into account the number of Agates in the household. The chance of encountering Rosalind first was small. "I came to return some items to your son Severn."

The excuse sounded transparent to his own ears, so he added, handing the shirt and cravat over to Mrs. Agate, "And of course I'd love to greet Rosal—Rosie if she is nearby."

"She'll be in the scullery, scrubbing away at the dinner dishes." The plump smiling face smiled even more broadly. "May I get you some dinner, Mr. Nathaniel? Or something for your men?"

"They're my father's men now," he admitted. "Sir William is waiting in the carriage, and I promised—"

"There's a *baronet* on the road before us?" A hand fluttered to her bosom. "Oh, heavens, you must stay here! Truly, it would be an honor."

"No, it really wouldn't. Please believe me. He's so full of similes at present that—"

He stopped talking, because Rosalind had stepped into the corridor from the doorway Nathaniel knew led to the kitchen.

When she saw him, her eyes went wide. She froze like a statue.

A beautiful water-splashed statue in a gown the color of her eyes, with a damp apron and soap-reddened hands.

Before he realized, he had taken several steps toward her. How he had missed her face. Her smile. Her hands, whether or not they were reddened by soap. "Rosalind."

She snapped from her rigor with a deep, sputtering breath. "Nath—Mr. Chand—wha—how—why are you here?"

Mrs. Agate piped up. "He brought back Severn's shirt and cravat, Rosie. Wasn't that nice?"

"Yes—very nice."

"And he says his father is waiting in the carriage and they can't stay, but you see if you can't talk him into it." With a wink, Mrs. Agate bustled off.

They stared at one another, alone for the moment, surrounded by the constant sounds of a busy coaching inn.

All Nathaniel's glib charm seemed to have deserted him. "I am glad to see you," he said simply. "So glad."

"I didn't think I would ever see you again." She brushed back a fallen wisp of hair, tucking it behind one ear. "I had almost got used to the idea."

He could not stop looking at her. He had days upon days of looking to make up for. "I...ah, here." Clumsily, he thrust the wad of banknotes at her. "This is for you. You won the race. Did you know?"

"Did I? And I'm not even winded." She looked at the money as though she didn't recognize it. "This is a fortune. How much is here?"

"Since you trusted me to choose, I decided that you bet ten pounds on Epigram. And at fifteen to one odds—there's one hundred fifty there." He lowered his voice. "It's what you wanted. It's enough to pay your debt."

Her hands trembled as she tucked it into the pocket of her gown. "I never expected it. I didn't..." She seemed not to know where to look. "You did this for me? You didn't have to do this for me."

"Of course I didn't *have* to. You're a terrible negotiator. You've never forced my hand. What I've done for you has been my choice."

"Your choice," she echoed in barely more than a whisper. She placed a steadying hand against the plaster wall, looking not at Nathaniel but at the splay of her fingers. "You chose this, even after I left you with no hope."

"Maybe you had no hope. I managed to scrape a bit together, and I *hope*—ha—that it's enough for the both of us." The letter that sent her away; he should have asked about it at once. "How is your sister? Is everything all right?"

"As all right as it ever is."

"Then why didn't you come back?" He had to ask, though the answer could only be *because I didn't choose to*.

"Because I couldn't untangle myself," she said. "I told you, I have ties—old ties. I owe Aunt Annie a great deal."

"Surely you owe yourself something too. You don't have to be trapped here. If you think it's a trap. Which you might not. Because it's your family. And—"

"Your short sentences are charming." When she looked at him, her eyes were heavy with tears—yet she smiled. "I do think I owe myself something, yes."

Her eyes shone, her shoulders were squared, her mouth was a sweet, curved promise.

It would be wrong, completely wrong, to kiss her now. He knew that. This was neither a kissing sort of place, nor should it be a kissing sort of conversation.

But somehow with her they all became the kissing sort of conversation. There was always something new to admire in her. There was always some reason to want to touch her. To be near her.

He did not kiss her, but instead placed his hand over the spot on the wall where hers had just rested. "Do you owe yourself me?" *Love? A happiness unrationed?*

"I owe myself a clean breach."

Oh. *Oh*. Now that hurt, like a blow to the gut.

"Of course," he said, trying to find firm footing as the corridor rocked beneath him. "You—yes, that makes sense. You must—I'll just go back to the carriage, and…it was good to see…" He trailed off, turning to go. Somehow his feet became tangled, and he kept his balance only by catching himself heavily against the wall.

There he remained, struggling to pull breath into heaving lungs. Winded and blown as a horse that just lost the race of its life.

Slim arms wrapped about him from behind; hands clasped over his heart. A head lay between his shoulder blades. "Nathaniel. Not with you. Never with you."

With determined strength, she pulled him about to face her, and somehow she was in his arms just as he was in hers. "I couldn't manage to break with you when I thought my life depended on it," she said. "Mine, or someone else's. I still begged you for another kiss, and another."

Relief swamped him, making him unsteady again. "That wasn't a kiss you asked me for when we last parted," he teased, pleased to see her blush.

Then her other words sunk in. "But whose life depended on a letter? What happened? You said everyone was all right."

"Yes." Her blush faded; her mouth pressed into a grim line. "Everyone is. It has to do with that clean breach to which I referred." Gnawing on her lip, she seemed deep in thought—and then she nodded. "Your father is out in the carriage before the Eight Bells, my mother said. Would you ask him to enter the inn for a few minutes?"

"I can, yes. Do you need to speak to him?" There was something here he wasn't understanding.

"Not for my own sake." Her lips made a tight curve that was not quite a smile. "But I should like him to meet with his old friend Anne Jones."

Twenty-five

CARYS AGREED TO FETCH AUNT ANNIE TO THE FRONT parlor, which Alec promised to keep clear of customers. "Though of course I'm going to listen in to whatever you're talking about."

"I hope you will," said Rosalind. "I hope everyone will."

Since their conversation the previous day, Aunt Annie had skirted Rosalind again. Only once the widow tried to keep her distance did Rosalind realize how frequently she was there. Anne Jones had the run of the Eight Bells. They had all adopted the habit of thinking she was to be trusted, simply because she had been present for so long.

Sir William hefted himself up the steps while Alec brought in his wheelchair. From the vestibule, the baronet wheeled neatly into the front parlor, the more formal room across from the public room favored by diners and drunkards alike.

"I didn't expect to see you again, Miss Agate. I trust you've been well?" The baronet's courtesy was unexpected. Gracious.

She stood behind a chair, too agitated to sit. "Yes, Sir William. Quite well, thank you. I see that you are too. Travel agrees with you."

He looked at her narrowly from beneath his steely brows, which then lifted. "I believe it does. So, you want me to have some speech with Anne Jones?"

She laced her fingers together. "Yes, sir. But before she arrives, I must tell you—I never worked for you."

The baronet's brows yanked back down. "I was under a different impression."

Rosalind could feel Nathaniel's gaze on her. He stood near his father and had startled when Rosalind spoke, but she did not dare look at him directly. These words were difficult enough to speak without watching all warmth ebb from his expression. "Yes, you were meant to. I have been a thief for years. I steal and copy papers from the people in whose houses I work. For my true employer." Her heart thudded. "Anne Jones."

Nathaniel gave a short bark of laughter. "I've always known you were more than a secretary."

"I have always known I was less." She was ashamed to admit this before them both, before Alec and any of her other brothers who were listening. They had been so proud. The Chandlers had thought her so capable. "She paid for the medical treatments that saved my life, and I have been hers ever since. For ten years."

Even as a girl of thirteen, she had known the things she did were wrong. But she had hoped that in the end everything would be put right.

The silence was so long and heavy that Rosalind felt her wall of secrets had tumbled down on her.

"And what information did you steal from me?" Sir William asked in a measured tone.

"Nothing." Her mouth twisted. "I was sent to Epsom before I found what Aunt Annie sought."

"Which was?"

"Anything related to Spain, 1805." She was done keeping secrets that were not her own.

"And you found nothing." Sir William steepled his hands before his chin. "Miss Agate, you're a terrible thief."

"I believe I was a better secretary than thief, yes. But my heart was in the former role, never in the latter." She ventured a glance at Nathaniel. He looked…bemused.

She shook out her trembling hands, then clamped them onto the back of the chair in front of her. Bemused was all right. Bemusement was better than disappointment.

Not that she had a right to hope for either. She had told him she couldn't see him again, and here he was, an undeserved gift.

"I don't want to lie any longer," she said. "I finally have a chance to decide what sort of life I'll have."

Already she felt lighter. As though she had shoved free of some of that fallen stone wall of secrets.

Before either of the Chandlers could reply, Aunt Annie entered bearing a teacup. "My Cyfrinach, what is this all about? Carys said I had a caller, and I—*oh*." The two Chandlers faced her. One seated, one standing; one golden, one gray.

The widow paled. With the jetty fabric of her gown, she looked as fragile as the china cup she held.

When she turned on her heel, Nathaniel stepped to one side and blocked the doorway.

Sir William, by contrast, looked almost pleased. "Anne Jones! Look at you, all dressed up like a widow. I wouldn't have thought it would suit you."

She recovered a little of her fragile smile. "But it does?"

"No, I didn't say that." He folded his arms, considering.

Rosalind spoke up. "Sir William, I just want to make certain of the matter. This is the same Anne Jones you knew in Spain. You know this woman?"

"Yes, I once did. So did many other men."

Aunt Annie set the teacup down with a clatter.

"She was a courtesan," the baronet explained. "Though perhaps that is not the right word. A courtesan has but one protector."

"You promised me marriage," Aunt Annie blurted out at once. But not soon enough, not loudly enough, to stop the words from echoing about the room.

They were loud in Rosalind's ears, playing again and again. *A courtesan*. The proper widow she had trusted with a decade of her life was really nothing of the sort.

"Huh," she said as she eased around the back of the chair and collapsed into it. "Huh."

But no one was listening to her. Sir William, completely unfazed, was answering, "We were shifting around the edge of a war. We all said things we didn't mean. I don't suppose you loved me, did you? Yet you said that often enough to the officers you served. You told my friend Smithy you loved him too. And Chatteris and Jordan."

"You and I have a particular tie." Anne's cheeks had flushed. "I have a letter of yours with private messages. You would not wish me to reveal it, I am sure."

The baronet looked at his lap where his hands were folded. When he looked up, his features were resigned. "If it's the sort of letter I think, Annie, you may do what you like with it. People forget that a man in a wheelchair is still a man. It would not be so terrible if they were reminded."

Rosalind cleared her throat. "Sir William, is there a chance your affair had lasting consequences?"

"She did not give me a disease, if that is what you refer to."

Anne gasped. She still stood in the middle of the room as though repelled in all directions.

"No, not a disease. You had better tell it all, *Aunt Annie*." Rosalind could not help but give the nickname a mocking edge. "Tell all your secrets. I am a grown woman, not a hurt child, and I want to pay my debts. I owed the Chandlers the truth. I owe you money, but since you've taken most of my salary for the past ten years, I think I have paid that debt as well."

"You can never pay your debt." Anne drew herself up straight. "You owe me your life."

"This argument again." Ten years' worth of strain heaped upon Rosalind. "Take it, then, if it's yours. If it's not my life, I don't want any part of it."

"You make me sound like an ogre! I would never, never hurt you, my Cyfrinach."

"My name is Rosalind," she corrected. "All right, then have Tranc kill me. He likes that sort of thing, doesn't he?"

"Who is Tranc?" Sir William fumbled with the unfamiliar word. "Why must anyone be killed?"

Anne turned to her former lover. "He is a Welsh criminal who will stop at nothing to collect money and power."

"Is he the one who poisoned my horses?"

"Yes!" Anne's tone throbbed with relief. "His men are everywhere. He sent one to feed the horses sanded sugar."

"Sand colic," Nathaniel mused. "Peters was right. He'll be so pleased. And Lombard will spit."

The conversation was turning awry—and then in an instant, it tipped upside down. "But you told me that *you* had sent someone to sicken the horses." Rosalind's fingers tightened on the arms of her chair. "You did that, by your own admission. I've the letter."

Just because someone told her something didn't mean it was true.

But what if it was? What if Tranc had given the order to Aunt Annie? What if they worked together?

No, it could go further than that.

Unsteady, she pushed to her feet. "For years, you've told me to fear and obey Tranc lest he take my sister. But I've never seen him. I've never met him. I only know what you've told me. Maybe everything you say he requires is really what you want."

Anne took a step toward Rosalind. "No, Rosie. My Cyfrinach. I tried to protect you—"

"You never protected me. You used me. And I let you use me." Her hand lifted to cover her mouth. "My God. My God. There's no Tranc, is there? It's you. He's you."

Anne only shook her head. She knew the power of silence.

A Welsh criminal who will stop at nothing to collect money and power. If she had to, she would even stoop so far as to save a life. She, known as Tranc.

Rosalind backed up a step, finding the support of the chair against her legs. "My God. It was you, all these years." Her voice grew ragged, rising. "How many secret helpers do you have? Your foundling homes—are they for the harvest of more like me? How many others work for you?"

"Just you, my—Rosie. Just you. It has always been you and me."

Not everything people tell you is true. "It has always been you," Rosalind said. "Only you. Not me. It has been long since I helped you for any reason other than guilt and fear and shame. What else have you lied about? Is there even a child?"

"A child?" Sir William broke in.

Anne turned toward him, then took a step in his direction. "We have a daughter, Gwilym. She was born in December 1805. For her protection, she does not know she is illegitimate. That the people who are raising her aren't her real parents. I would never do anything to hurt her or her prospects."

"We had a child?" Sir William frowned, counting months on his fingers.

"Please say it could not be possible," Nathaniel said.

"In the biological sense, it would be possible." The baronet leveled a stern gaze at Anne. "How can you be sure the child is mine? You were with many men."

Another righteous gasp. "If you saw her, you would know in an instant she was yours."

"Then I want to see her."

"But if you introduce yourself, then she will know she is a bastard!"

"I'll be inconspicuous."

As a group, they looked doubtfully at the massive man in the ornate wheelchair.

In that moment of distraction, Anne pulled a tiny pistol from her pocket and leveled it at Rosalind.

From the doorway followed a tiny metallic *click*. "You ought not to point a gun at Miss Agate."

Nathaniel, speaking with perfect calm, had pulled forth his own gun. The one he had hoped never to use while traveling, but always brought just in case. "Especially not in here. This is a nice parlor. If you want to fire that thing, Mrs. Jones, go into the taproom opposite."

"Let me leave." Anne was breathing hard, her outstretched hand trembling. Rosalind watched it, wary, ready to dodge. Knowing she could not dodge quickly enough. "Let me leave this place. I will go to one of my other homes, and I'll never see you again."

One of her other homes, she said. To how many people was she *Aunt*? Was she a proper widow to them too?

Keeping her eyes fixed on the gun, Rosalind shifted to one side. "There are more people like me, aren't there? Others who think they're protecting you by finding secrets that instead line your pockets?"

Anne took a deep breath and steadied her aim.

"So, yes, then." Rosalind eyed the tiny barrel of the gun. Being shot could not hurt more than the agony of burns, but she didn't wish to experience it. "Will you promise not to—to indenture another child?"

A hollow laugh. "My dear, if I ever I see a burned little girl whose parents cannot afford medicine, I will let her die."

"Or you could write to me," interjected Sir William. "I will pay the debt rather than turn it over to you."

"Put the gun down. Please." Rosalind begged the other woman with voice and eyes. So often as a child, she had looked into the eyes of Aunt Annie, the neighborhood's saint on earth, and found them beautiful. Had they ever been what they seemed? Had she been Tranc even during the years of her marriage, or had she turned to secrets and lies only when her soldier-husband left her a widow in Spain?

The answer didn't matter now, in the face of a gun.

For years, Rosalind had been a lamb for slaughter. But that was not the fault of the lamb, who knew no better than to follow those who shepherded it.

She knew better now. At last.

"Aunt Annie," she tried again. "Please. Put the gun away, and leave us all."

For a long, trembling moment, the black-clad arm held its gun. And then with a nod, the widow lowered it and whirled away, shoving past Nathaniel through the doorway.

And Annwyl Jones was gone, leaving behind a silence as sharp and sudden as a falling icicle.

This once, she had chosen to draw back rather than hurt someone. *Thank God*.

Nathaniel let out a deep breath and released the

hammer on his pistol. "It wasn't loaded. Sorry. Foolish of me." He pocketed it.

"It's all right." Rosalind hardly knew what she was saying. "It's all right now. It's all right."

Sir William was looking toward the doorway with troubled eyes. "But the child. If there *is* a child. How will I find her?"

"I can help you," said Rosalind. "I am a thief and a spy. Sir William, this is my specialty."

Nathaniel's mouth dropped open.

She coughed. "Or you could hire a professional sort of person."

"That might be better, yes," said Nathaniel. "Here I thought you were going to make an honest woman of yourself."

"I will. I want to. I've always wanted to." Still shaky, she crossed the room and took his hands. "You must have so many questions, Nathaniel. Whatever you want to ask, I'll answer."

The smile that shone down at her was a little sad. "There's one question in particular I want to ask you. But not yet. I don't have a home, and I'm not sure about the state of my position either."

Were his father not here, worried and shocked, she would have embraced him. Yes, she ached all over from tiredness, from strain. But she ached from within, too, from having missed Nathaniel like a piece of her own self. "When you ask, I'll answer."

"And where shall I find you to ask?"

She considered. "For the near and foreseeable future, I think I will be in the scullery. I've many dishes to wash."

"Do you have more to do right now? I could come help you," he said. "If you'd like help, that is. I don't want to be an arse about it."

Laughing, she wiggled her hands within his grasp. "I've never been asked a question so politely."

Oh, the devil with it. She wrapped her arms around him tightly, breathing him in. "I would like your help very much, Nathaniel. Thank you."

As he followed her to the scullery, he began whistling.

❧

After this, of course, the Chandler party had to dine and sup and drink; to stable the horses and stay the night. Sir William allowed that travelers needed rest sometimes, though—as he hurried to add—*not* entire days of it.

Alec had overheard everything that passed in the front parlor, and he had not hesitated to share the intriguing developments with the other Agates.

In the family sitting room that evening, there were many things to discuss and think over and discuss once again. And when Mrs. Jones and her startling departure failed to cleave free any new facets of conversation, the biscuits were passed around and Carys huffed off to gather tea things and the talk turned in whichever way it wished.

Rosalind could not say who was most delighted by the travelers' arrival: her parents and Carys, to have illustrious company; Elder, to receive his first serving of port—which he hated; or Sir William, who regaled her brothers with anecdotes about the recent Derby.

No, it was surely she who loved this evening best. She from whom a barb had been drawn after a decade and who now stood by Nathaniel with no wall between them. No more secrets or half-truths. No more shame.

When she visited him in his room that night, she stripped her clothing with no hesitation. She had been bare for him in every way, and he had stayed with her. Had come back to her. Surely he had bared himself just as much.

With fingers and lips and whispered words, they rediscovered one another. And the most important of these words came as she untied Nathaniel's cravat, as he watched her with eyes that pierced and caressed at once.

"I love you," he said. "Which you probably suspected."

Though she was nude, she felt warm all through. "And I love you," she replied. "Which you probably knew."

"I didn't." He shut his eyes against the tease and tug of his clothing. "I hoped."

Rising to her tiptoes, she pressed a kiss against the hollow of his throat. A pulse pounded there, as steady and strong as it was vulnerable. "I hoped for you too. I hoped for you from the first time you made a Houyhnhnm joke and showed me laughter could be slipped into any moment."

"I hoped for you from the moment you declined to check the lucerne for mold. When you trusted me."

"I trust you," she said breathlessly.

He took her to bed. And it was sweet and hot as he moved within her, a blade of joy reforged into passion.

Because she knew it wasn't just tonight. It wasn't just for now.

Not yet, but soon, it would be for always.

Twenty-six

THE FOLLOWING MORNING, BEFORE NATHANIEL could haul himself into the crested carriage opposite his father, Sir William shut the carriage door and traveled in it alone. The next day, he did the same. And then next, and the next.

Nathaniel realized that the celebration of the first leg of the journey had come to an end. Now the baronet had more to think about than how quickly Epigram had taken the lead, or whether Pale Marauder could ever be coaxed to spend his energy during the race instead of at the starting line. It seemed that when one learned that one's secretary had been a spy, albeit an ineffective one, and that one might or might not have a previously unknown daughter, one required some time to become accustomed to these facts.

This suited Nathaniel, because he had much to think about too. And he never thought so well as when his hands were busy. Tinkering with a water pump or hauling around a trunk. Or in this case, holding Bumblebee's reins as they trotted up the road.

As England slid past them in familiar lines, Nathaniel brought his thoughts into order.

If he wanted Rosalind—and God, how he wanted her—he needed to support a wife. If he wanted to support a wife, he could no longer work in this half-formed job for his father. He didn't have a home. And he didn't want the role he had, which would only get smaller and smaller until he became less than he was.

But Chandlers knew nothing except horses, and Nathaniel knew no other places but the roads of England. What was he fit for except the same things he had always done?

The road was dusty, the wet spring promising a hot, dry summer. On Bumblebee's back, Nathaniel followed the carriages. Their wheels tossed clouds before his vision, and he dropped further and further behind.

And then, around a gentle bend in the road, he caught sight of a familiar hulk of scorched brick. He imagined he heard the whinny of a massive Suffolk chestnut horse, the call of a punter on a small river he could view in his mind's eye.

"We've reached Kelting," he realized. After a moment's hesitation, he urged Bumblebee into a canter. When they caught up to the rest of the party, he called for a halt. Sliding from the horse's back, he handed the reins off to Lombard and opened the door to the crested carriage.

Within, Sir William frowned. "You cannot keep calling for a halt whenever you have a shirt to return. For God's sake, Nathaniel, use the mail."

"It's not a shirt I want to leave here. It's me."

Sir William blinked. "You." He slid over on the

squabs to peer at his surroundings. "You want to stay here? Where *is* here? We're not to halt for the day until we reach the Dog and Pony."

"This is the village of Kelting. It's a fine spot along the road, with a river and—"

"Ah, the fete. This is where that fete was. The one that…"

When he trailed off, Nathaniel finished the sentence for him. "The one that Anne Jones wrote about to you, yes. It was a wonderful fete."

"Life in a tiny village isn't all fetes, you know."

"Of course I know that. Nor is life like that anywhere else. Sometimes life is sick horses or blocked pipes. Sometimes it's a broken felloes."

Sir William's brows knit. "When did my carriage have a broken felloes?"

Nathaniel hurried on. "And sometimes life is working in a scullery. Sometimes it involves pulling a pistol. Sometimes it's abandoning a house that doesn't suit one anymore." He squinted at the burned-out walls of the Cock and Bull. "And sometimes it's rebuilding."

"What exactly are you saying?"

Nathaniel gestured at the building. "I want to buy that inn. I want to rebuild it. And I want to live in it and return it to use."

He wanted to make it his home, and Rosalind's.

Someday, if they washed dishes together, he wanted those dishes to be for their own guests or family. When they cared for horses, ill or healthy, the horses would be sturdy geldings and cobs. Horses like Bumblebee and Jake, good-tempered and useful.

He still had more than thirteen hundred pounds.

Far more than enough to buy the land and its remaining building. Enough to rebuild, too, if he was careful with his money. And if he did much of the work himself.

His hands flexed, eager to begin.

"A fine dream, but not one to be taken up at impulse," said Sir William. "Remount, and let's be on our way again. We'll be home at Chandler Hall by nightfall tomorrow."

"That's your home. But it's not my home."

Sir William shifted the walking stick from one hand to the other and back before replying. "It could be, you know. If you wanted it to be."

Why, that was almost a declaration of fatherly affection.

In the late light of afternoon, the burned hulk of the Cock and Bull cast a slanted shadow across the road. In its shadow, Nathaniel had kissed Rosalind, who had been burned and who was strong. Who was herself always striving to be better than circumstance wanted to allow.

Maybe that kiss was when Nathaniel had begun to change. Or maybe he had begun to change long before—the first time he wanted a drink and decided not to take one.

Maybe both, and every moment in between and since.

"Thank you, Father, but I'll stay here," he decided. "Only let me fetch my trunk, and then you must continue as you like."

"And how will that be?" Sir William's hands went tight on the head of his cane.

The baronet had given up a great deal for his family, and now he would be alone in an echoing house. Built to suit him, yes, but just because one had everything the way one wanted it did not mean one wasn't lonely.

"That's for you to decide," Nathaniel said. "But once this inn is rebuilt and open for custom, you'll always be welcome here. I'll turn this inn into the sort of place horse-racing travelers need. Secure and safe and healthful, with generous stables."

"Hmm." Sir William set aside the cane, then drew himself up. "You're decided?"

"Yes."

Slowly, the baronet nodded. "Write to me if there's anything you need."

"Are you offering help?"

"If you're not too proud to take it."

"Oh, I'm proud. But not too proud for that." Nathaniel grinned. "Though I hope I won't need it."

"Maybe you won't. If you meet a milkmaid, you'll know what to do." After a moment, Sir William's stern expression cracked into something kind.

Nathaniel bowed farewell, then said his good-bye to the rest of the party. Once his trunk was unloaded, he turned away. He didn't need to watch them leave.

For once, he felt the road had brought him exactly where he ought to be.

❧

A month went by, a month of work that tired Nathaniel to the bone. A month of tracing the owners of the Cock and Bull, contacting them, and buying the property; of drawing up plans and ordering supplies. When it came time to build, Nathaniel hired all the help he could from among the people of Kelting, but he still did much of the work himself. He was good enough with a hammer or saw, and if he didn't understand some piece of the plans, he didn't mind asking around.

When he designed the family quarters, he built in a bathing room with piped water. That was the only bit of Chandler Hall he missed. Though there was something to be said for the charms of a copper tub, too.

June had turned dry and warm. In Newmarket, the Jockey Club would be preparing for the July Course races. The summer race meet would bring gamblers and jockeys and trainers and horses from all around England. From beyond.

He didn't miss the turf itself, though he'd have liked to visit the new crop of colts. And he couldn't help but wish his inn were ready to take some of those travelers' custom.

George Hutchins, who knew everything and everyone in Kelting, introduced Nathaniel to the inhabitants and shops. Everyone he met was friendly and delighted the inn was to be returned to use, to draw travelers and their business. Many people remembered Nathaniel and "his lady" from the Whit week fete. Not a few young women also inquired about Peters, whose feats of wrestling in his shirtsleeves had made quite an impression.

Throughout the month, Nathaniel wrote to Rosalind. A month of letters in which he told her of his plans and schemes, and took her advice on how their shape might be planed and smoothed. A month in which he wrote to ask her a question.

And she said yes.

I will ask you again when we see each other, he wrote back. *When I have a home for us both.*

I would be willing to live in a stall with you next to Old Toby's brewery, she replied.

He laughed. Old Toby would be happy to leave the cramped quarters of the Cock and Bull stables. He had sold them back to Nathaniel and would instead rent brewing space in the basement of the newly rebuilt coaching inn. Nathaniel would buy all the ale Toby was able to produce for the taproom.

He had spent some time with Toby to view the equipment and design the space. Once offered ale, Nathaniel had declined it. And then he explained that he didn't feel like himself when he drank, and he would rather not anymore.

Old Toby accepted this with a nod. "Canno' be someone besides y'self, Chandler."

Nathaniel grew used to the smell of ale again, and he neither minded it nor craved it. He didn't plan to test himself with a pint, but he thought he'd be quite all right having it around.

He wrote to Rosalind:

> *Until there is room at the inn, I am renting a chamber from Hutchins. Shall I get a marriage license from the bishop, or would you rather the banns be called in the Kelting church after your arrival?*

The answer came more quickly than ever before.

> *A license, please, so we may marry all the sooner. When you are ready for me, I will come to you.*

Though their letters made the trip in a day on the swift coaches of the Royal Mail, on horseback or in a carriage Rosalind would need several days to reach Kelting. So he summoned her once the inn's new roof was completed, then worked almost day and night to finish a room or two so they might begin to live there.

> Dear Rosie,
> If you come to Kelting I will give you a posy.

> Dear Nathaniel,
> When I come to Kelting I will bring a spaniel.

"She's as horrible a poet as I am." He smiled when he read this latest letter. They were spending a small fortune on postage, but Nathaniel knew Rosalind had a bit of money on hand. She had, after all, won her wager on Epigram.

He wondered whether Rosalind was being serious about traveling with a spaniel. He liked the sound of that. Every coaching inn should have a dog or two running about, keeping an eye and a nose on the people who traveled by.

Not a sheepdog, though. Customers wouldn't like being herded.

Rosalind arrived a few days later in a much-traveled carriage, with a large basket over one of her arms. Once she descended the carriage steps, her parents followed. Plump Mrs. Agate and lanky Mr. Agate looked travel weary but gave Nathaniel the warmest of greetings.

"They wanted to see us married," Rosalind explained. "My brother Severn was in transports over being given charge of the Eight Bells for a few days."

"We wouldn't have done it," Mrs. Agate explained, "except our oldest, Bert, came to visit."

"A good steady lad," Mr. Agate added. "Bert will make sure Severn keeps his eye on the business and not on the ladies."

With some rearranging of the building materials strewn around inside the half-restored inn, Nathaniel made a room for the Agates and stowed their luggage. They dutifully promised to be on their way after the wedding breakfast, leaving the bride and groom alone, which convinced Nathaniel anew of their goodwill and good sense.

Arriving at their destination seemed to bring back the Agates' energy, because Nathaniel's future mother- and father-in-law were eager to be shown around the inn and its outbuildings. After asking whether he wanted their advice—good Lord, these were fine people—they offered several hints based on their experience of operating a coaching inn. Which he noted with thanks.

"And of course Rosie knows everything about it too," said Mrs. Agate. "Anything from scullery to budgets, she'll chime in. With your hard work and her—"

"Hard head?" interrupted Rosalind.

Her mother gave her a fond smile. "If you like, yes. I think the two of you will rub on quite well."

"I have no doubt of it," replied Nathaniel, shooting Rosalind a look that was intended to convey all sorts of salacious meanings.

She colored. "Not to change the subject, but you have not yet seen what's in the basket I brought." While Nathaniel had been assisting her parents with their luggage, she had stowed the lidded basket in the stables.

The foursome trooped in that direction. The low-slung building had long since lost the scent of horses, and Nathaniel looked forward to bringing it back. Instead, the smell of yeast and wet grain overlaid the air. Old Toby was seated on a bale of hay, cleaning some piece of brewing equipment with a cloth. After the introductions to Mr. and Mrs. Agate, he turned to Rosalind with a wink. "Your little fellow's been exploring. He's in that stall."

"Oh!" She darted behind the wooden partition.

When she emerged, it was with a bundle of puppy in her arms. White face and silky brown ears, pink tongue and bright eyes. It yipped a greeting at Nathaniel, who rubbed its little head until the puppy squeezed its eyes shut, wagging its tiny tail in canine delight.

"Is this a water spaniel?" Nathaniel asked. "He'll want to be splashing in the river all the time."

"*She* will." Rosalind smiled. "Look, she has a green ribbon to match mine, so obviously she is a girl."

Nathaniel apologized for overlooking this transparent cue. Indeed, there was a bow around the little spaniel's neck, the same shade as the one on Rosalind's bonnet. "The color of your eyes," he said, loving the way she blushed.

"It makes me feel pretty to wear this ribbon you chose."

"I probably ought to say it makes you look pretty too, but I don't think you need the help of a ribbon to be lovely."

She offered him a wicked smile. "I will wear my lace fichu with my wedding clothes. Only wait until you see that."

Mr. Agate cleared his throat. "Ah, let's have that little pup and, ah, we'll walk her about a bit. Toby, maybe you could show us around? Outside?"

They collected the spaniel from Rosalind and left her laughing and alone with Nathaniel. "I've named her Sheltie, by the way. I liked the idea of having our own Sheltie about the stable. Do you mind?"

"It's perfect." He kissed her lightly on the lips. "And now I must show you something too. For the inn."

At present, he was using the stable to store some items, including a few papers. Once he found the correct stall, he shuffled through a stack until he laid hands on the right one. "I was thinking of a new name. To make the inn truly ours, not the Cock and Bull anymore. How do you like this for a sign?"

He handed over the paper.

She studied it for a moment. "A red deer. I do like the image. Is that what you wish to call the place? The Red Deer?"

"Ah, not quite. It's the Rosy Hart."

Her brows knit. When the words clicked—*Rosie Heart*—she turned a most lovely shade of pink. "I can't think of a better name. It's perfect."

"I'm glad you like it." Nathaniel set the paper down, then took her hands in his. "Because it's yours.

The inn. My heart. This stable. Well—not Old Toby's brewing equipment, but every other part of the stable. Oh, and this."

Releasing her hands, he pulled something free from his waistcoat pocket and handed it to her.

She held it up to the light. "Is this your medal? From Whit Tuesday?"

"Yes. Because I can't think of anything you would want to win that you could not."

With a smile, she hung it around her neck. "I love you. Thank you. And what of you? How may I win you?"

"I am already yours, as I said. I love you dearly, Rosalind. You've agreed in writing, so I'm going to hold you to it. But I'd like to hear your answer with my own ears. Will you marry me?"

She reached for him. "'I'll have no husband if you be not he.'"

Nathaniel took her in his arms. "So that's a yes?"

"That's a yes from two Rosalinds at once."

"Ah, your namesake from *As You Like It*. I once thought it a foolish play, but it does end with a wedding. I got the license of the bishop four days ago, so we have only three more to wait before we can be married."

"Three days." She pushed back her bonnet. "That's not long to wait. I suppose."

"As always, your short sentences are unconvincing." He lowered his head to the curve of her neck, kissing the line of it. She smelled of soap, the sort he'd used at the Eight Bells when having a bath. Just before he and Rosalind made love for the first time.

He would not have thought a plain soap could be erotic, but the mere scent made him want to strip her bare. "We've already waited weeks."

"Three days isn't much longer."

Had she not sounded so breathless, he would have found it easier to agree. When he found her lips, though, there wasn't a prayer of waiting. Not with her sweet whispers in his ear, the firm curve of her waist in his hands, her breasts soft against his chest. He sank into their kiss, letting it build. Become the foundation of their home.

And then he leaned back just a bit to reach for one of the little horn buttons that marched down the front of her bodice. "May I undo them? Just one?"

"Or all?"

A halloo from the doorway made them snap apart in an instant. George Hutchins, eyes determinedly fastened on the ceiling, held out a letter. "Go' your mo'ning mail, Chandler."

After handing it over, he left with a tip of his hat and a knowing smile.

Nathaniel turned over the paper. "This letter can't be from you. It has a frank on it."

"Also, any letters I sent would have beaten me here." Pressing hands to her heated cheeks, Rosalind peered over his forearm to look at the paper. "That's your father's handwriting. Did you tell him of our plans to wed?"

"I did." Nathaniel cracked the seal and skimmed the firmly scripted lines.

A knot loosened within him, one he had not realized still hardened his heart. "He offers his congratulations to us both."

"That's kind. I wondered if he'd accept your marriage to his disgraced former secretary."

"Disgrace? I think there's more than enough of that to go around in the Chandler family. No, he says everything that is polite. And then—all business as usual. His investigator has found some information in London about Anne Jones and a possible child of hers that he should like to see. He plans to travel south, and if he is able, he would like to stay here. He asks when our coaching inn will be ready to accommodate travelers."

He handed the paper to Rosalind to read. "I knew he loved traveling. He missed it."

"Maybe he misses you too."

"Maybe," he granted. "I must write him we can't accommodate him as a traveler this time. But he could visit as family."

In Nathaniel's own home. On his own terms. With his own wife, his own life, all about him, strong and true.

"If he likes traveling so much, maybe he will come to the wedding." Rosalind handed back the letter.

"We must invite him, certainly. If he comes, he will be welcome."

And if he did not, that would be all right. The wheeled chair was difficult to pack into the carriage, and the stables were difficult to leave when so many horses demanded attention.

Even so. Sir William would like to be invited.

"Do you think he will find out anything about the child?" Nathaniel wondered. "If there is truly a child."

Rosalind looked surprised. "Aunt—Anne Jones told many lies." She fiddled with the ribbon of her bonnet.

"But I think she had a child, yes. She defended that secret when she stood up for no others."

"There is no place for a child in the life of a criminal genius, I suppose."

"I would hardly call her that. She had to give up something she loved very much; that was clear to me. Maybe that something was your father. Or a child. Or both. Maybe nothing but power. But how can it be genius if it leaves one with a sense of loss?"

He accepted this. "And now?"

"And now she wants power again. Power through information. If she wanted love, she'd have it."

"Is that so? Can such things be had only for the asking?" He folded his arms. "You once looked at me as though I were a madman for buying you sweets when you said you wanted them."

She smiled. "I should have put that differently. If she wanted love, she would seek it."

"Ah, I see. Nicely worded. That lets you make perfect sense yet still look at me as though I'm a madman."

She curtsied. "Secretaries can do that sort of thing."

"Oh, can they? I like this sort of talk much more than when you told me about what they don't do and don't have. Tell me, what else can secretaries do?" He extended a questing finger to untie the bow of her bonnet.

She let it fall to the floor of the stable. "We have years to find out."

"I look forward to them all," he said, and took her in his arms.

*Keep reading for an excerpt from the first book
in Romain's Matchmaker Trilogy*

It Takes Two
to Tangle

July 1815
Tallant House, London

IT WAS NO GOOD. THE CANVAS STILL LOOKED AS
though a chicken had been killed on it.

Henry Middlebrook grimaced and stepped back,
casting his eye over his work. In the cooling light of
early evening, his vermilion paint looked ghastly.

He dragged his brush over one corner of the canvas
and regarded it again. A slight improvement. Now it
looked as if someone had killed a chicken on it, then
tried to clean up the evidence.

No matter. He could fix it later somehow. Or hide
it in an attic.

As he stepped forward again, ready for another artistic
attack, Henry's foot bumped the fussy baroque table on
which he'd set his palette. The palette rattled perilously
close to the edge of the table, and Henry swooped for
it before it tipped. He lost his grip on his paintbrush and
could only watch, dismayed, as the wide brush flipped
end over end and landed with a faint thump on the carpet.

Well, damn.

"How lovely!" came a cry behind him, and Henry turned.

His sister-in-law Emily, the Countess of Tallant, was standing in the morning room doorway smiling at him. She wore a gown the watery, fragile pink of rose madder, with some part of it pinstriped and some other part of it beaded, and her auburn hair arranged with a quantity of pink-headed pins.

Henry did not understand all the details of women's fashion, having spent the past three years learning the significance of shoulder epaulets, forage caps, and stovepipe shakos. Still, the effect of Emily's ensemble was pleasing to anyone with the slightest eye for color—which Henry had, though no one looking at his canvas would possibly think so.

"Good evening, Emily," he said, shifting his foot to hide the fallen paintbrush. "I might say the same to you. You look very well."

"Nonsense, Hal," she said. "This gown is a full year out of fashion and is suitable for nothing but lolling around the house. I must go change for the ball, as must you. What I meant was that it's lovely to see you painting again."

She craned her neck to look behind him. "And it's even lovelier to see you resting your palette on that dreadful table. Jemmy's Aunt Matilda gave it to us as a wedding gift. I can only conclude she must have hated me."

Emily walked over to Henry and held out her hand for the paintbrush, which he sheepishly retrieved from the floor. She scrutinized it, then began to daub the gilded table at Henry's side with red curlicues.

"I'm not the expert you are, of course, but the texture of this red seems a bit off."

"Yes, it's too oily. I'm out of practice."

"Well, that's easily enough fixed by time. I'm glad we still had some of your supplies left from... well, before." Emily signed her name with fat, bold brush-strokes to the ruined tabletop. "There, that's the best this table has ever looked. If you can stand the sight of the beastly thing, then you must have it for your own use while you paint. Surely we can find a studio for you somewhere in the house. You could even keep painting here in the morning room if you don't mind rolling back the Axminster, of which I'm rather fond."

Henry looked at the heavy carpet guiltily. A splotch of warm red paint marred the fine sepia pattern of scrolls and bouquets. "I should have done that first thing. I'm sorry, Em."

She waved a hand. "I understand artists are remarkably forgetful creatures. Once the creative mood seizes you, you cannot be responsible for your actions."

"Are you giving me an excuse to be an aggravating guest? This could be entertaining."

Emily's mouth curled into the cunning smile that meant she was plotting something. "You're much more than a guest, as you know. But you're right. I should demand that you pay me a favor for spilling paint all over my possessions."

Henry took the brush from her and laid it carefully across the palette, atop the newly adorned table. "Let me guess. You already have a favor in mind, and you are delighted I have ruined your carpet, since now you can be sure I'll agree to whatever you ask."

Emily looked prouder than ever. "Excellent! We shall slip you back into polite society more easily than

I could ever have hoped. Already you are speaking its secret language again, for you are correct in every particular of your guess."

"I'm overjoyed to be such a prodigy. What, precisely, have I guessed?"

"Tonight, I am going to introduce you to your future wife. What do you think?" She beamed at him, as though she expected him to jump up and start applauding. Which was, of course, impossible.

Henry gripped the edge of the fussy little table tightly. It was difficult to imagine feeling comfortable amidst the *ton* again—as difficult as it had seemed to leave it three years ago.

But he was just as determined on the former as he'd once been on the latter. Choosing the right wife could be exactly the key he needed to unlock London.

Emily passed a hand in front of his face. "You didn't answer me, Hal."

Henry blinked; stalled. "Don't call me Hal, please."

She raised her eyes to heaven. "You know perfectly well that I shall never be able to stop calling you Hal in my lifetime, just as you cannot stop calling your brother Jem. We are all far too set in our ways. But that's not the answer I wanted. What do you think of my idea about finding you a wife? Actually, it was Jemmy's suggestion, but if you like it, I shall claim it for my own."

Fortunately, Henry's elder brother Jeremy, the Earl of Tallant, poked his dark head into the doorway at that moment, saving Henry from a reply. "Em? Aren't you ready yet? I've already had the carriage brought around."

In his sleek black tailcoat, mathematical-tied linens, and waistcoat of bronze silk, Jem looked every inch the earl. Every inch, that is, except the one between his forehead and nose. His eyes—a bright lapis-blue, the only feature the brothers had in common—held an ignoble amount of doubt just now. "Hal? Are you sure you're ready for this?"

Henry decided on deliberate obtuseness. "For Lady Applewood's ball? No, I still have to change my clothing."

"I'll send my man up to help you," Jem replied too quickly.

Emily crossed her arms and regarded her husband slowly, up and down. "You look very elegant, Jemmy. But why are you ready? We aren't leaving for an hour."

Jem's expression turned puzzled. "An hour? But I thought—"

"We must make a grand entrance," Emily said in a hurried hush. "I told you we shan't leave until nine."

Jem shrugged, squeezed by his wife, and came to stand next to Henry. "It's too dim in here," he decided as he regarded the painting. "I can't tell what you've painted."

Henry swept his arm to indicate the baroque table. "This table, for a start. And your carpet. And my breeches a bit." He regarded his garments ruefully.

Jem nodded. "Rather ambitious for your first effort."

"Yes. It's served me well to be ambitious, hasn't it?"

Jem managed a smile as his eyes found Henry's. "I suppose it has. Well, best get ready. Em's told you about our grand plan, hasn't she?"

"If you mean the plan to marry me off, then yes. I can't say I'm shocked. I'm only surprised it took her two weeks to broach the subject."

"She's been plotting it for weeks." Jem sighed. "Quite proud of the scheme."

"I'm still *right here*," Emily said from the doorway. "And I *am* proud of it. It's just…"

When she trailed off, both brothers turned to her. Emily's merry face looked sober all of a sudden. "We think you'd be happier, Hal. If you were married."

Henry pasted a smile across his face. "Don't worry about me. I'm quite as happy as can be expected."

Emily studied him for a long moment, then nodded. "One hour, Hal. Jemmy, do come with me. You may help me decide which dress to wear."

The earl followed his wife. "It doesn't matter, Em. You always look marvelous. Besides which, you never wear what I choose."

"That's because you'd send me out with no bodice. Honestly, Jem!"

Their voices quieted as they moved down the corridor, and Henry allowed the smile to drop from his face. He could guess what they'd begun talking about: just how happy *was* he?

He'd given them a truthful answer on the surface of it. He was as happy as could be expected. But a man in his situation had little enough reason for happiness.

Still, he had determination. Surely that was even more important. With enough determination, happiness might one day follow.

He dragged his easel to the edge of the morning room and gave his painting one last look.

Just as horrible as he'd thought. But in time, it would get better.

With a rueful shake of the head, he left behind his first foray back into painting and went upstairs to prepare for his first foray back into London society.

Acknowledgments

I could never complete a book without the help of many people. My deepest thanks go to...

My agent, Paige Wheeler, who guided me through the development of the Romance of the Turf series.

My editor, Deb Werksman, whose feedback was just what Rosalind and Nathaniel's story needed to shine.

The talented marketing, publicity, production, and art teams at Sourcebooks for launching this series so beautifully.

Amanda, whose patience as a critique partner was put to the test like never before.

My readers, who said they were excited to read romances set in the horse-racing world.

And my husband and daughter, who are my happily-ever-after.

About the Author

Historical romance author Theresa Romain pursued an impractical education that allowed her to read everything she could get her hands on. She then worked for universities and libraries, where she got to read even more. Eventually she started writing too. *A Gentleman's Game* is the first book in her new Romance of the Turf Regency series. Theresa lives with her family in the Midwest.